Cornered and severely outnumbered by the Association's navy, Syreen tries to reunite with her living ship. While her enemies blackmail her with an asteroid tossed down on an inhabited planet, the real danger hasn't even shown up yet — the fabric of space itself is torn apart, and within the ruptures, not only does space travel fail, but stars will die . . . together with their planets.

On her own, she can't win. But where can she find help?

Time of Wisdom
Copyright © 2020 Valerie J. Long
ISBN: 978-1-4874-2937-9
Cover art by Martine Jardin

Published by eXtasy Books Inc or
Devine Destinies, an imprint of eXtasy Books Inc

Look for us online at:
www.eXtasybooks.com or www.devinedestinies.com

Time of Wisdom
Forgotten People 4

By

Valerie J. Long

DEDICATION

In memory of Jonathan Swift, whose stories are still stirring our imagination today

PART ONE—REUNION

CHAPTER ONE

Mo stared at the green-golden U-shape on his board.
"This is *Assiduous,* a living ship — *my* living ship."
Syreen's last line was on replay in his mind.

He hadn't heard of *Forgotten People,* or if he had, he didn't
remember. He'd accepted her claim to the title *Navigator* as a
quirk — although she indeed was the best navigator ever — but
he had heard of *living ships* . . . in fairytales.

"How did you know it's here?"

Klondike certainly wasn't the first place he'd expect to find
materialized old lore — a remote place, at the outskirts of
known space, but still a place with regular traffic.

"I brought *Assiduous* here. He needed time to recover — in
a safe place, where the AP wouldn't find him."

"He. Okay. And how did you know how to fly such a
ship?"

"He taught me what I didn't know already, but I'm a Navigator, remember?"

"You mentioned that often enough, but what does it really
mean?"

"It means I'm born to fly living ships. Only females of the
People can integrate with them and take control."

"I don't get it." His mind stubbornly refused to draw conclusions from her statements. *It can't be.*

"Mo, I'm not human. I'm a descendant of an ancient race
few of your people remember, and those who do call us the
Forgotten People. Sadly, *Assiduous* is one of the only two connections to my past I have. I was raised by Duchy Navy as an

orphan—a foundling, dropped on a busy orbital station. I never met my parents. I have no one to ask about my legacy."

"What is the other connection?"

"The head of the Associated Planets Navy. He's of the People, too. He wants me—he needs me to control *Assiduous,* because he could never do it himself."

"He couldn't? Why?"

"*Assiduous* won't accept a male. It's impossible. You'll see."

Yusef listened. Everything she said sounded odd—but in an odd way, it made sense. It explained what she did—finding new routes, calculating seven-sigma jumps, dodging pulse shots, shooting more precisely than anyone else, or going dirtside with a spaceship—and left room for even more miracles.

He just couldn't imagine what kind of miracle they'd need to fend off those three battle groups with a total of three battle cruisers, nine light cruisers, nineteen destroyers, and a yet unknown number of stingships and missiles, that had arrived shortly after *Bumblebee.*

He'd grown fond of the ship they'd arrived with. *Bumblebee* was a swift and tough little warship, everything a solo pilot could ask for, but in the upcoming battle she was outclassed and outnumbered. There was no way for a single frigate to survive.

Their enemy had surely come to the same assessment. While his flagship was trying to catch up and his smaller units were cutting off their potential escape routes, the enemy signaled again.

"APS Bumblebee, *this is Admiral Cortez of* APS Vindicator. *You failed to follow my instructions. Unless you surrender instantly, I'm no longer in a position to give you quarter.*"

This time, Syreen decided to answer. "Admiral Cortez, unfortunately I can't give you what you want. However, should you at least be willing to formally declare war, I'll be ready to accept your capitulation any time. Just don't wait too long."

Yusef raised his eyebrows. *No way. They didn't come in numbers to say hi and bye. Too bad for them — they didn't see her fight. Or — wait.*

"Skipper?"

"What is it, Yusef?"

"What if they got data from our convoy, and know you can dodge pulse shots?"

"That won't help them."

Syreen kept her attention on the board. *Until we reach Assiduous, we're vulnerable. They won't be able to catch up, but I'd credit them for trying anything else. Like . . .*

She quickly entered a few parameters, rechecked them, and hit the button.

Bumblebee's two aft lasers fired, three times each, with reduced power. Six explosions indicated the successful elimination of six long-range missiles that had almost reached their frigate.

"Nice try," she said. "Okay, Admiral Cortez, you're playing your game well. Let's see how you deal with my next move."

"What are you up to?" Yusef asked. "You think you can hit him across this distance?"

"I could, but it would only be a tickle — or I could ruin our guns and burn a hole through his armor. Surely his repair crews would appreciate the drill. No. I didn't want to show him my tricks, but we need time for boarding *Assiduous,* and if he's willing to spend some more of his missiles, he might get at us at the very worst moment. No, I'll have to do something unconventional." The parameters for which she was entering right this moment.

"More unconventional than scoring impossible hits? I'm curious."

"In that case, check this out." She pushed her new solution over to his board.

Yusef glanced at it. "Seriously? No, of course you are. Again, you make the impossible possible. I wouldn't have thought of that."

"Neither did Cortez." She frowned and pulled her stick. *Bumblebee* changed course. "But he's learning fast — too fast for my taste."

"What was that?"

"Pulse shots from his destroyers. They must have used a kind of triangulation algorithm, or whatever it's called for nineteen instead of three angles, to shoot at us. Not precise enough to hit, and in any case, their shots couldn't have killed us, but — crap!"

She pulled again and dodged another bouquet of nineteen well-aimed shots. "Yes, he knows — Crew, prepare for jump *now*."

Bumblebee jumped.

CHAPTER TWO

Syreen gritted her teeth and fought for clear vision. "Ouch. That was rough."

Still, they'd been lucky to survive a jump so close to a star. It wasn't advisable to do such a jump, it required a tremendous amount of energy, was likely to burn the emitters up—if the ship managed to leave hyperspace in one piece at all—and it felt almost like a two-sigma jump.

Her board showed red. Indeed, their emitters had suffered. Without major repairs, *Bumblebee* would never do another hyperjump.

"That was it," Haiki said. "I can't fix that damage before they get us."

"Maneuverability is severely limited," Yusef added. "Plus, we're too close to the star now. The outer hull is already heating up."

Syreen nodded. "Agreed, but taking those destroyer shots would have peeled our shields and armor away before we reached the rendezvous point. We've won precious time."

Her board showed a new rendezvous point. While she rechecked her calculation, her flagship swiftly closed the distance.

She activated her radio. "*Assiduous*, pick us up."

Yusef checked his board again. "What? That close?"

The living ship's U-shape closed up around *Bumblebee*, and Syreen turned the frigate's outer hatch toward the central hangar door.

"Crew, passengers, prepare to change ship—Yusef, I must

go ahead. Please watch our back until I'm active."

When she reached the bridge door, she heard his reply.

"Sure."

Yusef examined his board. "Yeah, I'll watch our back."

What could I do? While the two ships were connected, maneuvering was out of the question. Their current position rendered the six guns useless. *The only thing I can do is watch what will come for us.*

Plus, he could watch their progress regarding the transfer.

The skipper had obviously overridden airlock operation — inner and outer hatch were open, and girls and crew were hastily passing through, urged on by Mo's reassuring but determined instructions.

The number of people aboard Bumblebee decreased quickly. Yusef nodded at Haiki, and the engineer left for the lock, too.

He'd stay as long as necessary, preparing for — yes, what?

Their jump must have caught Cortez by surprise. His missiles couldn't reach them yet. His lasers and pulse cannons could, once his gunners had calculated new solutions for their new target location. But even those, traveling at light speed, needed time to reach them. How long?

Another centicycle, perhaps?

"Yusef, get your ass over here!"

"Yessir!"

Syreen left her bridge, left her loyal pilot behind, and dashed for the airlock.

"Give way!" she commanded, reinforced by a mental instruction. Her passengers moved to both sides of the corridor and let her pass.

She had to reach *Assiduous'* pilot seat as fast as possible —

only she could make the impossible happen and get her people to safety—and she couldn't do that by queuing in line.

Inside her living ship, she ran for an elevator, cast her uniform off, let herself be sucked upward and raced toward her bridge, leaped for the seat and dropped into it.

She allowed herself a deep breath before adjusting her sitting position, impaling herself on his large, firm, and warm phallus and the no less firm butt plug—*Ouch! I'm not wet*—and leaning back into the neck pimples, while two more pricks hurt her thighs. *Ouch.*

— Welcome back. —

I feel — strong. You're larger than last time, mate.

— I've grown back to my normal size. —

Yeah. Everywhere.

Syreen welcomed the long missed, now so familiar sensations—Klondike's light, Klondike's heat, Klondike's gravity, Klondike's song . . . oh yes, that wonderful boner in her crotch, the warm hug of her chair—the delicate and yet so powerful little creature in his embrace, her wet and welcoming vagina—but also noticed the presence of a few nuisances that tossed little stabs of energy in her general direction.

We need to do something about them soon.

— They pose no threat to us. —

We need to protect Raydancer.

— We do not need its support any longer. —

I need its passengers. They support me.

— You brought more than enough new livestock. —

I need their knowledge.

— In that case, we should get rid of that wreck at our lock first. —

Give us another moment.

"Yusef, get your ass over here!"

CHAPTER THREE

Syreen felt *Bumblebee's* slender shape intimately connected to her center door. She felt remorse for what she had to do—the frigate had served her well, but after all, it had only been a useful tool, and with the damage suffered, it was a useless tool now, mostly a burden.

It can do us a last service. Let's get it under remote control. It'll attract some of our enemies' attention, and perhaps some of their shots, too.

— In that case, it won't last long. —

Longer than they'll expect, as we'll make it dodge their shots.

She knew her time was running out. Cortez' battle group was closing the distance fast, attempting a decisive first strike. Plus, his destroyers had turned and were coming in now. Worse, they had learned to make those *impossible* long-range shots count—interplanetary distances could no longer protect her.

There came their next volley.

She knew Yusef was aboard *Assiduous,* both ships ready for separation, all airlocks sealed, and steered the frigate clear before letting her living ship strafe away.

Are you still hungry?

— I am well fed, but I can make good use of organic nutrients. —

Let's get some.

Syreen entered deep integration.

The difference wasn't as striking as the last time—her *normal* integration with her ship was deeper than before, either due

8

to her own development or due to his greater power — but still near to overwhelming.

Syreen focused on the most imminent threats. Cortez had deployed sixteen more missiles against them, and the destroyers were trying to hit *Bumblebee* again — probably in order to dispose of that secondary target quickly.

APS Vindicator had deployed twelve stingships, which were attempting to intercept *Raydancer.*

No, you won't.

Finally, the larger warships would soon reach their maximum effective shooting distance, unless *Assiduous* would accelerate away from them — and from *Raydancer.*

No, we won't.

We will accept your gift and put your missiles to better use.

Ick.

Wading through *Bumblebee's* primitive computer controls was no fun. Trying to make it move with its damaged emitters was tiresome.

Cracking the missiles' target computers offered no challenge, though, as they weren't any better than those hacked at RAK-11 before.

Of course, *Raydancer's* controls were already well integrated.

We did this before.

Bumblebee evaded eleven hostile shots, while the other eight hadn't been on target anyway. With the triangulation data of *Raydancer, Bumblebee,* and *Assiduous* together, she picked her own targets — the corvette's single pulse cannon and two of the frigate's four forward cannons took out four AP stingships each.

Next, the frigate hit one AP destroyer twice, flipped, and shot another.

Precision rules!

Sixteen missiles were now heading for sixteen destroyers that were frantically trying to evade or shoot them, while useless commands from *APS Vindicator* failed to trigger their self-destruction.

Meanwhile, *Assiduous* approached the battle cruiser, dodging its well-aimed shots effortlessly.

Their enemy would eventually come up with the idea of scattershots that wouldn't be as easy to avoid. It was advisable to act first.

Yusef finally found Mo in a strange dome-like room, the walls covered with warts and strands pulsating in green and gold. Mo was sitting in a chair that looked like it had grown from the floor and yet didn't really belong there. He was gazing at a large sculpture in the dome center.

Only it was no sculpture, it was their skipper wrapped in a kind of reclining chair, stark naked, with a pulsating *something* penetrating her vagina. If not for the expression of bliss on her face, he'd have pulled her from that chair instantly.

Another chair grew from the floor behind him. He felt the urge to sit down and buckle up.

"What's going on here?" he asked.

"Watch," Mo said.

"Watch what?" Yusef asked. "That — abomination?"

"Watch the plot."

Now the pilot recognized the lights above the large seat, and the symbols next to them. "Crap."

The battle cruiser and three light cruisers were coming close, no longer in one line, but spreading out to bring all their forward guns to bear. A volley of twelve missiles preceded them, and eleven destroyers were coming from all directions.

Crimson red symbols told of eight severely damaged destroyers, one wrecked frigate, and twelve killed stingships.

The lights in the room flashed four times in quick succession.

The symbols of the four large warships turned crimson.
Next, their own ship trembled.

Oops.

Seven shots dodged, but one destroyer had hit home.

It felt like a tickle. A minor bruise that would soon be healed.

The small vessels seemed unable to recognize their inevitable defeat, though. Would they be worth salvaging? Would their crews of eight be worth preserving?

The plain numbers said *no, not with four much richer sources available.*

Her excitement said *no, not after they'd spoiled her orgasm just before.*

The tactical situation said no, not with twelve incoming missiles invulnerable against remote control attempts.

She turned and twisted around. Eight times, a shudder sprang from her *clit*—from the wart above her central door—and smashed one destroyer each.

Twelve more lighter shudders wiped the missiles from space and reinforced the joy of one wonderful, eight-fold orgasm.

Incoming calls demanded to spoil her happiness again. Those would have to wait, but she needed a break anyway, and slowly emerged from deep integration.

Syreen gazed at two puzzled male faces.

"Later, guys."

One thought opened a line and made the first caller audible. His signal was weak, most likely coming from a mobile device that had been inactive and thus had survived her EMP strike.

"*Unknown vessel, this is Admiral Cortez of* APS Vindicator. Vindicator, Badger, Fox, *and* Wolf *are unable to maneuver. I have to declare them non-combatants. Will you allow evac shuttle maneuvers?"*

"Admiral Cortez, this is Duchy Fleet Commander in Charge Syreen aboard *Assiduous*. You failed to declare war before opening fire. Your ships were then disabled during illegal combat action. I will not grant them non-combatant status after the fact. Instead, I claim them and all resources aboard my prize. Moreover, I cannot allow any uncontrolled ship activity while there are two more hostile battle groups active in this system."

"Cortez again. What do you mean, I failed to declare war? If you claim to be Duchy, we're at war since our initial operation against your home system."

"Admiral Cortez, I'm sorry you're misinformed, but Admiral Ravenport did not—I repeat, did not—declare war before shooting our orbital station, causing thousands of civil casualties. I will send you the recordings of my corvette, present during and after the attack."

Raydancer delivered its recordings. It wasn't entirely impossible to fake such data, but the AP had safeties in place against tampering, and those were unbroken. If Cortez found a working computer capable of checking their safeties, he'd recognize that.

There was a longer pause before Cortez called again, giving her time to prepare their rendezvous.

"Fleet Commander, I have no orders regarding such a situation, but before our computer failed, my records said we were at war. For the benefit of my men, I herewith formally declare war, thus making the situation match our records. I herewith instruct Commodore Gardner of APS Retaliator to transmit his records on the situation. I'm at your mercy, but ask you to accept his data, after the fact, as you put it, and grant us having acted in good faith regarding our formal situation."

He sounded sincere. She had to admit he was playing by the rules, even honorable, at least for AP standards.

— So what? We need organic substance eventually. —

I must consider the situation once our intervention ends. Criminals like Ravenport must eventually be replaced by honorable officers to reestablish order. I cannot recklessly waste the few good men I come across. However, I can't let them get away with their misdemeanor, either.

— Misdemeanor, huh? —

Syreen grinned.

"Admiral Cortez, I will check Commodore Gardner's data. For now, I assume it'll be acceptable. However, there are still hostile ships in this system. To use your own words — unless you and your fellows surrender instantly, I'm not in a position to give you quarter."

Instead, we'll soon be in a position to feed. We'll take Vindicator *first — it's the largest source.*

"What conditions would you offer?"

"You and your men will be spared. Your remaining ships may match your course and pick up your evac shuttles. After that, your shuttles may take you and your provisions down to Klondike. You may keep your shuttles, and I will keep your ships — all of your ships. You may wipe your records, if you like. Any hostile action from your side will void this agreement, and I will annihilate your entire fleet with every man aboard. Which I also have to do should you decline."

"You sound like you expect to win against my remaining two battle groups."

"That, and any reinforcement that might reach you. I will not hold you responsible for the actions of any AP ships arriving after our agreement, but I won't allow any threat in my back."

"I can only surrender my own battle group. I fear it's my fellow commandants' duty to continue the fight."

"He's playing for time," she said to Mo and Yusef. "He's anticipating reinforcements. We can expect Admiral Santiago to follow us from Appalahoo, but while Cortez came here, he probably sent for more ships."

"How can you tell?" Mo asked.

"He brought no corvettes. Santiago had one, and when he arrived at Klondike, it headed right for the departure point — as messenger, to confirm our presence to others. Those will follow, while Cortez is supposed to nail us down here."

"So what will you tell him?"

"Listen." She checked her position and opened the outside line again. "Admiral Cortez, you should know better than to play me for a fool. You're the one in charge, alive, in good health, and still able to transmit commands. Whatever your orders, as flag officer you're ultimately responsible — you've got the last word here. Note that I'm preparing to act on my announcement within the next five centicycles. Surrender now."

— We'll take the entire ship? —

Start with the aft section.

Cortez didn't answer. In the meantime, a data packet from *APS Retaliator* arrived. It contained the declaration of war Cortez had mentioned and Ravenport should have published in advance of his attack, with all safeties intact — and it contained a nasty Trojan, meant to mess with their programming.

— Skillfully written, but futile against us. —

I should be pissed off, but I feel rather entertained. We're in place — start the process.

Assiduous' legs spread out to reach around *Vindicator's* rear, found contact, and started the skimming process.

No surprise, Cortez' next call came soon. *"Fleet Commander, what's happening there?"*

"Admiral Cortez — as announced, I'm now collecting the valuable resources your flagship represents. I strongly recommend you evacuate your crew now — organic resources remaining aboard will not be spared. You may use your unarmed shuttles."

"Please — I need my assault shuttles, too, to save all of my crew.

We won't use their armament. Please!"

"He's desperate," Mo said.

She smiled grimly. "Granted, Cortez. Don't test my patience."

CHAPTER FOUR

Syreen kept a close watch on Cortez' assault shuttles. They were too close to allow them even an attempted shot — the easiest solution was to block their gun controls, the same way she and *Assiduous* had taken over the AP's missiles, but she didn't want to show her hand, so she withheld that option until she'd need it.

She also watched the two other battle groups, but those didn't move away from their positions around Klondike's main departure points.

Raydancer continued its silent approach. There was no need to announce the presence of potential hostages to their adversaries.

At the same time, she was well aware of the presence of the two men — Mo and Yusef — on her bridge. Haiki was with Gwen, and they had found the ship's lounge.

We shouldn't assimilate all resources. Can we separate provisions for our guests?

— That is what I always do. —

No, I mean, with their containers, so that they appear more familiar?

— I can do that, too. —

Please.

"Syreen?"

"Yes, Mo?"

"Are you still with us? You look absent."

She opened her eyes. "Sorry. I've been busy saving our asses. You've seen the plot?"

16

"Indeed. What happened to their ships?"

"My EMP cannon fried the big ones' wiring. On the destroyers, I used my concussion pulser."

"What's that?"

"That weapon causes a gravity vibration—strong enough to break ships of that size."

"Syreen . . . what's happening with you, if I may dare to ask?"

She smiled. "I'm currently integrated with *Assiduous*—with my ship. We are one, one body, one brain. We can see, hear, feel, smell what each other does, without delay. However, I could leave this seat any time I wanted—currently I don't, and that's for these nasty assault shuttles."

"It looks—awkward."

"To me, it feels natural, but I understand why you might see it that way. The physical contact is necessary for our integration."

"Physical contact . . . uh, I mean . . ."

"I know. It looks intimate, but our mental contact is so much more intimate that our physical union doesn't matter."

"But the—uh, punctures?"

"Oh—yes, our blood circuits are connected, too. After all, keeping his pilot alive and in good health is my partner's primary concern. My body must be fed, and all."

"So, it's a kind of drip feed?"

"Yes, and more. Anything I need."

Mo frowned. "And the ship is partially organic, so it can tend to your physical needs?"

"*Assiduous* is a living ship, Mo, not a semi-organic vehicle. A person with his own mind."

"A person . . . how? A copy or mirror of its pilot? Does it adapt to you?"

"*He* will eventually adapt to me, as I will adapt to him. Primarily, as the older and more experienced of us, he will teach me, and I will contribute my anarchic ideas."

"Older, huh? Much older?"

"Older, as in *ancient*, Mo. Many megacycles. Older than my Duchy — and that's one of the oldest star nations. Older than human expansion in space. He's seen it all."

The merchant captain shook his head. "I'm not sure I understand what you're talking about."

"Perhaps that will come later." She sensed new data and frowned. "New arrivals."

CHAPTER FIVE

Yusef quietly listened to the conversation of his old skipper with his most recent skipper. He wasn't sure if she still considered herself his current skipper, if she still had a task for him after their frigate *Bumblebee* was gone.

He wasn't sure if he'd still call her skipper. Too alien was her current appearance, too alien the way she *connected* to her ship — too frivolous for his taste. To publicly insert a tool into her most private parts — no, that was too much for him.

Okay, she'd told him about her skirmisher rides — but inside a one-seater, it was a kind of private act, not as public as *this*.

And this ship — it felt wrong. It smelled wrong. It looked wrong. Perhaps he was too traditional, too old-fashioned, but ships should smell of paint, rust and sweat, should look functional and square, should feel firm, cold, and edgy.

He smiled at this thought. Who was old-fashioned, if this ship indeed was many megacycles old?

No, not *if*. This ship *was* old, stinking old. No one could deny that. Was it jealousy? That this *vehicle* was allowed to stick its tool in where he couldn't? That she obviously enjoyed it — in public, before his eyes?

Or was it jealousy about the fact that his services as pilot weren't asked for anymore? He felt the weight of the decoration on his chest. That he could no longer assist her, because this ship could do everything better, not even counting its superior firepower?

I had better think of how we get out of this mess alive.

"New arrivals," she announced, and new lights appeared

in the three-dimensional plot above her seat.

He wasn't surprised to recognize another battle cruiser, three light cruisers and four destroyers. "This Santiago fellow?"

Syreen smiled. "The *Valkyrie*, yes."

"We're still outnumbered. What are your plans?"

"For now, we're feeding. Once we've picked up my corvette, we're on our way."

The new symbols turned toward Klondike's planet. He pointed at *Valkyrie*. "That doesn't look good."

Mo shook his head. "No—and this world has no AP CEOs for their protection."

"I only wonder how much time it'll take him to make his announcement."

"He'll first review the battle recordings."

"I doubt they'll teach him anything he's ready to learn."

On the plot, he could see their ship disconnecting from the powerless battle cruiser and turning toward a smaller symbol.

"We better get prepared," Syreen said. "He's up to no good."

Other symbols lit up. The two battle groups that had come with Cortez were leaving their interception positions and heading inward.

He pointed up. "They're coming for us."

"They think so, yes." The Navigator wiggled her toes.

Yusef tried to relate the casual movement to their dangerous situation. How could she appear so relaxed?

"Time's playing in our favor," she said. "Once we're reunited, nothing can stop us. Um—I'm repeating myself, am I?"

Another thought came to his mind. "Oh, Syreen—I don't know, did all of us leave the entrance hall, or whatever you call it? I didn't see a second airlock hatch."

"We don't need any. Relax, they're all in the lounge, all but the two of you, and the hangar won't be airless at any time."

CHAPTER SIX

Syreen counted down the centicycles for their rendezvous with *Raydancer*. She knew Santiago could estimate the right moment as precisely as she could, but he didn't have access to her programming.

She knew he'd try something nasty on her.

We're prepared.

"*Raydancer*, prepare for docking in two."

Assiduous leaped forward, saving eight centicycles of its original vector.

She felt the small ship penetrate her center door, felt a slight tingle in her own crotch, but discarded that feeling. *Later.*

Once *Raydancer* was safely settled and locked in place, she directed *Assiduous* on a new course.

"Welcome back, guys. Say hello to each other while I take care of some AP rogues."

"Rogues?" Mo echoed.

"Rogues." She highlighted a new item in the plot.

"No! But—he can't . . ." the merchant exclaimed.

And here comes the message.

"*Duchy Fleet* Assiduous, *this is APS Valkyrie, Admiral Santiago speaking. You may have tricked Cortez into surrender, but you won't play your tricks on me. We've launched a kinetic strike against Klondike One. Once you surrender and allow our boarding party in, we'll do our best to redirect the projectile. Of course, should you attack our ships, the planet will suffer the consequences.*"

Synchronized with the end of his transmission, the three

battle cruisers launched their stingships.

The next message was from Cortez. *"Santiago, you can't do that. Kinetic strikes against civil worlds are under edict!"*

That was exactly what the AP regulations aboard *Raydancer* told her. It was the same as her teachers had told her about Duchy regulations.

Now *Assiduous'* memories told her more.

— We, the People are supposed to enforce this edict. —

We will.

"APS *Valkyrie,* Admiral Santiago, this is Syreen, Navigator of *Assiduous.* I have evidence of a launched kinetic strike against an inhabited world. You're found guilty of a violation against Edict Number Two. *Valkyrie's* crew failed to stop you from doing so or even assisted you in your misdoing and thus is found guilty, too. It is my duty to sanction this violation. Other AP ships, you are given one and only one opportunity to stand back, by cutting your engines immediately after receiving this message and announcing your unconditional surrender. Note that a collective failure to comply may subject your fleet and your home world to coercive measures."

Prepare two gauge torpedoes.

— Ready. —

She took a deep breath and counted to ten.

Launch.

"Watch."

"We've launched a kinetic strike against Klondike One."

Yusef felt a clamp around his heart when he saw the highlighted projectile and its trajectory. Although he knew no one down on Klondike, he wished them spared from this nightmare.

How can an officer spend innocent lives so recklessly? Yusef clenched his fists.

Cortez' protest at least assured Yusef his expectations

weren't entirely wrong, and Syreen's instant and grim reply helped him feel a little better — he was on the right side of this conflict. *But will her strong words help in the end? She surely could destroy the battle cruiser as she did with* Vindicator, *but what can she do with the massive asteroid Santiago brought?*

His eyes widened. *Santiago planned this from the beginning! Warships don't carry rocks around for fun. What kind of people are they?*

Her deep breath brought him back. Poor woman — now she had to watch innocent people die only because she had picked this inhabited system to park her ship.

"Watch," the Navigator announced.

He saw two golden symbols travel toward *Valkyrie* and the asteroid, covering several light seconds within a blink. The symbols of both ship and asteroid disappeared.

"The sentence has been executed," she said aloud and over the lines. "There will be no kinetic strike. The public will be instructed on the reestablishment of effective edicts enforcement in due time."

Mo wasn't sure about those edicts — he knew there were some regulations on armed conflicts, but he'd never bothered to dig deeper into them. Merchant guild rules were what mattered to him.

"What was that?" he asked.

"Gauge torpedoes," she said absently. "Weapons of enforcement. The edict must not be violated."

"What does a gauge torpedo do?"

"It destroys the ties of matter."

He wasn't entirely sure what that meant, but the single line indicated something final. It sent a shiver down his spine.

"I assume there's not much to salvage then?"

"You'd have a hard time proving there's ever been something substantial."

He considered that and shivered again.

Meanwhile, first reactions to Santiago's announcement began to trickle in. Syreen prepared her next move while listening.

"Here's Klondike Port Authority. What do you mean, kinetic strike? This is madness — can someone help us? By all ghosts in space, what's going on here?"

"Admiral Santiago, this is Commodore Gardner. Sir, I must formally protest. This operation expressly violates our regulations. Return to appropriate rules of engagement immediately. Valkyrie *bridge crew, it is my duty to remind you of our rules for relief of command.* Assiduous, *neither I nor the crews of my battle group have any part in this."*

They'd soon enough see the result of her reply. Gardner's protest came too late for *Valkyrie's* crew, anyway. But the others — was she willing to grant them a little time for making up their minds, or would she insist on her claim of *immediate* surrender?

Enough people died today. Gardner may be another of those officers I'd like to keep in command.

But what of Santiago's battle group?

The three light cruisers, as well as four destroyers, had indeed cut their engines. Their transponders signaled surrender.

"Assiduous, this is Captain Bakr of AP light cruiser Squirrel, *second in command of* Valkyrie's *battle group. I herewith formally surrender the ships of our battle group. Please allow us a course correction so that we won't run into the planet. Planned parameters of this correction follow."*

"Captain Bakr, you're allowed to enter orbit around Klondike One, and you're also allowed to collect your stingships and their pilots before doing so."

"Here's Klondike port authority again. Can someone please explain what's going on here?"

"Klondike port authority, this is Syreen. I have to apologize for drawing the AP's attention to your world. I hadn't foreseen them resorting to such actions. Whether you file a formal complaint or not is up to you, but be assured I will follow up on this crime."

And here came the next caller — Gardner.

"Assiduous, *please clarify the meaning of* coercive actions *against our homeworld.*"

"Commodore Gardner, you were aware of the kinetic projectile *Valkyrie* carried, and you failed to act against its deployment. This is the second time I requested your surrender, and you're still playing for time. My patience has come to an end. I will not ask again."

What am I waiting for?

No message from the other remaining battle group. They kept perfect silence and showed no sign of surrender, either.

She closed her eyes and listened. Klondike sang a song of troubles. Tiny troubles, tinier troubles, and nuisances.

Syreen sighed and set course for Gardner's *Retaliator.*

We will need seven gauge torpedoes.

— EMP cannon or concussion pulser are more than sufficient to deal with a few light cruisers. —

I will not waste those torpedoes.

— What do you see? —

Nothing yet. Klondike told me of five worthy targets.

— My Navigator! —

Again, something her ship wasn't used to? There seemed to be no limit to new surprises.

"Crew and guests, prepare for battle action."

CHAPTER SEVEN

Syreen ignored Gardner's next two queries for more details about *coercive actions* like the first. She didn't bother to answer at all — she already knew what the commodore was waiting for, what kind of reinforcements Santiago had promised.

She had to be quick — and yet, she shouldn't give too much of *Assiduous'* abilities away, as Captain Bakr's ships were surely recording her every single move.

So she limited herself to frigate parameters. *Assiduous* wasn't happy with this *crawl,* but accepted her reasoning.

When *Retaliator* called again, Gardner sounded less confident than before.

"Assiduous, *you're not answering my calls. If you continue your approach like this, I have no choice but to resume battle."*

— We're reaching effective targeting range. —

No need to delay the inevitable.

She entered deep integration.

Fire.

The gauge torpedo hit *Retaliator* dead center. Like *Valkyrie* before, the large battle cruiser simply vanished.

There was some surprised chatter on the radio — panicking calls from the battle group's light cruisers, demanding calls from Klondike's orbit, and a single short transmission from the last intact battle group. It was skillfully encrypted — for human standards — and translated into *break up.*

She noticed their increasing engine activity and futile attempt to change course before she dealt out three casual concussion pulses, smashing their sturdy hulls into pieces, and turned toward her last targets.

The sharp turn she had to perform at high relativistic speed would give some more of *Assiduous'* skills away. She couldn't help it if she wanted to be done with all her current enemies before their reinforcements arrived.

"Assiduous — *this is Commodore Hernandez of* APS *Indefati-gable. Why do you refuse to communicate? Can't we negotiate?"*

Finally!

Syreen surfaced from her integration. Speaking was easier this way.

"Commodore Hernandez, like Commodore Gardner, you witnessed Santiago's violation of the edict, and unlike him, you did not even oppose it. You received my order to stand back, cut your engines, and signal your surrender, and you failed to comply. I cannot fail to execute my sentence, so I must incapacitate your ships. However, I'm in a good mood. Should you decide to declare your surrender now and evacuate your crews to the shuttles, I will not hurt them, and as with Cortez, this includes your assault shuttles. Don't mistake my mercy for weakness, though — make me regret my generosity, and you and your crews will pay the price."

She gazed at Mo. "What do you think? Will he accept my offer?"

"He should. He watched what you did with Gardner's ships. He can't be that dense." Mo frowned. "He could have called earlier."

"Yes — that's what worries me."

"He must have a hidden agenda."

"He *is* the hidden agenda. I doubt he pays heed to my last warning." She shook her head. "No. I should put it differ-ently — I'm sure he'll try a dirty trick. The question is, which one."

Only, he doesn't know what we can do.

"I must be ready."

CHAPTER EIGHT

Syreen sank back into deep integration.
— We must not expend ourselves. —
We won't.

She watched tiny objects appear around the four AP ships. Their size, drive signatures, scanner echoes, matched those of other AP shuttles. Other than Cortez, Hernandez could evacuate an intact battle cruiser, which would explain the greater number of small vessels.

Their drive signatures almost *match a shuttle's.*

— The cruisers' reactors are shutting down, but their guns are still hot. —

Running on capacitors. Against us, they wouldn't get more than one shot off anyway. So they'd have to make that one count. However, that's a decoy.

— A decoy? —

We're incapacitating their big ships anyway, so Hernandez is showing us something to catch our attention. Meanwhile, he's bringing his snipers into position.

— The assault shuttles? —

They're decoys, too. A minor threat to hide the real nasties — what do we think about where his stingships are? Their hangar is empty.

— We can't see stingships. —

No. But we can see twelve shuttles more than Cortez had. Twelve drive signatures with a strange jitter, and twelve hot guns.

— We see. —

We told him not to try tricks.

— What will we do? —

First we'll take out the tanks. They may be decoys, but their guns are still hot. Then we'll swat the stingships. And then — we'll get into position for their main force.

— Will we let Hernandez get away? —

No. We will feed on them later, as dessert. When we're done with the main body.

— We agree with this prioritization. —

Of course we do. By the way, we seem to get the hang of talking with ourselves.

She smiled. In deep integration, when the outer world seemed to slow down, she needed something to cling to, lest she be lost in the vast expanse of *Assiduous'* perceptions.

Launch.

The gauge torpedo shot forward. To her, time seemed to expand while it covered the distance. *So slow!*

Indefatigable was no more.

The three light cruisers were waiting in line.

We don't think so.

The tension between her thighs grew.

— They still could hurt us. —

We're not close enough yet.

Three light cruisers suddenly fired all they had — a dangerous amount of energy, enough to kill much larger ships.

She casually swayed out of the path of danger and triggered a prepared message.

"To whom it may concern — the AP just violated the declared terms of surrender by reintroducing an abandoned ship into battle. Their crews are no longer protected by universal laws of war. "

How long would Hernandez hold his stingships back?

Small as they were, operating as a pack they could take out a much larger ship. In this regard, they were no different from the skirmishers Syreen had grown up with. Their key success factor was coming close enough to make their shot count, though — whereas their size made them hard to hit.

It was a cynical deal — sacrificing a significant share to get a few guns through, in order to score a critical hit. The odds of survival were bad for skirmisher jockeys. Her own fate — and that of her former wingmates — was proof enough. She alone had survived, but her skirmisher hadn't.

No more time.

The spark sprang from her clit, jumped toward the foremost shuttle, split in three, struck three more — split again, hit nine, split and struck . . . and then, there was peace.

We must get into position.

CHAPTER NINE

M o let out a deep breath. "Jeez, it's over."
The Navigator didn't react. Instead, the plot showed them changing course again.

Should I be glad I can see what's happening, or would I rather be oblivious of our situation? One thing's for sure, though – she *doesn't need the three-dimensional display.*

He felt for his own seat — warm, and perfectly adapted to his shape and size. Too perfect to make him feel comfortable.

"It's over, right?"

She seemed to look right through him. Her voice sounded distant. "The hard part's still to come. Look."

The plot shrank. New symbols were added, approaching fast.

"Hyperspace?" he asked. "You can look through the planes?"

"We can't. The stars can, and they tell us."

"Well." He pointed at the symbols. "Do they also tell you what's coming there?"

"Sure. Tiny troubles, tinier troubles, and nuisances. Nuisances like light cruisers or destroyers. Tinier troubles like battle cruisers."

A cold fist seemed to grasp his heart. "What are tiny troubles, then?"

"Why, dreadnaughts, of course."

Syreen felt Mo's consternation. She also felt Yusef's fatalistic silence.

"Don't worry, guys. I'll get you through these troubles alive and well. I know how to deal with AP dreadnaughts."

She was confident in that regard — what worried her were the nuisances. There were simply too many of them.

No. Many, but not too many. We just have to play our cards well.

— Cards? —

Never mind.

"I remember," Mo said. "You abandoned your ship and entered the dreadnaught. Very reassuring for us."

— That approach is not advisable. —

He's joking. We must focus on battle preparations now. Can we have a spark ready and still launch the gauge torpedoes?

No, she wouldn't have had to ask — the respective process unfolded in her mind. Charging their legs separately would feel less comfortable, but it was supposed to work.

Syreen listened once again, and this time, together with *Assiduous*.

Here they come.

— We are ready. —

First, one battle group dropped from hyperspace, consisting of one battle cruiser with three light cruisers, four destroyers and two corvettes. Destroyers and corvettes immediately spread outward, opening the way system-inward for the larger warships. Targeting lasers reached out with searching fingers. Their lasers and pulse cannons were hot, ready for the kill.

Two dreadnaughts followed next. They, too, arrived with hot cannons, and immediately started to spill clouds of stingships.

Behind them, two more battle groups arrived, comprising two battle cruisers, six light cruisers, eight destroyers and four corvettes.

So a total of twenty-six full-size warships, six corvettes, and forty-eight stingships were approaching positions in an impressive pattern—well suited for the ships providing cover for each other while leaving an open firing range.

This AP fleet was much larger than the one that had invaded her home. They were prepared to face substantial resistance and crush it anyway.

They weren't prepared to meet a living ship at full power.

Launch.

Five gauge torpedoes dashed toward five large and slow targets. Slow but not defenseless—their computer had acquired that strange, U-shaped target and opened fire with pulse cannons, lasers and a score of missiles.

Assiduous swayed upward. Most of the energy beams and packets missed, but a few grazed the living ship's skin.

Ouch.

— Nothing serious. Just a few scratches. —

The torpedoes didn't miss their designated targets, and five powerful AP warships ceased to exist.

Assiduous and Syreen dodged another few of the better-aimed shots before she released the painful charge in her thighs.

The electromagnetic pulse covered a large part of the enemy formation. Computers, reactors, guns, aggregates, and wiring of stingships and missiles were fried. The light cruisers fared little better—their lights went dark, their active machinery died. Secondary aggregates kicked in, kept them habitable, would allow them to eventually rejoin battle.

Destroyers and corvettes had survived the strike, had been outside the affected area. Some seemed to be stunned anyway—their crews perhaps shocked by their opponent's ferocity?

Others stubbornly continued the fight. Some shots hit home.

Ouch!

Syreen and her partner struck back. Concussion pulses smashed one insolent destroyer after the other.

Five didn't shoot, so they were spared.

The corvettes were running toward an exit point. Syreen sent them another prepared message.

"AP ships—unless you cut your engines immediately, you're considered legitimate targets."

They quickly obeyed.

— What now? —

We'll collect valuable resources in our path, namely those who took part in the violation of the edict. Do we have room enough to harbor my frigate?

— It is damaged, so why bother? —

The situation has changed. Its memory now contains authentic evidence of the course of events. People would rather trust an AP ship's record than ours. By the way, couldn't we repair it?

— I understand. The answer is Yes, for both questions. —

CHAPTER TEN

M o turned around when four new persons arrived on the bridge. Two wore green uniforms similar to Syreen's, so they had to be Duchy personnel. They had to be *Raydancer's* crew, then.

The other two must have arrived with the corvette, too. The tall athlete radiated *bodyguard,* and the last had to be his protégé.

Mo rose and reached out a hand.

"Mo — ex-merchant captain, now Syreen's staff captain. Nice to meet you."

The uniformed men saluted casually.

"Private Stephan Smith. Hi, Mo."

"Private Herman Doeken. Welcome, Sir."

The last man took his hand. "Dragutin Petran. Call me Drake. In case you wonder what I'm doing here — I'm an archaeologist. I helped Syreen find this formidable ship. This is my bodyguard, Crow."

"Hello, Mo," Crow said.

Mo waved at Yusef. "Yusef, my former pilot, and until recently pilot of Duchy frigate *Bumblebee.*"

Private Smith gazed at Yusef's chest. "Two kills and a Silver Star? Wow. Congratulations."

Mo wouldn't let go of Drake's hand. "Can you tell me some more about *this?*"

"You mean *Assiduous?*"

"Yes, and what this is all about. It seems the Associated Planets are desperate to get hold of Syreen. She repeatedly called herself a *Navigator,* with a capital N, and there's no doubt she's exceptional, but I still don't see the whole picture."

Drake glanced at her nude figure, entangled in her seat. "You might already have noticed she's not entirely human, although she's got the looks. She is a member of a race we archaeologists call the *Forgotten People,* because there's so little information on them. To be honest, I didn't come across that name myself until I found that ancient star map. That map ultimately led us to this living ship, and you can't imagine the surprise when we found out she's the key to its activation."

Mo smirked and gestured at her. "Well, we were quite surprised when we found her in this seat like this."

"Yes. They're connected — also mentally." Drake pointed up. "She probably doesn't need this map, it's just for us. You've noticed that she can dodge shots traveling at light speed?"

"Yes. As she doesn't really need a computer to find jumps. If she didn't look so — so female . . . I don't know." He shook his head, then focused on Drake again. "How old is she?"

"As far as we know, she's twenty-four now."

"And this ship?"

"Some millennia. Enough to make star formations significantly different."

Mo tried to imagine how much time stars needed to *significantly* move. For navigation purposes, their positions could be assumed to be fixed.

The map caught his attention. "What's happening there?"

Drake looked up, where their own symbol was approaching another. "I assume we're feeding now."

CHAPTER ELEVEN

Klondike didn't sing of additional hyperspace travelers, so Syreen decided she could leave her seat. Sharing *Assiduous'* feeding sensations was *disturbing*.

She felt itches in her crotch, at her thighs, at her neck.

There's always a price to pay.

The men were watching her placing her bare feet on the deck.

Drake spoke up first. "The ship appears larger to me."

"Yes," she agreed and rose. "Welcome back aboard. Assiduous has regrown to full size and full power. You've seen what we can do."

"It looked easy."

"It was easy." She sighed. "Too easy for such a massacre. They weren't ready to listen to reason. I'm still not sure whether the Association's officers are generally so fanatic or whether their master sent only his most dedicated followers."

Another memory came up, images about her unpleasant encounter with the head of the AP's forces. Had their supreme commander, a member of the *People* like her, meddled with his subordinates' minds the way he had tried to with her? Had he *forced* them to violate the edict?

I must be sure.

"*Assiduous*, once you're finished with this one, take us to Hernandez. I must interrogate him."

– *Do we want to answer the incoming call?* –

So they could communicate without the seat now, too? *Yes.*

"Assiduous, *this is Captain Bakr. What are you doing with our*

37

ships and crews? I must protest!"

Transmit. "Captain Bakr, any ship which has taken part in violation of Edict Number Two will contribute its resources. *All* resources."

"You didn't even warn them!"

"Does he have a point there?" Mo asked.

Syreen shook her head. "No."

Put me up again.

"Captain Bakr, I do not negotiate with a fleet popping out of hyperspace with hot guns and active targeting lasers. They were prepared to enter a battle, and they got their battle. Note that AP Commodore Hernandez violated the terms of surrender after I announced the sanctions. Listen."

Replay.

Assiduous produced her voice on the radio and internal speakers. *"Other AP ships, you are given one and only one opportunity to stand back, by cutting your engines immediately after receiving this message and announcing your unconditional surrender. Note that a collective failure to comply may subject your fleet and your home world to coercive measures."*

Syreen nodded, although Bakr couldn't see her. "Captain Bakr, I hope I can still count on your word, more than I could count on Hernandez' surrender. Don't give me reason to reconsider."

Cut the line.

She gazed through Mo. "The question remains what to do next. Right now, I can't carry prisoners, and I can't let them run wild. In the long term, I still have to chase the AP out of the Duchy — and by doing that, perhaps teach them to leave others alone."

"Won't work," Mo said. "From what I've seen so far, they won't stop."

"Just the opposite," Drake said. "Attack their fleet in your home system, and they'll start throwing asteroids there. How many such attacks can you repel, even with this impressively powerful *single* ship?"

"But what can I do? How can I make the AP stop their wrongdoing without shooting down each and every one of their ships?"

Drake shook his head. "I have no clue."

"But you're a historian."

"In the past, there have been wars. The missionary wars, later the guild wars—whoever won could establish new rules."

Syreen shook her head. "I must find a way to pacify the AP without war. Who could I ask?"

Herman gestured toward the historian. "That's it. You mentioned the guild wars. That's who we need—the guild."

"The guild?" Drake echoed.

"The merchants' guild. Tell them. They have no military power, but with the violation of your edict—they established similar rules, if I recall my lessons rightly, and they could proclaim an embargo over the AP."

"What will that be good for?" Drake asked.

"Oh, a lot," Mo chimed in. "Violate an embargo, and you can't register your cargo with the guild. You can't advertise free capacity. On many stations, you can't dock, you can't transship, you can't rent space. Worse, you can't draw bills on the guild, you can't pay your crew. You don't cross the guild."

"They're that powerful?" Drake asked. "What if they abuse their power?"

"Oh—should they play foul, merchants would unite and tell them. But merchants won't fight an embargo against a space nation that throws rocks on inhabited planets. They will do as the guild says and tell the AP *hey, we're sorry, but our funds are tied up with the guild.*" He turned to Syreen. "Do you have any contacts in the guild?"

"No." She frowned. That wasn't true. "Yes, I do. Herman, do you remember Jacomo?"

CHAPTER TWELVE

O*uch.*

Syreen woke up to a firm poke.

Herman's face lingered above her. "Sorry, skipper. When I started telling our story, you fell asleep. We let you, but there are several calls, and we think some might be urgent."

She found herself lying on the floor of *Assiduous'* bridge. She grabbed one arm rest of her pilot seat and pulled herself up. "Yeah, okay, I'm coming. Who's first?"

"Can I get you anything?"

"Uh, yes. It might be time for breakfast, and a hot forwine, please." She sat down on the edge of her seat, which gave in to provide her with better comfort. "Thanks, *Assiduous.* Who are the callers?"

Herman nodded and left.

– The planetary authorities demand explanations, especially regarding the hostile fleet in orbit. In short, Admiral Cortez asks for mercy and assistance. In addition, there are distress signals from many of the smaller vessels. –

"Okay, put me through to Cortez first."

She briefly considered her next line.

"Admiral Cortez, what are your concerns?"

The signal delay alone, caused by the limits of light speed, told her that he was still quite far away. She didn't have to check her plot.

"Thank you for accepting my call, Fleet Commander. I'm receiving distress calls from all sides – in many cases, from emergency suits only. My shuttles are already stuffed to the max. I ask for your

mercy – please let us help."

"Admiral Cortez, I'm no longer acting as Duchy Fleet Commander. In my role as enforcer of the edicts, please address me as *Navigator*. Having said that, I've taken note of your message to Santiago and appreciate it. You may assume command of Captain Bakr's light cruisers and deploy them and their shuttles for search-and-rescue operations throughout the system. You may accelerate up to ten percent light speed, and you will refrain from heating up your guns, otherwise this agreement will be void. Within these limits, you may act at your own discretion. Meanwhile, Commodore Hernandez and yourself will be my guests. We need to talk face to face."

Again, she had to wait for his reply.

"Navigator, I'm grateful for your generosity. I will instruct my crews to strictly comply with your rules, and I will have my shuttle pilot set course for a rendezvous with your remarkable ship immediately. I'm looking forward to meeting you."

She made *Assiduous* cut the line and let her gaze sweep across Drake, Yusef, and Mo. "Of course he is. He can't miss the chance to have a peek inside."

The three men nodded. None of them offered a comment — they seemed perfectly happy just gazing at her.

She was happy with any or all of them, but her duties weren't done, yet. *No time for a welcome party yet.* At least the next call wouldn't require those long delays.

"Klondike port authority, this is Navigator Syreen aboard the living ship *Assiduous*. I'm sorry for ignoring you for so long — I was somewhat busy protecting your world."

"Heck, navigator, what's a living ship? And what are all these warships doing here? They didn't come for our chicks, did they?"

"No. They came for one chick — me — and it wasn't about entertainment. It's all about power. I'd like to invite a delegation from Klondike to my ship, to show you around and explain what it's about. I've also invited two AP officers. They will have to answer questions, and you'll surely be interested in their statements." She frowned. "For the records, I herewith declare the enforcement of edicts reestablished in this system. Edict Number One proscribes deliberate damage to the fabric of space. Edict Number Two proscribes deliberate destruction, sterilization or rendering uninhabitable of worlds, especially, but not limited to, kinetic strikes, large-scale application of nuclear or biological weapons, and systematic destruction of geological stability. Edict Number Three proscribes deliberate interference with the genetic code of intelligent beings. These three edicts are non-negotiable."

"Navigator, I'm still not sure what you're talking about, but yeah, thanks for the invitation. May I bring along my second-in-command?"

"You may bring as many as your shuttle can carry, or, if you don't own a shuttle, I'll send you my corvette."

"Uh — yes, that would be kind. We don't have much need for shuttles down here, so I fear, well, the one we ought to use might be a bit worn down."

She shook her head. *You mean you didn't care about maintenance.*

"Okay, Klondike, *Raydancer* will pick you up in two cycles."

This time, she wouldn't wade through the small ship's computer. "Yusef, you can surely pilot a corvette. *Raydancer* is easy to handle. Would you be so kind?"

His face lit up. "Your corvette? The pirate killer? Sure."

Chapter Thirteen

Syreen met her guests in a room adjacent to the bridge. She wore her uniform with updated decorations — the sixty larger stars for confirmed kills of tanks alone made her chest look like a parade ground.

The two AP officers, Cortez and Hernandez, and the two civilians from Klondike had chosen opposite sides of the room and were silently gazing at each other.

"Welcome aboard, Admiral Cortez, Commodore Hernandez." She saluted and turned around. "Welcome, Mr. Lupus, Mr. Wong. I'm Syreen, Navigator of the living ship *Assiduous*. Please, have a seat."

The four men looked puzzled, even more so when five seats and a table literally grew out of the floor.

"May I offer you a drink? Would hot forwine be okay for you? Yes?"

The four men nodded.

"Fine. *Assiduous,* please."

Five mugs with steaming content appeared at the table center and moved outward. Syreen took her mug and raised it. "Please. Feel comfortable. Enough people were hurt today."

"Yeah." Hernandez stared at her. "You massacred them."

Syreen stared back. "Yes, and I enjoyed it. I feel satisfied because I relieved the galaxy, in particular this system, of people able and willing to commit the most atrocious crime thinkable. A kinetic strike against an inhabited world is a capital offense by all known standards, including your own AP regulations, and it's even worse that it wasn't attempted against a military target, but purely as blackmail. It's frightening to recognize it not as the act of one misled madman, but as a maneuver widely supported by many AP crews and officers — including you, Commodore Hernandez. This — the attempt to annihilate an entire world of non-combatants — is what *I* call a massacre."

Hernandez leaned forward and opened his mouth to protest.

Shut up. Her mental command silenced him.

"Your situation wasn't improved by your violation of parole. While you're both my guests, Admiral Cortez may look forward to becoming a prisoner of war. You, Hernandez, cannot claim this status anymore. By your own regulations, you've forfeited any legal rights you and your men might have had. As accomplices in a violation of Edict Number Two, you are an organic resource, available for digestion." She could sense fear rising within him. *Calm down.* "However, you're alive and invited to this discussion, because your sentence isn't nailed down yet. So, as long as you participate in a civilized discussion, you're free to voice your opinions and interpretations, even if you disagree with me. But, in order to disagree, you must hear my point of view first."

She glanced to the other side. "This will also enlighten our guests from Klondike, I'm sure. They have every right to hear what made their peaceful world subject to your attack, and they have every right to hear it from you."

The Navigator clapped her hands. "Okay — before we start, I want to point out one more fact. Again quoting your own AP regulations, any warship entering a foreign system with heated guns must be considered hostile and a legitimate target. The same applies to warships entering an ongoing battle of their own navy. So, all of your ships arriving after the first shot were legitimate targets for me, even disregarding the previous violation of Edict Number Two."

"I understand," Cortez said. "Can you explain your view on the edict anyway?"

"Of course. You know your own regulations include such an edict, too. I don't know anything about its origin or whether our regulations are related, but effectively, they proscribe the same thing. There are two major differences. First, your regulations require a court-martial, mine don't. You could say, the culprit picks his own sentence. Second, your regulations condemn the actor. The People's Edict ultimately condemns the society providing the culprit with the means of violation—that is, giving him command over his ship."

Cortez paled.

Syreen nodded. "Yes, you've got it. It's no longer just an unprovoked attack on a civil space station with thousands of innocent victims. It's a whole navy gone rogue, and this evil must be eradicated before the entire galaxy suffers—no, in fact, it's a bit late to say that. Have you heard about the way many AP crews perform their *inspections* of merchant ships, and what they do when they find a ship's cat?" She didn't have to wait for his reply. "Yes, you've heard. You've surely also heard of *polite* AP visits to independent star nations? The arrogance of power in action? It's a disease. Your navy is deeply infested."

Cortez slowly nodded. "I see."

"As in *I hear what you're saying?*"

"No. I see—I've witnessed the misbehavior you're talking about, even among my crew, and I've let it happen. Our superiors told us that a certain level of fear would help keep things under control. And—who would care about a ship's cat? Everyone knows what job they've chosen." He raised both hands. "Don't get me wrong—I'm just quoting. No."

Cortez shook his head, took his hands down again, and replied to himself. "To be true, I've bought into that crap. It worked, and it helped my crew to some stress relief, if you know what I mean."

"I know," Syreen said. "I've traveled as a ship's cat a few times. It's not easy to get a lift with a hauler."

"And what's that got to do with us?" Hernandez asked.

Mr. Lupus and Mr. Wong glanced at him, then focused on Syreen.

"Good question," she said. "The short answer is—you're members of that same navy. You've witnessed the violation of the edict, and personally, you, Hernandez, provided more proof of the foulness inside your navy when you violated your parole."

Both officers frowned.

The Navigator smiled. "Nevertheless, you tried to do the best for your crew and still get your mission done. You showed initiative and courage, and set up an almost perfect trap. The best you could do in your situation. You showed bad judgment by trying to cheat *me*—but even that's somehow understandable."

Hernandez stared at her. "What do you want to tell me?"

"I don't want to hold grudges. I can't say I'm sorry for what I did to stop you, but that's over. I must be looking forward."

Mr. Lupus cleared his throat. "Excuse me, but before you start looking forward, can someone *please* explain what all this crap's been about?"

"Well." Syreen leaned forward. "I'm willing to take half the blame. A while ago, I parked my ship here in Klondike's corona to recharge. Like today, I was short of shuttles, so I used my corvette instead to travel dirtside. From here, different merchants took me to Nysa, the AP's main world."

"Why? Doesn't seem to be a nice place—or, better put, a place of nice people."

"It is a nice place, with nice people, not-so-nice people, and a few truly mean bastards—which I had to learn the hard way. Originally, I came to learn why they had attacked my home world, the Duchy, in the first place."

"Did you find out?"

"Yes. Their supreme commander — he demands to be called *master* — wants to get his hands on some ancient *relic,* which he hoped to find on my home world."

"A relic? What would that be good for?" Lupus ignored the two AP officers, who were very attentively listening.

She went on, "He expected such a relic to give him power. The power to control a living ship."

"Oh." Lupus raised both eyebrows. "A ship like yours, right? Capable of defeating a whole fleet of warships — under control of a man who'd just drop asteroids on civilized worlds? That's a nightmare. Please tell me he didn't find it."

"He did, only he didn't recognize it when he had it — and then, he lost it."

"And you found it, came back, and took the ship."

"Nah." Wong shook his head. "She brought the ship here. She had it before. Did you take it along on your journey?"

"Close." Syreen opened her arms. "This is the *relic.*"

All four men made puzzled faces.

"He didn't understand either. All you need to fly a living ship is a Navigator. Me."

CHAPTER FOURTEEN

Yusef walked along *Raydancer's* left flank. Here and there, scratches, pits, and blisters told of the corvette's lively past. A quick browse through the small ship's log had told him of several interesting encounters, and the reprogrammed controls for jumps and targeting clearly showed Syreen's precise style.

It was easy to fly, swift and fast, but it felt wrong to him.

He gazed across the hangar, or entrance hall—he wasn't sure what to call the spacious room in the living ship's center.

At the far end, he could spot a much bulkier shape, wrapped in a cocoon of green and golden threads—or branches?

Inside the cocoon, *his* severely damaged and worn-out frigate *Bumblebee* was enjoying a strange repair process, and as much as he disliked many of this living ship's aspects, he admired the way *Assiduous* treated the ship that had earned him his first military decorations.

The frigate felt almost as swift and fast as the much smaller corvette, was at least as easy to fly, but had much more jump capacity and firepower. He couldn't imagine returning to the old haulers he'd piloted before.

Chiara nudged his elbow.

He turned to her. "Oh, hey, I didn't notice you coming. Sorry."

"Brooding over your secret love?"

How had she learned about his soft spot for Syreen? "Hey, Chiara, I—uh . . ."

"No worries, friend. Each pilot I knew was married to his ship first, second, and third. I won't change that." She pointed at the cocoon. "She's beautiful. I won't forget the moment I first saw her — my escape from a fate surely worse than death. She came down to the surface to rescue me, offered me shelter and took me with her." Chiara snuggled into his arms. "She fought well. If Syreen will allow you to keep *Bumblebee,* I hope you'll take me along. I'll keep her tidy."

"Uh, well . . ."

"Hush." She pulled his head close and sealed his lips with a kiss.

CHAPTER FIFTEEN

Syreen watched the comprehension grow in her audience. Cortez was the first to speak up. "You mean, there is no token or key or anything? Just a skilled pilot?"

"Yes, and no. There is no technical device, but this ship wouldn't open up even for the best pilot ever. You need a key, and that key must be a descendant of the same race that built living ships around a hundred megacycles ago."

"But you just said all you need is you yourself."

She nodded and waited.

Mr. Lupus picked up the thread. "You said, you are a navigator—no, you said, you're to be addressed as Navigator. You also said these AP guys came for a chick—for you, while they obviously thought they came for a key, right? A moment ago, you said you're all that's needed to fly this ship, just before you explained it takes a descendant of the original builders. The only conclusion is—you are such a descendant. But you also look perfectly human to me—no offense meant. Does that mean a specific family of humans built this ship?"

"Close, except for your last conclusion. No, I'm not human. I'm a member of those folks nowadays called the Forgotten People, and only a member of the People can fly this ship."

She focused on Cortez and Hernandez again, who were both still struggling to digest her last statement. "To be precise, only a skilled female pilot of the People can fly this ship. No male. Not even your *master*."

"Our master? What's he got to do with this?" Cortez asked.

"He's of the People, too."

"How can you tell?"

"We met on Nysa. I could sense he's my kind. He could have recognized me for what I am, too—only he was too busy basking in his own haughtiness."

Cortez smirked. "I can imagine. Didn't he ask you?"

"His primary intent was to break me first—by torture—and interrogate me after."

The four men's faces showed disgust.

"Torture?" Hernandez finally asked, staring into his mug.

"Hammer, whip, pinchers, a scalpel to skin me—he employed a very skilled torturer."

The commodore shook his head. "He can't do that—such behavior is illegal even for a supreme officer. No, especially for an officer."

Cortez clenched his right fist and stared at his fellow officer. "But such behavior matches the orders we received all too well. Secret orders, of course, and by even mentioning them I'm violating my vow."

"You shouldn't—" Hernandez began.

Cortez shook his head. "You know it's all wrong. You could call sending our entire fleet out to hunt a single rogue woman down a kind of folly—but everything after that primary goal was fishy from the start."

He focused on the two locals. "Our instructions are quite explicit. Nothing should stop us. If necessary, we are expected to crush local resistance either by pure firepower or by taking coercive measures against the general populace. When I first read my orders, I thought my superiors were just trying to make a point. But no, they were to be taken literally. When I last met Santiago, he told me of a meeting with Admiral Horace."

He glanced at Hernandez. "You remember Horace?"

"Yes—old school, a good man. He'd never accepted those orders at face value."

"Until he was sent a special instructor. Santiago told of a guy who always stayed close to Horace. Lieutenant stripes, untidy, smelly, but with a gaze that made Santiago shiver — at least that's what he said. He also said Horace flinched each time that instructor moved."

"Scary." Hernandez turned to Syreen. "What do you make of that?"

"I met one of them. The master's puppets. Not nice. I had to have him shot down."

"Lucky moment."

"Yes, you could say so." Syreen wouldn't tell him that her mental command had urged the two AP marine soldiers to shoot the ugly creature in his back.

Mr Lupus put down his mug. "Did I understand right? You were basically ordered to threaten or kill us in order to make her comply with your demands?"

Cortez met his gaze and nodded. "Yes, in essence, that's exactly what we were supposed to do."

"And if she had given in, you'd have taken her and that ship to your master?"

"Such are my orders, yes."

"To give even more power to a man who's already ignoring each and every rule mankind has agreed upon." Lupus turned to Syreen. "I'm glad you won. I'm glad we're still alive, but I'm not sure if I'd have been happy if you'd given in."

"Klondike would probably be one of the last worlds to suffer from his oppression," Wong said. "But by then, we'd have already seen scores of refugees trying to escape his grasp. I mean, our people are no angels, but as long as you know how to handle them, there's no serious trouble."

Lupus nodded. "In any case, the more I learn about this master, the less I like the thought of him having access to this impressive ship you call a living ship. By the way, why — because some parts are organic?"

"Nah, because he *is* alive. *Assiduous,* welcome our guests."

His deep male voice seemed to come from everywhere. *"Welcome, Mr. Lupus, Mr. Wong, Admiral Cortez, Commodore Hernandez. Would you like a refill of your mugs?"*

CHAPTER SIXTEEN

M o leaned back and patted his armrest. "One thing's for sure. This fellow knows how to grow comfortable chairs out of nothing."

Drake grinned. "Not exactly out of nothing."

"Yeah, but you know what I mean. Very convenient."

"I know." Drake glanced at his bodyguard, Crow, then at Herman and Stephan, the two soldiers their skipper had brought with her from her home world.

If that term really applies, Mo thought. *Who knows for sure?*

Drake pointed at Herman, but watched the merchant skipper. "How sure can we be your proposal works? Will the guild listen? The Associated Planets are the most powerful star nation on this side of the galaxy."

"We can't be sure," Mo said. "But what's the alternative? This madness must be stopped."

"Agreed. And yet—"

"Yet it's a dangerous path we're about to follow, yes. If the AP doesn't listen to reason, if they decide to add insult to injury, we might stir intergalactic war."

"That's what I was about to say. History teaches us you need more than brave traders to stop a totalitarian regime."

Mo smiled. "We do have more than that. We have a Navigator."

"Indeed, and I've seen her making miracles happen with regard to navigation. Plus we all witnessed her outstanding performance in the recent battle. But all that won't help her against the AP in its entirety. What if they tell her to stand down or watch a dozen planets be blown to pieces?"

Mo shook his head. "I don't know what would happen —
but I'd expect her to save at least half of them, and should
anything like that really happen, I'd expect every other warship captain coming to her aid."

"That won't help the billions of people killed."

"No, and believe me, I'm scared. But the guild managed to
stop a war before."

"You needn't tell me of the guild wars, but the situation
back then was different. I could tell you of at least a dozen
factors . . ."

"And I'd tell you of the one decisive factor."

Drake smiled. "I already said, I know she's good. But that
just won't do."

"You saw her when she started. From when we met her
until today, she surprised us again every day. If there's one
person able to clear up this mess, it's her. Did you hear what
she said? The stars are singing to her."

"How would that help?"

"I don't know. I only know one thing. I'm going with her.
Anywhere."

CHAPTER SEVENTEEN

Syreen waited.

Again, her guests needed time to digest that new piece of information.

Again, Cortez was the first to gather his wits. After a sip from his mug, he cleared his throat and said, "And that's why no one else could fly this ship. It wouldn't accept anyone else, right?"

She waited.

Cortez smiled. "You wouldn't accept anyone else, right?"

"*My sole purpose is to serve a Navigator, a woman of the People.*"

"And if our master would force you?"

"*There is no way a male could get control over me.*"

"And if he had captured your pilot? He could have blackmailed you into accepting him."

"*Without my Navigator aboard, I couldn't serve him even if I wanted to. So there is no point.*"

The admiral gazed at her. "Sounds like a foolproof safety. However, such a ship is useless without a pilot."

"*I am not useless, only waiting for my next Navigator, even if it takes a few millennia.*"

Cortez stared at Syreen. "How old are your people?"

She shrugged. "*Assiduous* says about a hundred megacycles."

"And he's been waiting for you all that time?"

"Since his last pilot left him, yes."

The admiral shook his head and gazed into his mug.

"And then she came," Lupus said. "I wonder what twist of fate made her show up during that master's lifetime?"

"Fate is a bitch," Wong said.

"Aye," Lupus agreed and took his mug. "A toast to fate."

"Yeah." Wong raised his mug, too, and glanced at Cortez. First Cortez, then Hernandez joined in.

"Cheers." Syreen took a sip.

Cortez set his mug down first. "What are you going to do with us now?"

"Yes, I'm curious about that, too," Hernandez said.

She focused on Cortez. "Your man, your jurisdiction. Your problem. Deal with him as you deem appropriate."

Cortez frowned. "You said I'm your prisoner."

"Indeed. However, I couldn't fit all your crews into this ship. So I'm left with three choices. Firstly, I could hand you over to the local authorities."

"No!" Lupus and Wong said almost simultaneously.

"Secondly, I could take the officers aboard and consume your crew."

Cortez squinted. "What do you mean, *consume?*"

"Assimilate valuable resources and discard waste, like your converters do, only way more effectively. After all, this is a *living* ship. It needs nutrients from time to time."

"That's — that's —"

"Tasty? In fact, I haven't considered the issue of taste yet. I prefer not to share *Assiduous'* feeding sensations." She glanced up at the ceiling. "Sorry, mate." Then she turned back to Cortez. "However, I already said that sentence isn't nailed down yet. There is a third option."

"Which would be?"

"Once I'm finished with your master, once the Associated Planets are willing to return to civilized behavior instead of bullying other star nations, and once the edicts have been reestablished, your navy needs officers with high ethical

standards and courage, officers willing to challenge their superiors and make changes happen."

Cortez stared at her. "I'm not sure I get you."

"I'm talking of letting you leave not just on parole, but as a
free man—if you are ready to accept the responsibility. You
will have to act against your explicit orders, but not against
your regulations. Of course, you must not try to attack me
again—in that case, I wouldn't hesitate to return to option
two."

"Of course." He gazed at Hernandez. "I'm not sure . . ."

Syreen smiled. "You needn't tell me now. Return to your
crews and discuss with your other officers."

"Whether they prefer consumption or mutiny?" Cortez
asked.

"Not mutiny. Extended parole. You are already defeated.
Consider that."

"I already considered that. According to our regulations,
we're supposed to remain under parole as long as the enemy
is able to control it. We can be released, freed, bought out, or
simply left unguarded—in each case, we're free to rejoin the
fight. Once we're in control of our own fate and aboard a func-
tioning warship, we're supposed to resume following our orders." Cortez shook his head. "There's no such thing as extended parole. There's a mutiny, or there's a fight—where we
both know the only possible outcome."

CHAPTER EIGHTEEN

M o handed one mug each to Herman and Stephan. "What was it like, down on Klondike? How long have you been stuck there?"

"Two winters," Herman said. "It was, well, interesting."

"We knew her mission would take time," Stephan said. "We were prepared for a long wait."

"What did you do?" Mo asked.

Stephan sat up straight. "Well, we agreed on a plan for the regular chores. Discipline is important for a soldier, you know?"

"I know."

"And especially where four people must get along in a very tight space. No, I'm kidding, no soldier likes to do those chores. But we wanted to keep *Raydancer* tidy — for her. So we agreed on the basics, you know?"

"We set some time aside for learning and training, too," Herman said. "Fitness training, simulator training, and so on."

Drake nodded. "Everyone had to learn the basics of everything — just in case."

"The Klondike countryside is a dangerous place," Stephan said. "Hostile, hungry wildlife, uneven ground with pits and tunnels, sharp-edged and poisonous plants, you name it. But we had to go out for hunting, foraging, and for some exercises, too."

"We decided to build a shack," Herman said. "We didn't want to bring the fresh meat inside, and we didn't want to leave it out in the open. The first shack didn't survive the first storm. We had to rebuild it. Crow said a shelter would be convenient, so that we didn't have to pass the airlock and decontamination procedures every time. Think big, Drake said — what if we need a guard outside to scare scavengers away? Indeed, we had lost our game to the vermin a few times — getting outside takes time, too. So we built a shed for the game and a bigger log cabin for us, with a main room and a porch, tables, chairs, bed frames and all. That project kept us busy, and it was fun, too."

"It was a good basis for some research," Drake said. "But I agree, it was a very challenging and rewarding pastime. In the end, sitting on the porch, watching the sunset and all the little critters coming out—knowing you've built that chair with your own hands, yeah, that's something. Of course, there's all the data I had to dig through . . ."

"He's been teaching us history," Stephan said. "Telling us stories about the Forgotten People, about space exploration, the first expansion . . ."

Herman waved a hand at Drake. "He knows how to tell stories. First there was too much new stuff, but the more he told, the more pieces fell into place."

CHAPTER NINETEEN

Syreen gazed at Cortez while listening to Klondike's song. It told of no signs of new arrivals, only of loneliness.

"You don't really have an offer for us," Cortez complained. "Death or mutiny, what kind of choice is that?"

Syreen shrugged. "I didn't start this war, or the recent battle. It's not my job to make things easy for you. Okay — what's your proposal?"

"Mine?" He turned to Hernandez, to Lupus, to Wong, and back to her. "Well . . . you could surrender to me."

She laughed, then gave him a stern look. "Won't happen."

Wong pushed his mug to the side and leaned forward. "Admiral, we all understand you're an honorable man with high ethical standards. You don't want to deliberately neglect your duties as you see them, while at the same time, your responsibility for your crews demands you can't waste their lives for nothing."

Cortez frowned. "Go on."

"Perhaps I might help you to find a different way to judge your own situation. Only as a thought experiment, let us assume you find out your orders are illegitimate, what would be your duty?"

"I'd have to challenge that finding, as orders aren't easy to forge."

"And if your investigations support the finding?"

"I'd have to ask my superiors for new orders."

Wong smiled. "Until you can reach them, what were you supposed to do?"

"Follow the regulations and do what I deem best for the AP."

Wong nodded. "We'll let that stand for the time being. Now, as you said, orders aren't easy to forge. Let's say they are technically legitimate, that is, no one has tampered with them, but their wording is illegitimate. Like, for example, demanding mutiny."

Cortez shook his head. "I don't know where that would take us."

"Please," Hernandez said. "Let's continue with that experiment. I agree that it's possible to issue orders with illegitimate, ambiguous or contradictory content. However, the officer receiving those orders is expected to read his orders and ask for clarification."

"Unless they're sealed," Cortez said.

"Indeed."

"Were your orders sealed?" Wong asked. "If you may reveal that fact."

Cortez shook his head. "No, they weren't. Nor were they contradictory or unclear—well, there's always a little leeway, but in essence, they didn't leave much open to interpretation."

"Thanks, and sorry for the sidetrack. Back to the experiment. Can orders be technically sound, their wording clear and straightforward, and their content still be illegitimate? That is, orders that shouldn't be issued, according to your own regulations?"

"Yes, although—" Cortez paused when Wong raised a hand.

"Like ordering you to violate an edict?"

"Yes."

"And you're not supposed to follow this part of your orders?"

"True."

"But all other orders are still valid, right?"

Cortez nodded. "Yes, that's the problem."

"No, it's not, but let's look at that detail. How can such an illegitimate item slip into your orders? Wouldn't your superiors be aware of the violation?"

"I'd say so, yes."

"What does that tell you about the process of putting down those orders—or about its issuer?"

"Nothing good, but orders are orders anyway. I might raise a formal complaint and have the issue investigated. Until then, I'm still supposed to do what I'm told—the legitimate part, at least."

Wong gazed around. "Within this experiment, we've established the possibility that sound and clear orders may incorporate illegitimate content. We've also just found out that such illegitimate content may provide evidence against its issuer—to what end, would be subject to investigation. Let's follow that thread and see where it leads—what if your alleged superior turns out to be an impostor?"

"How could that happen? It's impossible to forge an AP navy ID—or cheat our systems."

"Not true," Syreen chimed in and glanced at Wong. She began to understand where he was heading. "Sorry to interrupt your reasoning, but it *is* possible. I did it twice. First, as Lieutenant Merigo Luquin aboard *APS Illustrious,* where I convinced Admiral Ravenport to give the AP corvette *Raydancer* to me. The second time I joined Admiral Ersan Tas of the 97th expeditionary corps on his flagship *Oppression,* playing the role of Captain Ishtar Gryf. I can confirm security is tight on Nysa Four—that's the AP navy's main base—but I got out unmolested."

"Impossible," Cortez said.

"Yes. Escape should be impossible for a chained and tortured prisoner, but I managed anyway. Evidence—I'm here, not there."

"But how?"

"Let's save that for later—this is still Mr. Wong's experiment. Please, Mr. Wong."

"Thank you, Navigator. My last question was—if you found out your orders were written by an impostor, would they still be legitimate, overall or partially?"

The admiral shook his head. "No. They'd be void as a whole. Only true AP navy officers can issue legitimate orders."

Wong spread his hands. "Well. We've just established that sound and clear orders may be illegitimate if their issuer is illegitimate. Earlier we found out that illegitimate content may provide evidence against the issuer. Our Navigator provided evidence that the existence of an illegitimate officer in the heart of the AP navy can't be ruled out. Do we all agree to this point?"

"For the experiment's sake, yes," Cortez said.

"Thank you, Admiral." Wong folded his hands. "Let's get to the end. Sorry if I'm touching a sore spot, but we've heard of torture before, and that it's a severe violation of AP regulations. Correct?"

"It would be."

"Thank you. Do we have reason to doubt the Navigator's statement on this topic, or can we accept it as evidence?"

Hernandez raised a hand. "Sorry to say that, but I don't see traces of torture."

"No," Syreen said. "We of the People can heal fast, even from severe injuries. Otherwise I wouldn't have been able to leave."

Wong nodded. "Either we accept your statement as truth or discard it as lie. There's no in-between." He turned back to Cortez. "Next—we heard of some illegitimate parts within otherwise sound and legitimate orders. I didn't see these orders, but I have no reason to doubt your word, so I regard this as hard evidence."

He glanced around. "There's a third fact, and as the first, it's a question of credibility. The Navigator said that the AP navy's supreme leader is of her own kin, of the People, as she said. Admiral Cortez, please tell me one thing. Can a member of a foreign nation legitimately become member of the AP navy?"

Cortez raised an eyebrow. "I don't know. There might be exceptions to the regulations in some annex, but I assume that would require additional administrative procedures."

"Let me rephrase my question. Can a member of a foreign nation, of a different race, legitimately become member of the AP navy without disclosing this fact?"

"If you put it like this, I'd say, no, that wouldn't be in accordance with our laws."

"And if such a member of a different race assumes the role of an AP officer without proper administrative procedures, or worse, in a clandestine way, would it be okay to call him an impostor?"

"Uh, yes." Cortez leaned forward. "What are you up to?"

"Well." Wong smiled. "Should you find out your orders were issued by an impostor, supported by reliable evidence, would discarding those orders still have to be considered mutiny? Or could you decide to put your responsibilities toward your nation, your navy and your men first, and return to your home world to demand an investigation, or even raise this issue to the attention of your political leaders?"

It took a while, but a smile crept into the admiral's face, too.

Chapter Twenty

Syreen felt alone in her seat, with the lights around her dimmed. Even her tight connection with *Assiduous* or Klondike's distant song didn't change that.

There's too much responsibility on my shoulders. I don't know how long I can bear it. I don't know how to handle it all. Even with such a splendid ship, I can't be everywhere.

She sensed — *Assiduous* sensed — Mo's familiar steps approach the bridge. *Light.*

The former merchant entered and accepted the seat that grew out of the floor without hesitation.

"Hello, Syreen."

"Hello, Mo. What can I do for my staff captain?"

"Nothing, thank you. Your crew and passengers are easy to handle — everyone is grateful to be alive, everyone knows what a hard job you're doing, and everyone is fascinated by the prospect of making history, or better, of watching you shape history. I'm here to ask what we can do for you."

"Oh — nothing, thank you."

Mo smiled. "I know — you've done your job, we're approaching a seven-sigma jump, the first of many. Everything's settled for now. The Klondike guys and the AP officers made peace with each other, perhaps even became friends . . . I've heard they planned a little detour to the local venues before their departure. AP credits are welcome dirtside."

"From the little I've seen, I'm not surprised."

"I've listened in to local communication. Three ships crowded with survivors — each one glad to be alive, each one praising your mercy and their officers' wisdom — they'll probably spend their last credit down there. A warm shower of rain for the locals."

"As if they weren't used to rain."

"I've heard of that regular afternoon downpour."

They grinned at each other.

Mo briefly glanced at her crotch, where *Assiduous* penetrated her, then focused on her face. "I know — we know — you're the only one. One Navigator, one living ship. One woman of the People against one of the largest space nations of this side of the galaxy. You must feel very lonely. I'm here to let you know — you're not alone. We're here to support you any way we can. Yusef, Haiki, me, Jona, even Chiara and Gwen, are ready to board *Bumblebee* and become part of your fleet. Stephan and Herman told me they'd take *Raydancer* and do whatever you need. We go wherever you send us, do whatever you tell us. That's what I came for — to tell you we're not just your passengers."

She felt a tear running down her cheek. "Thank you, Mo."

"You're welcome." He scratched his chin. "Will we do any stops on our way to Kyris?"

"*Assiduous* assures me we're fully charged. We're confident that we could do the entire sequence without stops. I'm tempted to try it, but I'm used to recharging early and often. So I've scheduled a stop in an unnamed pivot system close to Kyris."

"Just to recharge?"

"No, for everything. A mug of forwine, a decent meal, a comfort stop, time to rethink our approach — and listen around."

"The stars? A song of troubles and nuisances?"

"Yes. I'd prefer not to run into a fleet of dreadnaughts."

"Do you expect to find them there?"

"Not really." She waved a hand. "Their fleet is large, but

they can't place a dreadnaught in every system — not even at each of the major trade nodes. Perhaps a battle group, perhaps just a corvette as observer."

"Which will run for help once we show up."

"If I let them go. I'll have to think about that, too — starting a shoot-out in a friendly system isn't the best imaginable introduction."

— No, but we could fry their computer. —

She grinned at Mo. "I've just got a better idea. It's obvious, once you think of it, but I'm still not used to *Assiduous'* numerous talents."

"Is it secret, or would you tell me?"

"Nah, it's okay. If it's just a small ship, we'll take them under remote control, like we did with *Raydancer* and *Bumblebee.*"

She shrugged. "If I'd have to fight a battle group — with their missile capacity, I couldn't take risks. And if it's a dreadnaught, we won't go there anyway."

"Sounds fine to me."

"Yes. Dealing with the local authorities won't be as easy. They might feel the need to stay on the AP's good side. I must consider that — but for now, I must focus on the jump sequence."

"Mind if I stay?"

"No, that's fine. Crew, prepare for jump sequence in five."

Focusing on the feeling of that firm object inside her privates, she entered deep integration.

PART TWO—RUPTURES

CHAPTER TWENTY-ONE

Accompanied by the songs of stars distant and close, the union of pilot and ship slipped through the barriers between the planes.

I can see.

– This is unheard of. –

Syreen gave herself to this strange kind of perception. It wasn't vision, it wasn't hearing, it wasn't smelling, it wasn't tactile sensation, and it was all of them.

They sailed past a peppery, cool red dwarf, made a turn around a bright and fluffy giant, then aimed at a crisp yellow youngling, all accompanied by their choir of interwoven, elegiac harmonies.

She felt their path through between dissonances, fractions and ruptures, danced and swung on toward their destination.

The more she listened to their environment, the better she understood its structure, the deeper she became immersed into her perceptions, the less she liked the scratches, ruptures, entanglements, and scars she found everywhere around them.

This is sad. So much damage.

– There's nothing we can do about it. –

There must be.

Syreen reached out, tried to get hold of the image of a broken strand, then of its opposite, and held both loose ends together.

With a bright silvery glow, they mended and straightened.

There is a way. We can help.

— I witness the unfathomable. —

Hear their song.

There was a new quality in the stars' choir—a cheerful spirit had snuck into their mournful melodies.

With new confidence, she ran her mind across a scratch and evened it out, then another.

She tried to touch a minor rupture, but a sudden sting made her withdraw.

I'm not ready for this. Yet. But this is what we're truly made for.

— We've almost arrived. —

Yes. Goodbye hyperspace.

As gently as they had started their journey, they left hyperspace. Next, she surfaced from her deep integration with *Assiduous*. She paused before she opened her eyes. Her vision, all her senses, had to adjust to the limitations of her physical existence first.

The merchant captain gazed at her for a while, as if waiting for something. "Are you okay?"

"Yes, I'm fine."

"I ask because you said you'd do a sequence of jumps. New ideas, then?"

"No. Mo, we're already where we're supposed to be."

"In one jump?"

"I wouldn't call it a jump, but yes, we didn't have to leave hyperspace in-between. It was one single flight."

He shook his head. "You're taking it so lightly—what about all the obstacles in hyperspace? Are your calculations so precise?"

"They don't have to be, Mo. What you're doing, what we've done together, those were jumps indeed, with blindfolds on. But I'm a Navigator, and *Assiduous* is a full capacity living ship. We did a fully controlled hyperflight."

"What do you call *fully controlled*?"

"When you're walking down a twisted corridor without running into the walls—each step placed where you want it, subconsciously, while you're planning ahead for your next turn."

"You can *see* in hyperspace?"

"Whatever you'd call this perception, yes."

"Girl, you're not of this world."

She nodded. "True. Now, let's have a decent lunch."

CHAPTER TWENTY-TWO

Curious faces watched their arrival in the mess. Conversations around the tables paused, people turned to the door.

Mo followed their gazes. "Uh, Syreen?"

She turned to him with a smile. "Yes, Mo?"

"You didn't—you're not wearing your uniform."

The Navigator glanced down her nude body. "Oh, that. I won't need it now anyway."

He shook his head. *Women!*

Jona rose from her chair, blew a kiss in his direction, and took Syreen in her arms. She, like most of the other women, wore a towel as improvised miniskirt around her hips with uniform boots and a bare chest. "No worries, dear. Our staff captain is just a bit old-fashioned. No one will be hurt by the sight of a beautiful young woman. You've got more important stuff than clothes to worry about, I'm sure. However, now's time to relax and enjoy your meal. Sit down, and I'll get you a mug of forwine, okay?"

The former entertainer led Syreen to a free seat and left for the counter.

Mo saw Drake waving and joined the historian. He knocked on the table before sitting down. "Solid."

"Yes," Drake said. "*Assiduous* asked about variable furniture. I told him to leave it like this. All these *living* installations can be disturbing. We need something unchanging to cling to sometimes."

"Indeed," Mo said. "Now more than ever."

"What's troubling you?"

"I don't know ... maybe, well, uh, I'm not sure." He pointed across the room. "I fear we're losing her."

"Losing—how?" Drake pushed his mug over. "Here, take this. I only just fetched it."

Mo accepted the mug with a nod and drank of the hot forwine. The warmth soothed some of his tension. "She's changing, Drake. Did you notice—we only made one jump?"

"Not really. Her jumps are so smooth I hardly notice any— if not for her announcements. But she announced a sequence, didn't she?"

"Yes." Mo took another sip. "I need that now, thank you. Yes, she announced a sequence, we did a jump—and then she told me we're already there. Instead of doing the planned sequence, she did it all in one single hyperflight."

"Which obviously worked fine. She knows what she's doing, Mo. Trust her."

"Oh, that I do. But—when she opened her eyes, she told me she can see in hyperspace."

The historian raised an eyebrow. "That's extraordinary."

Mo shook his head. "From all I've learned, it's impossible. No human mind can comprehend the fifth dimension."

"But she's no human being. We already know that."

"Yes—and she's becoming less human every day. That's what frightens me."

Drake nodded at the naked body. "She's looking very human now. No, I must disagree. She's not becoming *less*. She's becoming *more* than just a mere human every day."

Mo tried to remember the woman he had allowed aboard his ship. Pretty, confident—commanding. Indeed, she was still there, somewhere under that tremendous burden she'd taken upon her shoulders.

CHAPTER TWENTY-THREE

Syreen had carefully considered their approach to Kyris — and then discarded all her creative ideas. She had found no signs of AP warships from the distance, and now that they had arrived at the system's outskirts, *Assiduous'* sensors told her no different.

"Warship Assiduous, *this is Kyris port authority. Please identify yourself and your origin, and state your business here."*

"Kyris port authority, this is the living ship *Assiduous* of the People. I'm Navigator Syreen, previously known to you as Duchy Fleet Commander in Charge. I came to meet guild secretary Jacomo again."

While she waited for their reply, she set course for Kyris' orbital station.

"Warship Assiduous, *this is Kyris port authority. Welcome back, Fleet Commander Syreen. Pardon me, but your message is confusing — are you part of Duchy Fleet, which surrendered to the Associated Planets, or which other navy? What is a living ship, and what people do you belong to?"*

"Kyris port authority, while I won't fail my responsibilities toward the Duchy until formal transfer of command, I'm currently not acting as Duchy Fleet officer. Nevertheless, for the records, I hereby state that I as current Duchy Fleet Commander in Charge did not surrender to the Associated Planets. I came here as Navigator of the People, nowadays called the *Forgotten People,* as most of my kin have disappeared during the last hundred megacycles, and together with my living ship, I am acting as an enforcer of edicts."

She smiled, even though her contact couldn't see it. "A living ship, as the name says, is a sentient, living being, capable of travelling through space and hyperspace and able to take crew, passengers and freight along. *Assiduous'* hangar currently harbors the well-known corvette *Raydancer* as well as the frigate *Bumblebee,* both re-registered as Duchy warships, and both bearing evidence of violations of Edict Number Two by the AP navy. I require docking capacity for both smaller ships, preferably at adjacent docks. *Assiduous* will enter an independent parking orbit, for which I'd appreciate your proposal."

She knew how long her message and their answer had to travel. How much more time would they need to digest her news?

Their message came surprisingly fast.

"Navigator Syreen, while the presence of a warship in our orbit would make us worry under other circumstances, your reputation as triple star angel precedes you, and we feel honored by your visit. You will be assigned docking bays alpha one and alpha two, both free of charge. We will assign an honor guard to the docks — feel free to ask them for any assistance you and your crew might need. Should you feel so inclined, both the Duchy ambassador and our harbor director would welcome you for a cup of tea or forwine. Secretary Jacomo has already cancelled his appointments for today, and you're welcome to his office any time."

She shrugged. *Does that sound fishy? Docking free of charge? No. I must not expect the worst everywhere. The Kyris people were kind last time. However, something I said must have triggered their attention — aside from the visit of a living ship itself.*

CHAPTER TWENTY-FOUR

Syreen watched Herman absently gazing at her chest through the corvette's cockpit door. She didn't have to focus on his mind to know about his thoughts. Reclining in her pilot chair, she turned toward him and placed her boots to both sides of the doorframe.

"All okay?" she asked.

"Huh? Oh—sure, okay. It's that number of decorations that looks odd. Unbalanced, if you allow. But it's surely impressive."

"Plus, you'd like to look at my chest without the decorations or the fabric."

"Uh. Sir, I don't want to—"

"Hush. You know we did it before. It's a pleasant memory for me, too."

She pointed at *Raydancer's* communications panel. "No sign from *Bumblebee* yet. With such a huge flock of excited girls, Mo and Yusef will have a hard time getting them all aboard and seated, so I'd guess we can put a little time aside."

She placed one hand to her collar and slowly pulled the zipper down all the way. The uniform jacket opened and unveiled her firm breasts and erect nipples.

"This is so wrong," she said, rose, and pulled her pants down. "I'm your commanding officer. But I'm also wet and horny. So—this is not an order, but you're welcome to push your hard cock deep into my tight pussy."

He smiled. "Stress relief for my skipper can't be wrong."

With a chime and a flash, the comm panel begged for attention. Herman tightened his grip around her hips, pushed his cock firmly in three more times, and shot his load.

She squealed, panted twice, and then tapped a symbol.

"Yes, Yusef? Ready to go?"

"*Bumblebee is ready for a shuttle run, yes. I've prepared an optimized solution for both of us, if you don't mind. Here, you got it.*"

She tapped another symbol and checked his data. "I'm fine with that. Thank you, Yusef. Proceed as proposed. We'll meet at the dock."

After she cut the comm line, she squeezed her pelvis muscles. "Can I have another load, please?"

CHAPTER TWENTY-FIVE

R *aydancer* trembled, accompanied by a loud *bump.*
Syreen smiled at Herman, who was just arranging his clothes.

The soldier smiled back. "Not as smooth as I'm used to —
but I'm spoiled from traveling with you."

She nodded and closed her jacket. "Primitive computer programming can never replace true skill. Ready?"

He picked an imaginary speck from his sleeve and pointed at the door. "Please."

Her breast brushed along his arm, her hip touched his genitals. "Oh. I'm so sorry — not."

"Good. I like that spirit in you."

"It's like I've found a bit of my younger self here. I hope it sticks."

"Oh, yes. I think you're still quite sticky."

They both laughed.

When the outer door opened, she put on a more serious face for the young Kyris honor guard captain waiting outside. The nervousness she sensed in his mind somewhat spoiled the professional attitude he tried to show.

Four ensigns presented their sidearms. They were trying hard to keep their heads straight forward, but couldn't keep their eyes from glancing in her direction.

Playing a game, are we? Okay, I won't spoil it for you.

She stepped through the outer doorframe and stopped.

Nothing happened.

The captain blushed, produced a pipe, and sounded it.

"Welcome aboard Kyris Orbital, Navigator Syreen!"

Only then did she salute. "Thank you, Captain."

"At your service."

"Thank you. You've surely been told that I've been here before. I'll find my way around, but you're welcome to join me, if you wish. Duties require me to meet with the guild secretary first, that's still level seven, correct?"

"Well, yes. Please, go ahead." He gestured her forward. "Ensign Arthur, follow me. Ensign Roscoe, guard the ship."

She wondered about the remaining two officer candidates, but the Kyris guards seemed to be organized in pairs — they didn't need further instructions to join their teammate.

Nor did they need instructions to let Herman pass before falling in line behind them.

The captain stayed close to her side when she started toward dock alpha two, where a similar group of guards had already welcomed Mo and Drake.

Both men and their honor guard joined her, and together, they walked down the hallway to the ring corridor of Kyris Orbital's second level. Mo moved to her side, Drake followed with Herman, so the nameless captain had to trail after them.

"You know where to go?" Mo asked.

"Inward, then up. The alpha docks are on level two. This is the passenger area, meant for liners and shuttles. Hotels on this level, bars and restaurants below, shopping above. The guild hall is on level seven, together with embassies and merchant offices. Gamma docks — where I docked last time — are on level ten. I know there's plenty of transship storage space between, but I didn't explore the other levels."

"You were here with *Raydancer* last time — why a Gamma dock?"

"I asked for a dock next to the *Light of Mandalay*."

"Ah, sure, the ship you saved from the pirates. Yeah, okay. How did you like Kyris?"

"My first impression was good, and now that I've had the opportunity to compare, it's even better. Tidy and peaceful, hospitable and happy."

"Really, eh?"

"Oh, there are a few dark side alleys, but those don't count."

"Hah, and you explored them all?"

"I've navigated only a few. They're reasonably clean, too."

"No vermin?"

"Two-legged only. Nothing to worry about."

They both laughed.

CHAPTER TWENTY-SIX

M o had visited countless guild halls in his days as merchant captain, and Kyris was no different — tastefully
decorated, with marble floor and walls, and golden, burgundy, and ebony furniture.

The guards at the entrance gave way the moment they
spotted their small entourage, and the doors opened. A short
man in a white robe stepped out with wide arms and an even
wider smile.

"Welcome, Navigator Syreen, welcome! Nice to see you
again and in good health! Oh, and I see, you even brought
your old company — welcome, Mr. Petran, welcome, Mr.
Doeken." He turned to Mo. "Sorry — you must be Mr. Mo . . ."

"Just Mo. And you are?"

"Jacomo. I'm the guild secretary on Kyris. Please, come in.
May I lead? Oh — Captain Jardin, you and your men are welcome to visit our guard mess for some refreshments." He
briefly glanced across Mo, Herman, Drake, and Syreen.
"Would you join me in the meeting room?"

Syreen smiled and walked past him. She obviously knew
her way.

Jacomo gazed at her bottom, shrugged, and smiled at Mo.
"Navigators don't need directions. Please."

The secretary let them all pass and fell into step behind
them, down a corridor with ivory-painted walls to a small
conference room with an oval table and eight chairs.

Syreen waited for them to spread around the table and
Jacomo to show each guest where to sit before sitting down.

The secretary approached an open panel in the wall and fetched a tray with five mugs. The aroma of an expensive hot forwine filled the small room.

When he had passed the mugs around, he took his own seat and nodded at them all. "Duke's health."

"Duke's health," Syreen and Herman echoed, and Drake and Mo followed.

"Now," the secretary began, and placed his mug down. "You've come a long way since we last met. We followed the news about you—your second and third registration as star angel, some rumors of battle, which must have been massively understated, compared to the count of stars on your chest, and your recent feat—reopening trade through the rift by exterminating a pirate's nest and re-charting the respective route."

"Re-charting?" Mo echoed.

Jacomo showed him a friendly smile. "Indeed. I've learned you were escorting a large convoy through there. The convoy captains unanimously voted to publish their navigation recordings and jump parameters—out of respect for the woman guiding them through the heart of a storm, as they said."

Mo raised an eyebrow. Merchant captains usually didn't volunteer details that could give them a competitive advantage.

The secretary seemed to guess his thoughts. "They stated, an increase in traffic could only help to improve the situation of the star nations around the rift, and deter pirates."

Mo nodded. That was a sensible move.

"Times are changing," Jacomo went on. "There are signs of a changing attitude all around—cooperation among merchants, an increase in filed complaints for misconduct during inspections, and last, but not least, a remarkable discussion with regard to ship's cats. Many skippers now say that taking advantage of women in such a way would discredit the deeds of the first triple star angel in recorded history. Others say, denying them the only option of leaving their planet, escaping from whatever bad fate, would be even worse. Some skippers say they'd hire a woman for regular ship-keeping work. It should be okay to enjoy her presence as long as she's given her own bunk. An ongoing discussion, but surely a sign for a change to the better."

Syreen shrugged and leaned forward. "That wasn't exactly part of my mission."

"Please," the secretary said. "Don't belittle what you did by example alone. Rumor has it you'd go for any rapist and shoot his balls across several light seconds."

They laughed out loud.

"Now tell me, if you may — does your joint return mean you found what you were looking for?"

"Most definitely so," Drake said. "To be honest, I didn't exactly know what we should find — an uncharted planet, some rusty and broken leftovers of an ancient race? Yes, we found that planet, Syreen found that planet. We found the legacy of an ancient race."

Jacomo listened very attentively now. Mo leaned back.

"We found what appeared to be a shipwreck — it was a large, regular object that on first impression couldn't have been built in that dusty cavern, or at least, that wouldn't have made any sense. From the scientific point of view, you could say it was a premature conclusion, but it was a workable hypothesis to be proven or disproven, and it was the most likely explanation of what we saw, so it met Ockham's criterion, if you know what I mean."

Jacomo nodded, so Drake didn't have to elaborate.

Mo wouldn't interrupt the historian's story, so he didn't ask, either.

"Well, it turned out to be anything but a wreck — it was a spaceship, true, but fully operational. Which we found out when our Navigator touched the door opener. It is a *living ship,* calling himself *Assiduous,* and it — he — had been waiting for a new pilot to claim him for megacycles."

Drake gestured to Syreen. "However, it wasn't the fact that she's a very good pilot that made him accept her. It's the fact that she's a member of the very same race that created this kind of spaceship. She's of the *Forgotten People* herself."

CHAPTER TWENTY-SEVEN

Herman had expected a moment of surprise from the secretary, although his skipper had announced her heritage to the authorities before. However, their host sat there for several centicycles with his mouth open, his hands frozen in mid-air, and almost unblinking.

After a while, Drake placed one hand on Jacomo's arm and asked, "Are you okay?"

Now the man blinked, let his arms drop on the table, and took several deep breaths. "Yes. I'm sorry, but I only just realized the full impact of your statement. You're a historian yourself — what do you know about the history of our guild?"

"It was founded four megacycles ago, as a result of the so-called guild wars. The guild established rules that are valid until today, such as *merchant ships cannot be armed.*"

"Correct, our codex. The most important rules of all are called edicts — can you guess why?"

"To distinguish them from other rules?" Drake asked.

Jacomo shook his head. "That's true, but it's not the rationale. After the war, the peace negotiations were set up in a neutral place, on a barren planet — a planet that must have been wiped clean by multiple kinetic strikes many megacycles before the guild wars. That planet hosts only one building, made from crystalline carbon, and that building hosts a sequence of three plates, each of which shows one engraved rule in several symbol sets. We can read one of these symbol sets — it's our Common, only slightly different from the way it looks today. These rules are labeled *edicts* — Edict Number

One, Edict Number Two, Edict Number Three. We made these edicts the foundation of our codex."

Drake frowned and glanced at Syreen. "Are they in any way related to your edicts?"

The Navigator shrugged. "I've never heard of them, but I must admit, I didn't read the guild codex."

Jacomo waved his arms. "The harbor master told me of your message regarding evidence of violations of an Edict Number Two—of course, I had assumed you meant the codex."

"No, I quoted the set of edicts my people established. Edict Number One proscribes deliberate damage of the fabric of space, or destruction of living stars. Edict Number Two proscribes deliberate destruction, sterilization or rendering uninhabitable of worlds, especially, but not limited to, kinetic strikes, large-scale application of nuclear or biological weapons, and systematic destruction of geological stability. Edict Number Three proscribes deliberate interference with the genetic code of intelligent beings."

The secretary answered with a very slow nod. "And that's exactly what we found engraved—the codex shows the original words, while our edicts are rephrased in much simpler words."

"And?" Drake asked.

"The way I see it, I'm currently facing a member of the very same people who wrote the original, fundamental rules of our codex."

CHAPTER TWENTY-EIGHT

Syreen sensed the secretary's unvoiced question and cocked her head. "You said your codex shows the original words — just the Common version, or all languages?"

Jacomo tapped the table. "The codex contains a three-dimensional model of the original engravings. I can show it to you."

"That won't help. Can you send that part of your codex to my ship? I'm sure *Assiduous* can confirm or deny your conclusion."

"Sure." He tapped an order, and a chime sounded.

"A confirmation." The secretary tapped once more.

Assiduous' voice filled the room. *"These engravings were made by the People."*

"Wow, that was quick," Jacomo said. "How did he even know what we wanted?"

She shrugged. "Why else would we send him such data?"

He must be following all electronic talk all over the station. If he can listen to our discussion, who else can? Where's the bug?

"Does that change anything?" she asked. "You're still the guild secretary on Kyris, right?"

"Yes, I am. And you represent everything the guild chose to stand for. When I chose to serve the guild, I devoted my life to the principles it's based on, that is, to these edicts — to you. I'm at your command."

She shook her head. "I didn't come to command, but to seek your advice. I could have picked any guild hall, but I preferred to meet someone I know. Before I ask my question, let's have a look at the evidence we brought. First, Appalahoo. *Assiduous* already sent it to you."

After the last replay, the room remained silent for a while. Syreen opened her mind for the emotions around her, ranging from disapproval to barely suppressed anger.

Finally, the secretary spoke up again. "Yes, there can't be any doubt. We've just witnessed two deliberate violations of Edict Number Two."

She nodded. "I brought further evidence this behavior was founded on secret orders by the Association's supreme commander."

Jacomo shook his head. "Where the violation is outrageous in itself, issuing such an order is insane. What does this *supreme commander* think the edicts mean?"

"He must think he's strong enough with his navy," Mo said.

"Yes. That's a point," the secretary said and reached for his mug. "I don't understand how the AP navy can afford so many dreadnaughts, but they're basically unmatched."

He smiled at Syreen. "Of course, I've heard they lost one at the Duchy, but that won't change the overall situation."

"They are no longer unmatched," she said drily. "*Assiduous* and I took out two at Klondike."

"One shot each," Mo added. "They hardly found time to return fire."

"But . . ." Jacomo began.

"*Assiduous* is an Enforcer of the People," Syreen said. "Built to enforce compliance with the edicts by all necessary means."

"Strong enough to eliminate even that asteroid with one shot," Mo added.

"I wondered about that part," Jacomo said. "So Klondike wasn't harmed?"

"No," Mo said.

The secretary sighed. "That's a big relief."

"It doesn't change the facts, though," Syreen said. "The attempt alone counts as violation. Now, what do the guild rules require you to do with a star nation gone rogue?"

Jacomo sighed again. "I saw this question coming. A star nation found guilty of violating one or more edicts must be sanctioned, and the two most powerful sanctions the guild can impose are bans on trade and funds, where it's hard to do one without the other."

"Before, you said there can't be any doubt. So this is settled?" She saw the *No* in his face before he voiced it.

"Sadly, no. A formal guild tribunal must officially determine the violation and decide on the sanctions. While I should have little doubt on the outcome, it's not that easy, I fear."

"Why?"

"Because guild tribunals are invoked by the regional guild commissar. Our commissar used to live on Nysa. I mean, he should still live there, unless your supreme commander decided to remove him from office."

"Why would he?" Mo asked. "Oh."

She nodded. "Yes. I wouldn't put that past him. He must know about the codex and how things work. By eliminating the commissar he doesn't have to fear sanctions."

She faced Jacomo. "Commissars can retire, become sick, or die. What would the guild do?"

"I know what you're up to. Yes, we could install a new commissar—once we know what happened to the current one. Would you go to Nysa to find out?"

"If I have to. Whatever it takes. Is the regional commissar the only one who could invoke a tribunal, or could another do the same?"

Jacomo made a sad face. "In principle, any commissar can do the necessary. Practically, no. You'd have to travel to another sector, and that's an impossible feat even for the best navigators, as you'd have to cross the great chasm."

"I wouldn't be so sure," Mo said.

"What is it about that great chasm?" Syreen asked.

"It's basically impassable," Jacomo said. "Nothing larger than message drones get through, and one in ten doesn't arrive at all. For larger ships, it's one-sigma or worse for a sequence of at least ten jumps. Impassable."

"A damaged hyperstructure?"

"Don't ask me, but if I had to guess what a violation of Edict Number One looks like . . ."

She squinted. "If I had to guess, it once must have been one of the most-frequented routes, easy to navigate. Everyone could have done six-sigma, but many pilots were happy with five, a quick-and-dirty solution."

Jacomo nodded. "Go on."

"By and by, the situation deteriorated. Good pilots could still do five-sigma, and of course, you could vary the route. A megacycle later, an entire region was damaged."

Mo stared at her.

Syreen glanced at him, then focused on Jacomo again. "Every time you do a bad jump, you feel pain. But that's nothing compared to the pain hyperspace suffers. Bad jumps rip holes in the structure of the universe. Those damages may heal over time—unless you tear at their edges. That's what happened—too many bad jumps resulted in damage space can't heal on its own."

"How could anyone have known?" Jacomo asked.

"You didn't have a Navigator," Syreen said. "But you didn't have to know. All you had to do was to navigate properly, to calculate your jumps by the Books. Because six-sigma jumps are like needles, pushing the fabric of space aside and letting it slip back into place. Now tell me—where do I have to go?"

Chapter Twenty-nine

Syreen expected protest. She didn't have to wait long.

"You can't be serious," Mo said. "I know you're good, but even you can't jump through ripped hyperspace."

Drake and Jacomo nodded. Only Herman radiated unconditional confidence in her.

"You're right, I can't simply jump through ripped hyperspace. But in hyperflight, I can see where I'm going. I will follow the narrow paths that are still passable."

It must work, somehow. I can't let them win.

"I thought hyperjump and hyperflight were the same," Jacomo said. "Are you saying you'll try to chart new routes, like you did through the rift?"

"No. I said I can see." She emptied her mug.

Jacomo smiled and exchanged it for a filled one.

Syreen nodded, picked it up and inhaled the rich smell. "Thank you. The hyperjump you all know feels like a singular event." She snapped her fingers. "And you're there. No feel for the time passed, but your computer can tell you there was a significant duration. Start, end, and path are determined before you go. For a passenger, hyperflight feels the same, but there are two major differences. First, you don't have to define the path before you depart, you only need a direction. Second, you can change your course mid-flight."

"Sounds easy, the way you describe it—like a shuttle flight," Jacomo said. "I wonder why people don't do it all the time."

"There are two minor complications," Syreen said. "First,

your ship's instruments must be capable of reading and presenting hyperspace structures. Second, your pilot must be
able to make the necessary decisions in a timely manner—
within nanocycles."

"Impossible." Jacomo shook his head.

"That's why nobody does it all the time. They can't do what
I can do when I'm integrated with my ship."

"Integrated?"

"One body, one mind—thinking at computer speed."

"Oh—that. Yes, I've heard the Duchy still uses such de-
vices. Your people have a similar technology."

"Much better." *I'd better leave it at that. How can you explain
vision to the blind?*

"In any case, it allows me to see the fabric of hyperspace
while traveling it. I don't need a pre-charted jump, I can sail
around sore spots."

Jacomo sighed and raised his own mug. "There's so much
you could teach us."

*If people would follow instructions, if people would do thorough
calculations, teaching would be fun. No, that's not fair. I've met so
many pilots who were excited to learn better jumps. Or beyond that.*

"You still have to tell me where to go," she repeated.

The secretary fixed his gaze on her chest for a moment.
"The Sirius sector, Crown system. That's the heart of the
guild. Tell them you're from the Duchy, and you'll have their
undivided attention."

CHAPTER THIRTY

Herman decided to fill the silence with his question. "What's your situation here? Our honor guard seemed to be on edge. Why?"

The guild secretary frowned. "You remember the trouble with the local representatives of your family when you left? Your complaint about them acting against the legitimate interests of your family's company? Your request was granted, and they were on their own. Only they didn't act defeated. They had—they have—individual connections on Kyris, and somehow, they remained in business, especially after most connections to the Duchy were cut. They had a contingency plan. Worse, they have their own protection racket going."

"A racket?" Herman asked. "Why would Kyris tolerate them?"

"Connections, as I said. Bribes, blackmail, favors to collect, whatever. However, nothing too obvious. Nothing the local authorities would have to explain to the general public. But you don't cross them, certainly not twice."

"How could that happen?"

"Well." Jacomo licked his lip. "Not long after you left, an AP battle group showed up, with a battle cruiser in the lead. They visited Kyris—not just Kyris Orbital, but the surface, too—and asked questions. Their behavior was neither pleasant nor polite, but the Doeken reps with their muscle stepped in and established boundaries. Perhaps out of fear for their own young, perhaps for their own hidden agenda, but they prevented the worst. That was something to build on, and they knew how to turn public opinion to their own advantage. However, since then, things are tense wherever they show up."

"A racket?" Mo asked.

Jacomo shrugged. "Officially not. Under the surface — well, you can't know for sure. Being cautious can't be wrong."

Herman shook his head. Another stain on his family's reputation. How could they have brought such people into power?

"We will be cautious," Syreen said. "Although they'd better not cross me. I'm running out of patience with bullies."

Herman wholeheartedly agreed with her. So close to his homeworld, he felt homesick.

"I think we're done here for now," his skipper said. "The Duchy ambassador asked for my visit. It's my duty to follow his invitation. Secretary Jacomo, thank you for your hospitality and advice. Oh, and should you have any messages you want me to deliver to Crown, physical or electronic, just let me know."

As a merchant's son, Herman knew her offer was priceless. Shipping electronic messages didn't count — one message drone lost out of ten was still calculable — but she'd just granted delivery of physical goods where ordinary merchant shipments had been a sure loss for generations. She could have asked any price.

Jacomo confirmed his thoughts. "You could ask any price."

"I know," Syreen said. "My needs are covered."

Herman pursed his lips. *But not ours. Well, she must know what she's doing.*

"There are messages that can't be trusted to drones, even encrypted. Given that once-in-a-lifetime opportunity, I must take the chance, and I trust you to deliver a data vault untouched," Jacomo said. "I must offer compensation, though, that's a question of guild honor."

"In that case, I will accept whatever you feel inclined to

offer."

"Thank you." He tapped a symbol. "Recording. In acceptance of the obligation placed on the guild, guild secretary Jacomo on Kyris, Northern Rim Sector, hereby grants Navigator Syreen of the Forgotten People—soon no longer forgotten—lifetime free access to any and all guild services."

Herman swallowed. Under any other circumstances, such a deal would have been priceless, too—but as compensation for her offer, it was barely appropriate. After all, most guild fees required no direct investment on behalf of the guild, they only covered day-to-day expenses that occurred anyway, like office space rental or employee salary.

Jacomo wasn't finished, though. "Accepting our *beholdenment* toward the aforementioned Navigator Syreen as an enforcer of the edicts, I herewith commit the guild to coverage of any and all docking or landing fees for any and all star systems with guild presence for the living ship *Assiduous* under command of Navigator Syreen, including any and all secondary vessels in her service, effective immediately. I am fully aware of the financial liability entered, but I reassure the guild that the services she already volunteered are more than worth the price. Recording completed."

Herman watched Mo's face mirroring his own amazement. Now, this was a deal! At the same time, he wondered whether the archaic term *beholdenment* touched specific guild regulations.

Plus, it was a smart move—Kyris didn't charge them anyway, so it wasn't his own purse he just had committed.

"That's very generous of you," Syreen said.

"It's not," Jacomo disagreed. "But it's all I can do, all I'm legally entitled to do, and under any other circumstances, my superiors would cut my head off for doing it without their prior agreement anyway. However, once you arrive on the other side of the chasm, they'll congratulate themselves for such a cheap deal. I will need about a tencycle to compile my data vault. Is that acceptable for you?"

"Oh yes. My passengers need a little time off, and the AP won't show up within the next two or three tencycles yet. As you just raised the burden of docking fees from my purse, you may as well take the time you need. No need to forego sleep. Better make sure you do it right—who knows how soon I could do the same run again."

Jacomo showed a smile, warmer than Herman had ever seen on his or any other merchant's face. Without jealousy, he recognized the secretary had fallen in love with her.

"Thank you for your understanding and your sound advice," the secretary said. "I will do as you say."

"In that case, we'd better leave you to your task now," the Navigator said. "Thank you again for your excellent forwine. We'll meet again before we depart."

When they rose, she added, "I'll find my way out, thank you."

Jacomo grinned. "Of course you will, *Navigator*."

CHAPTER THIRTY-ONE

While walking down the corridors to the embassy together with her entourage, Syreen sensed something foul aboard Kyris Orbital. She couldn't name it yet, so she shrugged and listened to Kyris' song instead.

It didn't sing of trouble. No AP ships approaching, no reason to leave soon.

Their honor guard captain had managed to slip to her side this time. "My parents told me tales of the past, of large fleets and battles in space, of dragons and ships that are alive. I can't believe it's all true. But now—do you have dragons aboard, too?"

"Not any I'd know of," she said. "In fact, I never met any dragons."

"But you heard of them, did you?"

"No, never."

"But . . . wouldn't your parents have told you?"

She shrugged. "Maybe they would. But I never met my parents. I'm an orphan, a foundling, raised by Duchy Fleet staff."

"Oh—I'm sorry."

"Never mind."

"And your ship, is it really alive?"

"That's why he's called a living ship."

"He?"

"His name is *Assiduous.*" She closed her eyes for a few steps. "We haven't had much time together yet. Most of the time, we had to fight."

The captain shook his head. "Your ship talks with you?"

"Occasionally, we're just talking, yes. But when we're flying, we're joined." *No need to tell the physical details.* "We're one. I can see through our sensors. I feel the sun on our skin. It is — very intense."

"Oh."

That was the last word he spoke before his limp body dropped to the floor.

Syreen sensed hatred, turned around, and faced the evil glare of a brawny man over the barrel of the stunner in his hand. She remembered the face — it was the same guy who'd guided her out of the Doeken office on her first visit to Kyris Orbital.

He smiled. "I see you remember me. Good. My employer would like to speak to you in private."

She returned the smile. "I'm not sorry at all to deny an invitation delivered so impolitely, but I'm on my way to a much more pleasant meeting."

"Your fashionable guards won't protect you."

"No." Her special senses, now focusing on the situation around her again, told her of their unconsciousness and of the five more men that now threatened Drake, Mo, and Herman. They had organized a good place and time for their ambush — there were no other people approaching. *How unusual for such a frequented area. But it tells a lot about their influence.*

"You're unarmed. You'd better come along."

"To spare you the effort of carrying our limp bodies around? That would be convenient for you. But I already told you no."

He raised his gun and waved his hand. "You think you have a choice?"

"Indeed I do."

Too late. His men had already shot her company. Drake, Mo, and Herman shared the same fate as their honor guards before.

Her own opponent's mouth twitched. She knew he'd shoot her, too. Too bad.

Freeze.

The man before her couldn't even blink when she showed him her teeth. She could sense and smell his fear when she sank her canines into his throat. His motionless companions had no choice but to watch her.

When Syreen was finished, she found herself surrounded by fourteen motionless bodies. Her six adversaries were pale, deprived of blood and strength, but would eventually recover and not remember anything.

Her friends and her guard would recover, too, but stunner aftereffects were bad if not treated properly. She searched the captain, retrieved his radio, and activated it.

"Kyris Orbital security for Navigator Syreen."

"Navigator — what happened to Captain Jardin?"

"He was stunned, together with his men and my friends. May I propose you send medical aid?"

"Stunned — but you're okay? Who attacked you? What happened to them?"

"Yes, I'm okay. Our attackers passed out, too."

"Okay, I'll send someone. Stay where you are."

"Negative. I have some urgent business to tend to. Bye."

She placed the radio down and left.

CHAPTER THIRTY-TWO

O*pen the door and ignore me.*
Upon Syreen's command, the guard's eyes and mind went blank. She entered the Doeken family office and marched straight through the anteroom to a certain back door.

The old man behind the desk turned to the door with a face showing dismay. "I said no interruptions—you!"

"I."

He tried to peek past her.

"I'm alone," she said. "Your muscle is out of sorts."

The man tried to reach under his desk.

Don't.

His hand froze.

"I'm not here to discuss manners," she said. "You could have sent me an invitation, Mr. Secretary. I might have been curious enough to follow it. Instead, you sent your men to shoot my friends down."

The Doeken secretary showed a thin smile. "Surely you can prove your accusation?"

Syreen shrugged. "It might be possible to find some records showing a remote connection between the men and this office. It might even be possible to trace payments after thorough investigation."

"Which wouldn't prove anything—if you managed to find anything."

"You have no clue what a living ship can do with this world's primitive computers—it wouldn't take more than a microcycle to dig up *all* data on your business transactions. However, I'm not here to waste my time with legal dodges. I found all the proof I need in your minions' minds, Mr. Allay — or should I call you Mr. Vascos?"

The so addressed man flinched. "What — how — I have no clue what you're talking about."

"You know. However, I don't care about your past. What matters to me is that you sent out six men, one of which shot down one of my men, Private Herman Doeken, Duchy infantry, currently under my command as Duchy Fleet Commander in Charge. You ordered and authorized an attack on Duchy Fleet. The Duchy is currently at war, and your attack is a direct attempt to weaken our defenses. Even in an independent star system, this would subject you to a court-martial."

Mr. Allay or Vascos shrank in his chair. "But . . ."

"I have no doubt of the outcome of such a court-martial. Do you?"

She could sense his mind racing — what could he do to delay or interrupt such a trial? Who could he call to intervene, to bribe or to blackmail judges?

"I won't waste my time with you," Syreen said. "But I can't let you go, either. I'm here to execute your sentence."

Die.

CHAPTER THIRTY-THREE

Walking down another corridor, Syreen contemplated her situation. She felt little remorse for her latest kill, instead, she regretted the waste of resources—but as announced, she hadn't been willing to waste any more time with that man. He had knowingly overstepped the border, not just a sign of poor judgment, but of placing himself above the rules.

She didn't like that attitude in the Association's *master*, and she liked it even less in a merchant company secretary. A supreme commander was supposed to interpret, even change rules, an employee wasn't.

That *master* could have changed all the rules in his world, she mused, but he had knowingly overstepped borders, too. Worse, he had found willing aides in his officers—people who had to be thoroughly put back into their place for the better of this sector with all its independent worlds.

Syreen sensed warm, welcoming thoughts directed at her. The Duchy marine soldier at the embassy door obviously had recognized her, watched her approach, turned to her, and saluted firmly.

She walked up to him and returned the salute with a smile.

He relaxed and opened the door for her. "Fleet Commander, welcome. Please, enter."

"Thank you."

Syreen wasn't surprised to find the Duchy ambassador to Kyris, Lord Hakon Persson, waiting in the anteroom.

"Milord," she said, and curtsied.

The ambassador bowed, took her hand and kissed it.

After a moment, he let her hand go and straightened himself. "Navigator Syreen, we are honored by your visit. Please, would you follow me?"

"Sure."

She took in his appearance and emotions. The same friendly face she remembered, deeper wrinkles, sad blue eyes, deeper worries.

"Here," he said and pointed through an open door. Two comfortable chairs, a low table, and two mugs of steaming forwine didn't seem appropriate for the serious topics she had to address. She accepted one of the offered chairs anyway, and waited for him to open the conversation.

"You've come a long way since you left," he said. "I still remember the young lieutenant, shaken and stirred from a recent battle, visibly fighting for her composure, seeking my advice — and, at the same time, showing astonishing determination and good judgment. I tried to follow the news about you, together with the guild secretary — I guess you met him already?" When she nodded, he smiled. "Good. He's a good man, very understanding — we owe him a lot, being cut off from our home world and all."

"I may be able to improve your situation," she said. "The escort services I offered proved fruitful. You heard of my passage through the rift?"

It was his turn to nod. "A remarkable feat indeed. But you had better keep your credits. Running a small fleet is expensive."

"No, it isn't. My storage is full of AP provisions, and a living ship's maintenance only requires raw material. I only have to pay my crew."

"Plus docking fees."

"No longer. The guild will pay my future docking fees."

The ambassador raised both eyebrows. "That's unheard of.

How did you manage that?"

"I promised Jacomo shipment across the chasm, to the Sirius sector."

"The chasm isn't passable."

"It is, for me. Let me fill you in about my people, the Forgotten People, and what it means to be a Navigator."

A cycle and three mugs of forwine later, Syreen finished, "And now I'm here again."

The ambassador unfolded his hands. "What a story. Yes, I understand now. It's a sensible move to put them under edict, even if it means severe hardship for their population — and, to some extent, for the trade of this sector, too. Merchants need contracts to run their ships and feed their crews. AP destinations make up a fifth of their business. Take that away, and . . ."

He shrugged. "Desperate people go desperate ways. Piracy suddenly might look like a good option. Or violating the embargo. In any case, in the short term, things will get worse. People like that Mr. Allay — the man who eased you out of his office last time, you remember — won't hesitate to profit from the situation."

She shook her head. "It's my sad duty to inform you Mr. Allay will no longer profit from any situation. He sent me an invitation I couldn't decline, but in the course of our conversation, he suffered a stroke."

"Kyris Orbital has a very good stroke unit."

"I fear the medical emergency teams were busy cleaning up the mess his thugs had created by stunning my honor guard and my friends."

"Stunning your guard? But *you* are here. What happened to his thugs?"

"They suffered a sudden weakness and passed out, too." She showed her predator smile, only without canines, and the ambassador flinched. "I think they underestimated the skills of a Navigator."

While he tried to digest this information, she took another sip from her mug.

"I'm unsure. Should I visit the Duchy and eliminate their fleet there?"

"No."

The firmness of his answer surprised her. "Why not?"

"Two reasons. One, that would show everyone there's still an emotional connection between you and the Duchy that could be used as blackmail. You can't leave and do what needs to be done and stay to protect the Duchy against another violation of Edict Number Two. Let the AP believe you're no longer connected to us."

"But I am. For the records, I'm still Fleet Commander in Charge, and I can't throw that responsibility away like a wet towel."

"That didn't prevent you from doing what was necessary for the last, what, eight kilocycles? Going after that edict is in the Duchy's best interest. Being stuck with guard duty on your home world isn't—at least no more than it was before you left. Which brings me to reason two. If I'd have to place a trap for you anywhere, for the same reasons mentioned before, I'd pick the Duchy, just in case you decide to return there. You don't want to spring that trap—that wouldn't do us any good, either."

She took a deep breath, leaned back, and offered him her warmest smile. "As always, your advice is sound and wise. However, perhaps you could file at least a minor complaint about me? Saying that I'm not caring enough about my home world? That might save both you and our home some trouble."

"And it would shed a bad light on you."

"I can stand the heat. Once I return and take care of the AP fleet and their supreme commander, that part of my reputation will be the least of my worries Do you know what's the ultimate sanction for a violation of Edict Number Two?"

"No—but I assume your people's rules aren't about trade embargos. Elimination of the culprit's fleet?"

"My people assume that only a rotten society can provide the circumstances allowing their navy to violate the edicts systematically—note I'm not talking about a single rogue. I must consider all facts. Larger parts of their navy are willing to execute those orders." She didn't mention Edict Number Three—deliberate interference with the genetic code of intelligent beings, which she had encountered twice already. "In order to discourage others, the countermeasures can be made to match the violation."

Lord Hakon shook his head. "I'm not sure I understand."

"You do. The ultimate sanction is elimination of roots— that is, their world."

"You couldn't do that."

"I'm commanding the means to do it, and I won't neglect my duties by failing to do the necessary. That doesn't mean I'd like it, so you're right."

"I admit I'm frightened."

"Me too. Being an *enforcer* of edicts isn't easy. However, not having to fear such consequences might have encouraged the AP to do what they did. As you indicated, they might consider more kinetic strikes as blackmail against me, and not just strikes at the Duchy. If necessary, I will have to make my point *ultimately* clear."

"Even if you break yourself in the process?"

"Perhaps. I'm a soldier. Such is my job."

"Bad job."

"Yeah." She raised her mug. "Duke's health."

CHAPTER THIRTY-FOUR

Under protection of four Duchy marine soldiers, Syreen should have felt safe. They radiated a lot more attentiveness than Kyris' gaudy honor guardsmen.

She couldn't relax. She could tell herself repeatedly the previous ambush wasn't her fault, but she felt responsible for her company's fate anyway, and she felt especially sorry for her crew.

This time, she had to watch their backs with open senses. Indeed, she could still sense something foul under Kyris' tidy surface, but she couldn't put her finger on it. Too many people, too many minds, too many mischievous thoughts—the local tradesman trying to cheat his partner, barkeepers selling watered forwine, drunk men looking for willing or not so willing women, women willing to offer their bodies and deprive their victims of more than the negotiated credits—all mixed into one hard-to-digest broth.

The ambassador at her side wasn't aware of her worries. He was looking forward to their meeting with the harbor director.

"I want to see his face when he learns about your next destination," he had announced.

She hadn't objected. Announcing her destination was a sensible move if she wanted to direct attention away from her home world. Moreover, she felt a childish joy over the prospect of another surprised face, too.

No evildoers were lurking along their way to the local authorities, located on the station's top level. Instead, they passed a few local guards with the same no-nonsense attitude as their marine soldiers who watched her with a lot of respect. After all, she was obviously unharmed, while she had defeated six armed opponents with her bare hands. Plus her canines, but they didn't know about them.

A tall man in business attire opened the door for them. "Navigator Syreen, Lord Hakon, welcome! Come in, the director is eager to meet you."

Their guards stayed behind. The ambassador gently nudged her shoulder, and she walked in first.

The most unusual feature of the harbor director's office was the large window into space, where the station's rotation slowly moved the planet into view.

Spacefaring people didn't need windows. For some, the sight of the void might even cause nausea—but she could understand why a dirtbug might want to see his home now and then. She had no trouble with either.

The large conference table in the room's center was undecorated. Instead, three chairs were placed in a semicircle before the window. Their host rose from one of the chairs and turned to them.

"Welcome! Welcome, Navigator, we're honored by your visit. And Lord Hakon—always a pleasure. Please, have a seat."

Syreen took the chair he adjusted for her—no surprise, the one next to his. The ambassador slipped into the remaining chair.

"May I offer you anything? Forwine, beer, juice?"

"Forwine, thank you," she said.

The ambassador nodded.

"You had a nice journey to Kyris?" their host made a futile attempt at small talk.

"It was a smooth flight, thank you. Relaxing, compared to the battle before."

"Oh, hmm. How do you like it here?"

She smiled coldly. "It's mostly the same tidy place I remember from my last visit — with the same brute private muscle I brought to the authorities' attention during my last visit. They seemed as if they've been encouraged to continue their misdemeanors rather than disciplined. I wouldn't accept such under my command."

The director's face froze. She sensed his anger and the ambassador's amusement.

"Are you trying to instruct me about my job?"

"You asked for my professional assessment about your station, from harbor director to fleet commander, and that's what I gave you. You didn't expect me to tell you lies, did you?"

"No, but I hadn't expected such a — uh — straightforward answer."

She shrugged. "I'm supreme commandant of a fleet at war. I had to witness an attempt to wipe out an entire planet. In order to defend their population's innocent lives, I had to destroy a hostile fleet, kill thousands of spacemen, make their wives widows, their children orphans by the score. Yes, I'm talking straight."

Syreen forced him to meet her gaze. "My fleet was wiped out when we met their first attack. All my fellow pilots died. My friends, my family died when the AP wiped out our orbital station. I continued the fight alone, destroyed one of their dreadnaughts from the inside. Even that didn't discourage them."

She sat up. "I've witnessed their navy bullying other independent systems, harassing merchants and their crews, abusing passengers — ship's cats, as you call them — and overstepping each and every rule of civilized behavior all around this sector. Their violation of the edict is only the last escalation in a long sequence of atrocities the AP navy committed. Such behavior happens if you allow people to establish their own set of rules, if you fail to put bullies back into place. I don't want to watch more of it."

Their host had a red face. "You *do* try to instruct me."

What is he afraid of? What is he trying to hide? "If you want to put it that way, yes. I'm talking about responsible execution of authority. Because that's what an enforcer does. And I'm talking to the man whose responsibility would have been to prevent the assault on my people's and my health only cycles ago. I'm talking to the man who assigned a flock of younglings to a serious escort job as cannon fodder while keeping his experienced staff behind." *There.* "Tell me, what did Mr. Allay pay you?"

Both men sat up straight. Lord Hakon showed sheer surprise.

The director opened his mouth to call his guards.

Shut up and freeze.

"Your thoughts gave you away. I'm sure my ship will dig up all the ugly detail from your computers."

"You can't do that," Lord Hakon said, eyeing the motionless harbor director. "Even if all you said is true — you can't interfere with their computers. You have no legal power here on Kyris."

He's right, from his point of view. I must take a wider view. "Let me put it this way. This man was part of a ploy to kidnap an enforcer, thus trying to prevent me from enforcing the edict. Whether they were aware of the fact or not, they made themselves obstacles to my mission. Violations of the edict and personal attacks on me both are under my jurisdiction."

"Usually such action requires joint agreements."

"Yes, interstellar politics, I know. I'm trying to play by your rules, as long as they don't interfere with my duties. The edicts aren't subject to negotiation."

"You're placing yourself above human legislation?"

"Yes, if I have to. The edicts *are* above human legislation."

Lord Hakon shook his head. "That won't make life easier for you."

Syreen put on her predator smile, mostly for the director's benefit. "What will the local government do when presented with overwhelming evidence — and his full confession?"

The ambassador gazed at their host. "He doesn't look very cooperative."

"He will do as I say. He'll do anything necessary — because otherwise, I might have to place this world under edict, too."

"For just one man?"

"The society that put him in his position might have failed to establish measures against corruption. I'm just one woman, one ship against an entire galaxy. I simply can't afford to leave backstabbers behind."

"It still feels, uh, like an overreaction to me."

Again, she smiled. "Trial and sentence aren't done yet. There are good people on Kyris Orbital, too."

She focused on the harbor director. "Why don't you call your guards in and make your confession?"

Speak the truth.

Her victim blinked, took a deep breath, squinted, and called out, "Guard!"

A moment later, two guards entered. "Yes, Director? Everything okay?"

Syreen sensed mischief, but wasn't quick enough.

"That woman accused me of corruption. Arrest her."

That could have gone better. Truth, but twisted.

The guards were already approaching her. *Wait and listen.*

She focused on the director again. *Now tell them about your part in this ploy. Everything, from the beginning.*

And he began to spill out his story. His guards listened, their minds radiating growing disgust. *Good men, not part of this foulness.* She relaxed her grip on them — it was no longer necessary.

CHAPTER THIRTY-FIVE

Syreen accompanied the ambassador back to his rooms. They marched across the station in silence. Only when the embassy doors had closed behind them did he speak up.

"You could control his mind?"

"Yes."

"I didn't want to touch that topic while we were in his office. The embassy should be safe against eavesdroppers."

"Thank you."

"You are more powerful than I expected."

"It is helpful." She shrugged. "Such power must be used responsibly, like my ship. But I feel no remorse for making him tell of all his misdoings."

"No, you needn't feel bad about him. He will get what he deserves. Overall, the people on Kyris are good people. I'm glad you found that solution — my heart nearly stopped when he voiced his accusation against you."

She shook her head. "What did he expect to gain? He had a good job, surely well paid, a good reputation — and gave it all away."

"You couldn't read that from his mind?"

"No. He didn't think of it. I could have made him tell me, but I didn't think of it, and once the guards were involved, it didn't look like a good idea anymore. I could have made them forget — but I prefer not to use my powers on innocent people."

"I'm glad you see it that way."

"Yes." When he offered her a seat, she dropped into it. "It's too easy to do it wrong. Tempting."

He slowly sank into another chair. "What is it that's holding you back? Discipline?"

She contemplated his question. "Yes and no. Discipline helps. You won't get your commission if you're found trigger-happy. No navy needs officers who shoot without proper reason. It's even worse for skirmisher pilots—you know, do you?"

"I know."

She remembered her first real flight lessons—alone in her skirmisher cockpit, the stimulator inside her privates, beginning to do its work with her first practice targets. Promising orgasm for more and better hits.

"The ultimate reward—pure lust, if you continue. Sexual frustration for holding yourself back. You must learn patience, learn to extend your lust, learn to enjoy the process, not the immediate climax. A hard lesson in self-control. Discipline, as you call it. It helps you to stay on the better side of bravery, without becoming reckless. It worked for me." She closed her eyes. "It worked, even though my wing commander chided me for not flying by the Books. He was shot, I'm alive. I knew how to control and direct my emotions."

The ambassador remained silent. She opened her eyes again.

"Discipline isn't all when you command true power. A skirmisher is a dangerous tool, but it's still a small bird. It can poke a dreadnaught, pierce a battle cruiser, damage a light cruiser, or kill a frigate. It can't wipe an asteroid or a small moon from existence. *Assiduous* and I together, we can."

"Wipe from existence sounds dramatic."

"But it's true. You'd have a hard time proving anything was there. It's a weapon of enforcement, built for just that purpose. *Assiduous* would remind me if I tried misuse—but ultimately, he'll follow my orders."

"So it's all about you."

"Yes. It's all about me. If I do wrong, it's on my bill alone."

Again, she closed her eyes. "There is another factor. Harmony."

"Harmony?"

"Yes. I'm not striving for perfection, I'm striving for harmony. That's what the edicts are about, after all. About keeping the fabric of space intact, about the nurturing of life, about natural evolution—about harmony. Violating an edict impedes harmony—enforcing an edict to reestablish harmony may create a temporary discord, too. I try to avoid discord. That's the primary factor holding me back."

She focused on him. He met her gaze and waited.

"Harmony's holding me back as long as I want it to. Harmony won't stop me. Discipline is what makes me go on, makes me distort harmony where I'd prefer to do nothing. Discipline, the virtue of a soldier, makes me kill. I've learned to live with it."

CHAPTER THIRTY-SIX

When she left the embassy, Syreen refused the offer of an armed escort.

"I can take care of myself," she said to the marine captain at the door. "But someone might have a bone to pick with you — watch out for the next few tencycles."

"Do you have anything specific for us, Navigator?"

"Only a bad feeling. I've stirred a few things up. Local muscle suddenly out of job, old bills presented, new faces trying to establish their business, such things as that."

"Oh, okay, we can handle that."

"Good luck."

"Good luck to you, Navigator."

"Thank you." She gave him a last smile and turned down the corridor. It was time to collect her friends from the sick bay.

Her senses were on alert. Whatever the reason for that foul feeling haunting her since she had arrived, eliminating two heads of local crime hadn't helped.

Which meant the real origin had to be even worse. That thought didn't cheer her up.

The sick bay — pardon, hospital — was on the eleventh or second-topmost floor, four levels above the embassies and merchant offices.

Level nine, where the foulness felt most intense, was deserted.

This is the place, she thought.

Next, four men turned around a corner in front of her. Without looking behind, she sensed three more blocking her retreat.

Three of the faces before her looked familiar — they belonged to the Doeken muscle she had sent to the hospital before. They had recovered amazingly fast despite the power she had drained from them.

Freeze, she commanded.

They dashed forward toward her.

CHAPTER THIRTY-SEVEN

Unarmed, outnumbered, her mental commands failing — Syreen's situation had gone down the drain rather quickly. However, her opponents weren't armed, either. No stunners this time.

Hand-to-hand combat, then?

She jumped forward. *Better fight only one group at a time.*

She reached her first opponent, lashed out — he dodged and grinned at her, baring his canines.

His two fellows threw themselves upon her, forced her against the wall.

This is going to be dirty.

Her head jerked forward, smashed one attacker's teeth, made him step back. She struggled to get one arm free, found enough room to lean forward — her canines dug into another man's throat, tore, ripped his windpipe apart. He went down with a gurgling sound. *Two out, five to go.*

They were too strong, though. Four of them pinned her arms and legs to the wall. The fifth man stood before her — the only one not of the Doeken muscle team she had met before.

He was all foulness — the source of all bad she had sensed before. He was wrong, not human, not of her People, and yet, a little bit of both. He was a violation of the third edict, a genetic bastard.

He seemed immune to her powers.

Who else could she call?

"You better keep your mouth shut, and your mind, too. Be nice, and I won't let them bite your arms and legs off. Cry for help, and I'll kill them all. Or better, I make them kill each other. Every single one of them. All of the station. Yes, I think I'd like that. Come on, give me a reason."

Her heart sank. She lowered her head. She wouldn't give in to blackmail — but what would it help to sacrifice innocents if she was dismembered anyway? *Lost.*

CHAPTER THIRTY-EIGHT

Syreen's mind raced. Her opponents were dragging her through a corridor toward one of the Gamma docks. Her options crumbled with every step. Once she was out of the public area, once they'd carried her aboard another ship, her chances to escape were close to zero.

They stopped before docking bay Gamma Four.

No, she couldn't call for help, at least not in a way her opponent could understand and thus would act upon. Unless that help came truly quick.

She closed her eyes and listened.

Kyris sang to her. The star sang, the planet echoed, and the fabric around them vibrated with their harmonic melody.

The Navigator could locate herself within that fabric by the width of a hair, and could calculate His Foulness' position just as precisely.

She knew where *Bumblebee* was docked, knew its gun positions, knew their precision parameters, their firing range.

All she needed was a sequence of numbers. Math.

Assiduous would listen. *Assiduous* would understand.

She double-checked her solution and sent her mental command — numbers.

"What's that gibberish?" His Foulness said. "I told you not to —"

A single laser shot, tightly focused, powerful enough to pierce station walls, floors, plumbing, wiring, flesh in its way, went through his crotch, torso, and head.

His four henchmen froze in surprise, only for a brief

moment, but long enough for her to pull her arms free, strike out to both sides, crushing two more windpipes, and then she had a go at the others. Her powerful bites tore their necks apart.

Free.

The station's klaxons wailed.

"*Hull breach,*" an artificial voice announced. "*Hull breach, Beta and Gamma docks. Keep clear, air seals are closing. Within affected sections, proceed to emergency bays.*"

Now she'd have to apologize for a major weapon malfunction and for eventual collateral damage. Hopefully, nobody had gotten into the laser's path in the beta dock corridors.

First, she had to worry about her section losing air. Flashing blue arrows pointed to alcoves framed in the same blue light. Red lights marked fire extinguishers and other emergency equipment—she spotted a set of emergency seal patches and pulled it from the wall.

Close to the opening in the floor, still glowing red from the laser heat, she could sense the draft of precious air rushing out. Breathing would become hard soon.

"*Hull breach, Gamma docks Three and Four. Air pressure dropping. Danger! Proceed to emergency bays now.*"

Better do something about it, tin brain. Like I do.

She adjusted one patch and held its sticky edge toward one side of the hole in the floor. When she let go, the draft sucked the patch down like a closing trap door.

Next. She looked up. The ceiling was out of reach, but of course, the patch set contained a telescope stick that could hold a patch.

Syreen held her breath, applied a patch to the stick and directed it up to the side of the upper hole. A switch released the patch, and again, the draft pulled it tight.

"*Low air pressure, Gamma docks Three and Four, stabilized. Please confirm emergency repair.*"

She focused on her next steps, toward the emergency bay,

one foot, the other. In thin air, she couldn't move fast, and she had to waste some of her remaining breath now.

"Gamma four, confirmed. Hull patched."

A human voice replaced the computer. *"Gamma four, emergency repair acknowledged. Re-pressurization initiated. Stand by for medevac team to pick you up. This is Kyris Orbital crisis team, Lieutenant Storgard speaking. If you can, please identify number of affected persons."*

She already felt the rush of air, the pressure rising again. Soon, habitable conditions had been reestablished.

"Lieutenant Storgard, this is Navigator Syreen speaking. For Gamma four, one survivor, five casualties. I owe you an explanation, and I must demand one, but not on this line."

"Navigator Syreen, I'm glad you're okay. Your ship — oh, okay, not on this line." A different voice replaced Storgard's. *"This is Major Harrod, Kyris security and acting director. I'm looking forward to meeting you. I will send you another escort. There's been way too much commotion around you lately, and I won't have any more of that on our peaceful station."*

Meaning his was an invitation she couldn't turn down.

"I agree. Please tell me—was anyone hurt on the beta docks?"

"Luckily, no. The corridor was empty. Excuse me for now."

Syreen could imagine what the lieutenant had been about to tell her. She had alerted her ship. *Assiduous* wouldn't like her being in danger while separated from him.

She directed her attention outward. The foulness on the station was gone.

Kyris sang of excitement, of power, of change. Syreen could sense the echo of *Assiduous'* presence woven into its melody. She could sense his alertness, could even sense his EMP cannon slowly charging.

Calm down, partner. All clear for now.

CHAPTER THIRTY-NINE

When Syreen sensed people approaching, she rose from the floor and stretched her legs.

Two men in airtight suits with repair gear were accompanied by four armed guards.

One guard stepped forward. "First Lieutenant Tomlin at your service, Navigator. I'm ordered to take care of your protection. Major Harrod kindly asks you to meet him as soon as your duties allow. If I may assist you in any other way, please say so."

She sensed fear in him and could guess the reason. There hadn't been any radio communication, but one of her ships had shot at the station—seemingly out of the blue, but very precisely, at the very corridor she had been in. Where she had reported five dead.

She pointed at the corpses behind her. "There are four men that had been arrested only few cycles before. Had they remained arrested, they'd be alive now." Next, she showed him the scorched limbs of her adversary. Nausea grew in the officer. Her mental command eased it. "This is to be collected as evidence for a violation of Edict Number Three."

He swallowed hard, leaned toward her, and whispered, "What is Edict Number Three?"

"A deliberate genetic modification, like in this case, creating a chimera."

His gaze fell on the four other victims with their ripped throats. They surely looked like some beast had attacked them. She wouldn't tell him that her own bite had caused their wounds.

"Uh, okay." He turned to his men. "Thomson, collect those limbs and all the rest."

Thomson didn't look happy. She eased his nausea, too.

Together, they waited for him to finish the gruesome task.

Meanwhile, one of the repairmen stepped up to them. "No damage other than the two already patched breaches, and those patches are well placed. They can remain until the outer hull is fixed. Good job."

She smiled at him. "Thank you."

The repairmen left.

Tomlin looked up and down. "That laser shot must have killed your chimera. A lucky hit?"

"Precise calculation."

He paled. "Without line of sight?"

"*I* could see him."

The lieutenant needed a moment to grasp the implications. She appeared unarmed, but her ships' guns could hit anyone on this station, anywhere.

Syreen nodded. "You and your men are here to make sure I don't have to pierce your hull again."

CHAPTER FORTY

Syreen sensed a mix of anger, fear, and worries.

When she and First Lieutenant Tomlin entered Major Harrod's office, she touched his mind very gently to calm him. Too much excitement would only burden their talk.

The lieutenant had to deliver his report first. He told of the corpses, of the scorched chimera, what he had learned about the precision shot. Finally, he was dismissed.

The major focused on her. "So this shot was no accident?"

"No. You could call it self-defense, and I must apologize for the collateral damage I caused. I'm also sorry for my harsh words before—now that I know what kind of opponent I faced, it's clear that you can't be held responsible even for his presence on Kyris, or for releasing his helpers—he must have been very convincing. I almost fell for his kind manners myself."

"It's been disturbing. A docked ship, a ship considered friendly, shooting at us. You understand that?"

"I surely can sympathize with that. The last few cycles have been disturbing for me, too. A station whose people gave me a friendly welcome, a station where I expected to find friends—but what I found were two kidnapping attempts, my friends shot down, my parade escort helpless, a local gang leader roaming free, a corrupt harbor director entangled in crime, and finally, a genetic experiment created by the AP . . . it wasn't my best day."

Major Harrod frowned. "You're holding that against us?"

"Not at all. I'm explaining my situation and can only ask

125

for your understanding. We were both driven by events beyond our control."

"I'm not sure whether that explanation will suffice for my government."

"What else would you need?"

The major folded his hands. "I need answers, substantial answers. What were those men after?"

She sighed. *It's not always as easy to get substantial answers. But for you, I have one.*

"Me. Me and my ship. While that local thug Allay probably only searched to please his own ego, the chimera would have taken me to Nysa, where their supreme commander in his quest for ultimate power would have had me tortured until I surrendered control over my living ship to him. Which mustn't happen."

"Because you want to keep that ultimate power for yourself?"

She met his demanding glare. "Yes. Exactly that. I want that ultimate power in my own hands. I must be sure the person in control will not foster piracy in order to make merchants accept abusive inspections. I must be sure the person in control will not bully independent star nations with *friendly* battle group visits. I must be sure the person in control will never again shoot an orbital station without prior declaration of war. I must be sure the person in control will never threaten kinetic strikes on inhabited worlds. I must be sure the person in control will not try to crush any potential opposition. I can't be sure of anyone else. So I must bear that burden myself."

His face had become more worried with every one of her statements. "But you do use your power."

"Yes. I must complete my mission. I must stop that man. In order to do that, I must defend myself." She leaned forward. "If necessary, I must accept collateral damage. I must accept and bear the grief coming with it. Major Harrod, this whole galaxy is sick." Her statement tuned in with Kyris' song, always present in the back of her mind, and she understood. With a sad face, she gazed at the major. Could he handle the truth? *He's an officer, so he has to.*

So she continued. "What will you do when the fabric of space is torn apart, when stars can no longer hold their planets? What will you do when stars die?"

CHAPTER FORTY-ONE

M o felt the weakness in his legs and sat down on the comfortable bench at the back of *Assiduous'* mess. Jona joined him and caressed his cheek. "Not better yet?"

"It doesn't hurt anymore. I'm just weak."

"Good. Bastards. Good they got what they deserved." She pulled him tight. "Good to have you back."

Mo had his doubts about Kyris' official statements, about what *they* had got, but didn't voice them. The crew of the ship Syreen should have been brought to had a lot to answer for, but he doubted they'd tell much before an AP dreadnaught would visit Kyris and demand their delivery.

"What do you think she'll tell us?" Jona asked.

"Perhaps something about the next leg on our journey."

Haiki and Gwen joined them, arms wrapped around each other.

"What's up?" the engineer asked.

"An announcement," Mo said.

"That much I've heard. What about?"

"Don't know. How was your tencycle?"

"Ah, nice. Quite a few people eager to offer us drinks in exchange for a story, asking about my medal, and all. Gwen and I had a good time, and the other girls, too, I reckon."

"They asked about the rift and the pirates," Gwen said. "Skippers and pilots—it's time someone does something about those pirates, they said. Asked if we'd shoot more, they did."

Haiki nodded and pulled her closer. "I said I couldn't

speak for her, but I also said I'm sure she'll shoot every pirate unlucky enough to cross her path, and I said I'll jump into a pirate's nest together with her any day again. You know what's strange about that? I meant it."

"You know what?" Mo said. "I've known you for many, many winters. You've been as much a weasel as I have, following the easy path. But I believe you. And I will follow her, too. Wherever we're going."

"What are you doing otherwise?" Jona asked.

"Well," Haiki said. "*Assiduous* doesn't need engineers. However, now and then, he asks about frigate and corvette design. While we both don't know much about the military stuff, I can explain how our ships basically work, and together, we can figure out the rest. I can go where he can't, aboard the ships, and can tell him what I need to fix things. You know, I've learned a lot about warships. Aside from the guns, they're not much different from haulers. Stephan knows about guns—everything else is my specialty. The principles are the same, where warships have more redundancy."

That was a long speech for Haiki, but the engineer Mo had known a long time had changed, like them all.

Mo pulled Jona tighter.

She patted his head. "Not now. We'll have our private time later."

Mo gave her a warm smile. After all these years, he had lost his ship and his command. Instead, he had found adventure, he had found a kind of meaning for his life beyond shipping cargo—and he had found a woman worth keeping.

Fate has a strange sense of humor, he thought, *but as long as Jona is part of the pun, I'm fine.*

Mo gave Gwen a nudge when their skipper arrived. She forwarded his hint to Haiki, and they turned to the counter just in time to watch her climb onto it.

The mess had filled—somehow word of her announcement

had spread around. The women were excited, chattering about their time on the station – nice, tidy, with so many kind people, some of them even interested in a little *entertainment* in a silent corner. All of them wore new clothing, new shoes, colors, a bracelet here, a necklace there. Syreen had granted each of them a generous credit limit. Their share of their earnings, she had said, for sharing the risk.

The lighting changed, dim in the background, bright where she stood, the only woman without boots. Her uniform had displayed blood stains on it when they had returned to the ship together. Now she was wearing a clean set of trousers and jacket.

When she raised one hand, all other talks faded away.

"Thank you." She glanced around. "I hope you enjoyed your stay on Kyris – well, most of you, at least. You might have heard of our encounter with some local thugs and of a few unplanned hospital visits. This wasn't the worst, though. I met a very inquisitive AP guy – he tried to snatch me away to his ship. I wasn't happy with that, and the Kyris authorities weren't either. However, right now it seems wiser to avoid further confrontation, so we're leaving."

So far, Mo knew the story.

Syreen went on, "On Kyris, I've learned where I must be going next. I need a guild commissar and a guild tribunal to formally decide about an edict against the AP. Sadly, the next commissar is located on Nysa, the heart of the Association. It seems unwise to go there."

That remark earned her a few laughs.

"The second-next central guild world is called Crown, located in the Sirius sector. In case you've never heard of it – neither had I – it's on the far side of a region called the chasm, which hasn't been navigable for generations. To make that entirely clear – there is no safe passage for any conventional spaceship. Even one out of ten message drones gets lost. For larger ships, it's a sequence of at least ten one-sigma jumps. That means, one out of three ships gets lost — per jump. Overall, one out of sixty may get through."

Mo already knew she'd be going. Jona pulled him tight. He patted her hand.

The Navigator smiled. "I'm not planning to get lost. I know what's wrong with the chasm. The fabric of space itself is damaged from too many extremely poor jumps there, threadbare, so to say, but that won't stop me — us. *Assiduous* and I will travel across the chasm, and, if necessary, I will repair broken hyperspace along my way."

"*Repair?*" Mo echoed.

She picked his remark up across the room. "If that's what it takes, yes. I will mend broken fabric, join broken threads, soothe rough terrain, and make hyperspace navigable again."

The audience stared at her.

She shrugged. "It's new for me, too — just like hyperflight. But I've learned that I can see the fabric of space, and *Assiduous* and I together can do something about it. I probably won't be able to do it all in one tencycle, but I'm sure I'll find my way."

Syreen gazed around. "Success isn't guaranteed, though. I can't make promises. The situation here hasn't changed, either — it's not safe to leave you behind. Most certainly not in a place where the AP knows I've been. Nevertheless, should any one of you wish to stay in this sector, I'll find a way to drop you where they won't find you easily, perhaps in a less frequented system, perhaps dirtside where they wouldn't expect you."

"Dirtside can be dangerous, too," Casey chimed in.

Her remark stirred laughter — everyone remembered Appalahoo with its large predators.

"Agreed," Martine called. "Gattaca wasn't guns and roses either."

Jona rose. "I made my decision back there. At your side, I feel safe. Any pilot who could pick me up from Gattaca will make that chasm tour look like a honeymoon cruise. Count me in — and if there's anything I can do, I will."

Aside from keeping me out of her hair? Mo thought. *Sweeping Assiduous' less-frequented corners, perhaps? Calling the occasional couple of girls to order?*

Not that he'd complain about spotting two pretty women making love to each other now and then, and if they didn't feel disturbed by his presence, he wouldn't turn away. If he had learned one thing on his journey with Syreen — life was precious, and you had to enjoy what you could as long as you still could.

Syreen watched the discussions about her offer, listened, and briefly sensed for emotions — only briefly, so as not to become overwhelmed by their trust and loyalty.

The overall consensus was to stay with her — if she would let them, if they were no burden for her, if, if, if . . .

She rose once again, and the mess fell silent again. "I want to make myself clear to you. Yes, I feel responsible for your fate since I rescued you. I wouldn't like sending you away. No, you are no burden to *Assiduous* or me. Just the opposite — your smiles, your laughs make us happy, entertain us, sometimes keep us from brooding too much over all the evil we've seen. Yes, you're welcome to stay. Don't try to second-guess my words, they're meant as I say them."

"It's settled, then," Jona said aloud. "We're coming along. Does anyone disagree?"

Syreen had just climbed down from her counter when Drake approached her, Crow in tow. He radiated concern and determination.

"Navigator," he began.

"Syreen to you. No need to be formal between us. I'm only

sorry — I returned you to Kyris but didn't let you go your own way."

He smiled. "I totally agree with your rationale. However, that doesn't change what needs to be done. You know I'm a historian."

"Yes — and you're watching it happen, right?"

"Indeed." He gazed down at her bare feet. "I'd like to follow along and watch your story evolve. But I fear my duty as a historian is to spread word of your mission now. Once you return, surely with a positive decision about your edict, you need support from the public. How can you expect support if nobody knows about your cause? I will be your herald, and Crow will defend us. So, if you find a place to let us disembark, we'll make our own way."

She nodded.

"As much as I regret seeing you go, I appreciate what you're willing to do for me. So I won't try to hold you back. Instead, I'll give you help along the way."

He looked up and eyed her curiously.

"First, you may choose any arms or equipment you need from *Bumblebee*. Second, as Duchy Fleet Commander, I will issue you a license for those guns, so you can legally carry them — and so that merchants will let you keep them when you travel with any of them. Third, I will provide you with your first ship. There's one merchant who owes me a favor."

"That's very generous of you."

"It's not, considering the risk you're taking. There's one more. You've already learned about my mental skills."

Drake frowned. "I've guessed about those, however . . ."

"You must know that the AP set creatures on my tracks who are able to control the minds of weaker people. They could easily make you drop your gun."

The historian paled. "Then . . ."

"You'd be helpless. Unless *I* order you not to follow their instructions. My command would be much stronger."

"In that case . . ."

"There's one drawback, though. Your immunity against their mental orders might force them to resort to more violent means."

Drake took a deep breath and pointed at Crow. "Of course. We had already discussed the latter—that's a risk we're both willing to take. We only weren't aware of the other. I'll gladly accept any protection you can give me."

"I do, too," the bodyguard said. "It'll help me do my job."

Drake waved a hand. "What do we have to do? Meditate or something?"

"No." She focused on the two. *Don't follow any mental command but mine.* "Done."

Drake shook his head. "That's all? I don't feel any different."

"You shouldn't."

The historian smiled. "Smooth like your navigation? I should have expected that."

Crow smiled, too. "A woman's touch, boss. Gentle, subtle, and compelling. You never notice until it's too late."

They all laughed.

CHAPTER FORTY-TWO

When the signature appeared, Syreen smiled. In time, on track. Almost seven-sigma, finely adjusted.

She activated *Assiduous'* identification and waited for a few moments. "*Narihira* for *Assiduous*. Captain Ubukata, this is Navigator Syreen, sending my praise to Philippe for this smooth jump."

"*This is* Narihira, *Captain Ubukata speaking. Assiduous, please declare your intentions.*"

Didn't he recognize me? His voice sounds close to panic.

"Captain Ubukata, my intentions are friendly. I'm Syreen, your star angel. Last time we met, on your way to Woo, I crawled down the aft duct for you. After that, you promised me to fly the route I need, with or without cargo. Do you remember me?"

This time, the answer took more time.

"*Syreen — yes, I remember, but what kind of ship is that?*"

"Captain, this is the living ship *Assiduous*, built by my people, until recently called the Forgotten People."

"*By all spirits in space! Pardon me, but this is something to digest — well, almost like finding out about seven-sigma jumps. Welcome, star angel. Be welcome aboard my ship, and if you would allow me to deliver my current cargo, I'll do whatever run you need, as promised.*"

"Would you allow me to bring two passengers along? I can vouch for them."

"*Be welcome, then.*"

"Fine. Await our shuttle in ten."

135

Yusef piloted Syreen, Drake, and Crow to the merchant ship with *Bumblebee's* boarding scooter.

The pilot felt a little sting in his heart when he remembered their good old *Molly Malone*.

Perhaps one day I'll fly another hauler. Can I forget directing a frigate then? This way or that, I'll never feel whole again. Not after leaving her *behind, or better, being left behind when she leaves.*

Concentration, now. That hauler looks like someone already ran a dent into its aft with his shuttle. I won't be the next one to mistreat her.

Yusef was too good at his job to add as much as a scratch. He gently attached the scooter to the shuttle airlock.

"Done."

He rose to help Crow and Drake with their luggage. Syreen was already operating their own airlock, a duffel bag over her shoulder.

Picking up another bag didn't stop Yusef from admiring her appearance. She wore her Duchy uniform—tight green pants and top, soft black boots, a green jacket with all her decorations, and the burgundy beret identifying her as starship captain.

As if she could sense his gaze, she turned to him and gave him a warm smile.

A smile to die for. Or better, to live for.

Syreen pushed Yusef's emotions aside. She had to focus on their meeting.

The hauler's inner door opened, and she faced Captain Ubukata, wearing his white dress uniform with sleeve stripes and everything—frozen with half-raised hand upon the sight of her.

She made one step forward to an imaginary line on the

deck that merchant ships didn't have. "Navigator Syreen with company asking for permission to come aboard."

"What? Uh—yes, sure, come." Ubukata waved her forward. "Welcome. Uh—I didn't expect to see you like this, but as you're commanding a ship . . ." He pointed at her chest. "What are these for?"

She gazed down and pointed to her ribbons in sequence. "Scoring first in my pilot test. Precision shooting. Exemplary conduct." Next came the Duchy Fleet badge, the five-ray silver star with halo for a hyperflight command, the four-ray silver star for a warfare command, several rows of small four-ray stars for acknowledged kills, and finally the silver spiral-galaxy symbol for the Duchy Fleet Commander in Charge.

"Fleet Commander?" Ubukata echoed.

"In Charge—that's the highest rank in Duchy Navy."

"More than admiral?" He frowned. "Yes, of course. You've come a long way since we last met."

Syreen smiled. He was adapting to the new situation surprisingly quickly. "I already was fleet commander when we last met. You couldn't know, because I didn't advertise it. So please don't feel bad for it."

The merchant captain shook his head. "I have to feel bad about it. After all, I had given an order to let you starve and die."

"What?" Drake called out from behind.

The Navigator shook her head. "You couldn't know about me because I didn't tell you. Back then, we had a little misunderstanding, but together with Horus, we found a fine solution—I remember well that you gave me credit and full rations even before we implemented it. How's your engineer doing?"

"Doing fine, doing fine. He's waiting in the mess, eager to meet you again—he's in for a surprise, too, I'd wager." Only now, he squinted past her. "I'm sorry, gentlemen, for letting myself be sidetracked. Welcome aboard my *Narihira*. Please follow me."

Syreen wouldn't have needed his guidance to find *Narihira's* mess, but she could sense the skipper's eagerness to present her to his crew. Both of them, engineer Horus and pilot Philippe, were waiting in the mess, obviously feeling safe enough to leave their bridge alone with a warship watching over them.

Ubukata entered the mess first, announcing, "Folks, see who's visiting us again."

When he stepped aside and she entered, the two men radiated surprise indeed. However, the engineer quickly overcame his amazement, and, ignoring her decorations, came forward to pull her into a firm hug. "Glad to see you well," he whispered into her ear.

Behind them, Drake and Crow and Yusef filed into the room and dropped their luggage.

Horus let her go, so that she could hand the bag she was carrying to Crow, and Philippe hugged her, too. "I'm doing seven-sigma wherever I can. It's so much smoother, and it almost feels as if hyperspace is sucking us forward."

Or as if the stars guide you. Which they probably do.

Horus nodded. "We've replaced all broken emitters anyway, checked the remaining ones for wear, and stocked up more spares than we had before. Plus I'm letting the crawler check the line clamps in the aft duct each time we're docked. It still can't mount new ones, but it can show me when it's time to crawl in. We're not running into such trouble again."

Ubukata shrugged. "I'd replace that line sooner rather than later — but I'd have to put her into dock to have the aft section refitted, and while we're saving considerable amounts on spares due to less wear with those seven-sigma jumps, I still can't afford that. I've promised Horus a more versatile crawler, though. Well — what have you been doing since we last met?"

Syreen pointed at the chairs. "Have a seat, and I'll give you a summary. Drake can fill you in on the whole story later."

They sat down.

"After I left you, I continued my journey to Nysa . . ."

" . . . and after we left Kyris, Drake proposed to spread the news on my mission and the edict throughout this sector. However, we don't want the AP to make the connection. Neither *Assiduous* nor *Bumblebee* nor *Raydancer* should appear in any inhabited system to drop him off there. So I decided to intercept you and *Narihira* to ask you whether you'd take them along."

Syreen focused on Ubukata. "It's not entirely without risk. An AP inspection while they're aboard might cause you a lot of trouble. AP spies learning about their passage might still lead to a rather unpleasant interrogation. However, should you manage to get them off your ship without the authorities noticing, that risk should be marginal."

The merchant captain nodded. "It's very kind of you to consider my safety. But remember, I promised you any route you needed, with or without cargo—or passengers, in this case—unconditionally. So if you asked me to take them to Nysa, I'd do it, despite the possible outcome."

She could feel Yusef's agreement, too. It had to be some code of honor between merchants that she hadn't completely understood, yet, but if Ubukata was willing to help her cause, she had no choice but to accept his aid.

"Believe me," he said. "After what you told me, I do have reason to fear the AP bullies even more—but I also see the need to do something about it. If you're the only one to put a stop to their crimes, you must get all the support anyone can give. And if you say the news must be spread, we'll do our part. Mr. Dragutin can tell me the details, and we'll pass them on, from guild world to guild world. Plus, I'll do my best to find another skipper willing to take him along. A double star angel's recommendation will surely help."

"Triple," Yusef said. "Triple star angel, after we made the trip through the rift."

Ubukata stared at her pilot. "That was her, too?"

"That was her, too," Yusef agreed. "Including her daring recapture of a ship taken by pirates, reinstating legal ownership and command, and shooting a few other warships with our frigate."

"So there's still only one star angel—I had first thought there'd be more to come. I didn't make the connection." The merchant half closed his eyes. "These are interesting times. I wish you luck with your mission, wherever you're going next."

"Oh, that's no secret," she said. "The Crown system, Sirius sector."

"That's behind the chasm."

"Yes. *Assiduous* and I, we'll meet that challenge."

"Everyone else I'd ask whether he's mad. But you—you have another trick up your sleeve, do you?"

"I do. I'll spread my wings, and my feathers will carry me across. That's what angels do, don't they?"

PART THREE—REPAIRS

CHAPTER FORTY-THREE

Syreen hesitated before climbing into her pilot's seat. Was it fear she felt?

If so, neither the double penetration by *Assiduous'* formidable phalluses nor the pricks in her thighs and neck were the reason. The little pain they caused were forgotten once she could be one with him, and she felt wet and ready enough for their glorious reunion.

Her nudity meant nothing. She had never understood why it had made her fellow pilots feel vulnerable—no clothing could truly replace a skirmisher's thin sheet of steel.

It was the task before them that troubled her. Each of their last legs had taken them closer to the chasm. Each hyperflight had shown her more damage, torn fabric, ripped threads, warped hyperspace, and decay in the foundation below. The area before them was on the brink of vanishing from existence—and once it did, pulling stars and planets with it, this entire galaxy was doomed. Like a gargantuan black hole, the chasm would suck up everything. The stars' sad songs bore evidence of what was and what would be.

There might be no more than a few megacycles left before the process became irreversible.

That wasn't her concern now—not yet. Right now, she only had to find a way past the damaged area, and from what she had seen, that task was even more complicated than she had expected.

Navigable hyperspace had become a maze of dead ends, allowing her to follow a passage for a few hundred light years, just to end in a system with only one way out—the one she had arrived through. It could be a task of more than a life-time finding the one connection to the other side. Meanwhile, Drake and Ubukata would spread their news of an edict never to come.

She had examined the message drones' passage. The threads those drones followed were too thin even for her.

Unless I can do something about it.

Assiduous' primary phallus pulsated invitingly. *Come,* it seemed to say. *Come and join me for a ride.*

"Well," she said aloud, and only to herself. "Well, idling around won't take me anywhere, either."

Then she reached for the phallus and stroked it firmly. "Be hard for me. We'll have fun together, now."

CHAPTER FORTY-FOUR

Weeping stars, holding on to frayed seams, watching the foundations of their existence fading away, were almost too much to bear.

Before her, only thin lines held together what once had been solid — each so frail that the slightest touch should rip it apart. What had appeared like the best passage across now almost caused her despair.

Syreen recalled her past. Three destroyers and eight skirmisher wings against a hostile fleet assembled around five dreadnaughts hadn't made her determination falter, not even after all her wingmates had been shot dead.

She had fought on, and she could do the same now.

If you can't win, change the rules.

— Pardon? —

Partner, we're changing the game.

The Navigator reached out to catch hold of a nearby star. Upon her touch, the star shivered, then cheered. Encouraged, she felt forward to three more stars.

She drew a fine string from each of them and began to weave these strings into a delicate pattern. Where they touched, they solidified. At the same time, each of her pulls tired her, each weaving made her ache, made her feel sore. She knew she couldn't let go, but the pain in her grew, too. Each new link felt like a stab, each pull cut deep. She felt like crying.

Finally, the entire structure felt strong enough to support her journey, and she guided *Assiduous* across her web.

Beyond, she found firmer support, held by a group of large red giants, whose songs welcomed her with glee — but she felt too weak to appreciate it. She had to let go, had to drop from hyperspace, had to find rest . . .

Herman noticed *Assiduous'* lights flicker.

"We've left hyperspace," he said aloud. "Something's wrong."

"Why? What's different?" Vivien asked, displeased by the interruption.

"Terribly wrong," he insisted. "Come along. You, too, Charlene."

He pulled the two girls with him, out of his bedroom, down the corridor to the elevator, and, despite their protests, all the way to the bridge.

He found Syreen wrapped into her chair, penetrated and connected as always, but where he'd expected to see her vivid, naked body, he found a skinny figure with ribs, hips, and cheekbones peeking forward through pale, paper-like skin.

"That's — horrible," Vivien said. "What's she doing in that, uh, monstrosity?"

"Shut up and come," he said and shoved them closer. Keeping a firm grip on both of them, he leaned forward and offered his neck to her lips.

"Bite me," he whispered. "You need it."

Her lips touched his neck, and he felt four tiny, pointy things slowly poking through his skin. *Ouch.*

The girls shrieked, but he wouldn't let them go. He knew what Syreen needed now, and he alone wasn't able to give it to her.

The Navigator's bite gained a little power, and the pain faded. His grip around the women faltered, but they had stopped shrieking and fighting. When he sank to the floor, Vivien leaned forward.

Charlene followed.

Vivien joined him on the floor. "I had no clue," she whispered, then reached to her neck. The tiny holes had already closed. "But if that's what she needs most . . ."

"It's the fastest way to regain her power," he said. "In an emergency like this . . ."

"I can feel her gratitude," Charlene said and sat down next to them. "She's so — so, uh, weak still."

"That chair," Vivien whispered. "She's bound to the ship?"

Herman only nodded.

Vivien tried to pull his head around, but didn't find enough strength. He turned to her, and she blew him a kiss. Next, he found her hand between his legs.

"I need you now," she whispered. "I'm feeling too weak to walk out, but I need you now. Can you do me now?"

"I don't know," he admitted, but then he felt Charlene's lips around his cock, a tingle, and a welcome reaction. "Uh, together we might get something done . . ."

CHAPTER FORTY-FIVE

Syreen still felt weakness in her legs when she climbed out of her pilot chair. *I can't do that every tencycle.*

For now, she didn't have to. *Assiduous* would need a few more tencycles to recharge by bathing in the star's light.

She gazed down on Herman with the two women, all sprawled on the floor, the juices of their lovemaking still drying. His blood had saved her from passing out for a long time. The two women's presence had saved her from sucking him dry — knowing there was more to have had saved his life.

Now she owed them an explanation.

Just then the dark-haired woman — Vivien — opened her eyes and gave her a weak smile. "That was — strange," she whispered. "I — I didn't expect that."

"I shouldn't have abused you like this," Syreen said. "I have to apologize."

"No — no, it's okay. I could feel you needed it dearly. After all you did for us, what's a little blood donation?"

Her emotions said the same — it was okay for her.

Well, if she doesn't feel horror, I shouldn't try to convince her otherwise, should I?

The blonde struggled to get up, then surprised Syreen with a tight hug. "Poor thing," she said. "You're expending yourself. You were looking like you were dried out. You should call for our aid in time, next time."

Being held by another nude woman, wearing the fresh smell of lovemaking, didn't feel bad at all. Syreen suppressed the urge to reach for her firm buttocks. "You're taking it surprisingly easy — uh, Charlie?"

"Charlene. Well, I think, Charlie is okay, too. Yes — it's been an ugly sight, you in that chair, but you've been looking so frail, so helpless, and you've been so grateful . . . and, well, the way you were connected . . . is it fun, sometimes?"

"Each time. Only not when it takes too long."

Charlene smiled. "But now you'd like to have more — gentler, like only a woman can give you. I could feel your hesitation when you let go."

Vivien now stood behind her, radiating weakness, but also lust. The dark-haired woman let her fingers run down Syreen's spine and into her butt crack.

Syreen felt her own gooseflesh and smelled fresh wetness — her own, Vivien's, Charlene's.

Charlene's hands gently followed the curve around Syreen's breasts, went up to her shoulders, then down again. The blonde bent her knees and kissed Syreen's nipples.

Vivien's hands were now at her hip bones, feeling their way inward and down, to the thighs, around her legs, across her buttocks, and into the crack again. One finger touched her labia. "Oh, dirty girl, you're dripping wet already."

Syreen noticed Herman stirring. The private was still reclining on the floor, but his member was firmly erect now. She smiled. If he enjoyed watching them, he deserved it, but indeed, she wasn't eager to feel anything penetrating her.

Charlene was busy sucking her right nipple now. Vivien was brushing her own nipples across Syreen's back, with one hand combing her pubic hair. The other hand was still exploring the wetness between her thighs.

When Vivien accidentally touched her clit, she came.

"Wow," Charlene commented. "That was fast."

"But only the first," Vivien said. "We're only getting started."

Syreen panted. "How . . ."

"Hush." Charlene placed a finger on Syreen's lips. "Re-member — we're professionals."

CHAPTER FORTY-SIX

Again, Syreen shivered in the face of ruined fabric with ruffled seams. Again, navigating hyperspace and recreating her path literally *on the fly* required great effort.

This time she felt no fear, though. She knew she could do it, she knew how to do it, she knew how much she could do without overspending herself, and the expected pain no longer worried her. Plus, she knew she had five women at her side, willing to give her whatever she'd need. Three for her immediate relief, two in reserve or to call for more. Not one of the twenty-four women aboard had refused to help after Charlene and Vivien had explained how important their task was — and how *good* it felt to help.

So she spent her time in hyperflight mending, knitting, weaving, splicing, accompanied by the stars' lament turning into rejoicing.

So she spent her time off-duty, when *Assiduous* had to recharge, listening to their welcoming tunes while enjoying gentle professional stress relief.

Occasionally, she had to eat. A rumbling belly wouldn't help her focus on her tasks.

During one lunch, Mo joined her at her table. "May I?"

She nodded, and he took a seat.

He came straight to the point. Points? He couldn't spot any indication of canines when she took the next bite of her meal. "Syreen — you should know, I may not look as tasty as the ladies, but I'm there if you need me."

"I know," she reassured him. "I also know you're doing your best for the ladies' comfort. I'm aware Haiki and Yusef are spending their time with *Bumblebee,* keeping the frigate in shape as well as exercising, just in case we might need that ship. You're keeping them occupied with little chores—not enough to make them complain, but enough to prevent boredom. That's a big help for me. Thank you."

"You're welcome—you know, sometimes I must remind myself of what we're doing, why we're here, but each time I see you, your serene determination, I know what I must do." He folded his hands. "I'm feeling better—did I tell you before? The old Mo, *Molly Malone's* skipper, didn't care about the universe, about the people around. Shipping young women to their doom—what a despicable guy that man was. Today, I can look into a mirror and be proud of what I see. I don't want that to change."

She nodded and slightly cocked her head.

"Yes, thank you. Can you already tell how far we've come? Or how many more legs we'll need?"

She swallowed and nodded again. "We're more than halfway through, by distance alone. But the hard part is still ahead of us. As it seems, there's been heavier travel on this side of the chasm even after it tore. Maybe because there were worlds to trade with, worlds not to be deserted. However, continuing their ways did those worlds a bad service—I've seen stars entirely disconnected."

"Bad for those worlds that aren't self-dependent."

She frowned. "Bad for those that were, too. Tearing the fabric of space weakened their stars, meaning their stars are fading. The habitable zone moves system-inward, but the planets' orbit remains. Those worlds are cold, probably lost their atmosphere within generations. Without a chance to leave, their population was doomed—unless they had another world, closer to their star, to retreat to."

Mo tried to imagine such a fate.

"But—that's horrible! In a way, that's even worse than—it makes a kinetic strike appear merciful."

Syreen spread her arms. "That's why the edicts are ordered the way they are. That's why the proscription of damage to the fabric of space comes before the destruction of worlds."

The old skipper suddenly felt a deep sadness. "And there's nothing we can do for them?"

The Navigator shook her head. "No. I'm trying to find us a way through less damaged zones, where I can do repairs with reasonable effort. I'm circumnavigating the worst places— those around the dying stars. Even I can't go there. It would take a fleet of living ships with their navigators to mend such severe damage."

"A fleet we don't have."

"No." Her face looked sad now, too. "No. I must bear that burden on top of all others. It's no relief that the damage is not on my conscience."

She gazed down on her plate, no longer eating.

Mo rose and left. *Making her sad like that preys on my conscience, now. Why did I ask?*

CHAPTER FORTY-SEVEN

Broken strings, dying stars everywhere ahead — Syreen couldn't spot a single safe thread to reinforce.

She surfaced from deep integration.

We'll have to weave a new mesh.

— My Navigator. —

"Call the others," she addressed Jona. "Quick."

No more than a centicycle later, her entire crew assembled around her.

— Servants. Livestock. —

Crew. They're supporting our cause willingly.

— As my Navigator wants. —

Let's get it done.

She felt a neck offered to her lips and accepted the donation. Another followed, and another, and a fourth one.

The fifth woman briefly radiated disappointment when the Navigator didn't bite.

"Soon," Syreen said. "Stay close."

For a moment, she focused on the phalluses inside her. Next, she sensed the warm and wet cavern welcoming her primary inseminator.

Let's get it done, she repeated.

She pulled a thread from the weave she had arrived through, split it into five and sent those lines to the next five stars ahead — five stars nearer to non-existence than any she had connected to before.

Her touch seemed to make them flash — a whimper became a cheer, mourning became a tune of hope.

With her embroidery growing, the stars' single chants became a canon, then a choir — with their song telling her where and how to knit and knot.

Syreen felt exhausted, but happy, and not as worn-out as on her previous flights, when she surfaced from deep integration and opened her eyes.

The first thing she saw was ginger hair and a smile.

"You okay?" Gwen asked.

"Okay," she whispered and returned the smile. "We made it."

"Hard work?"

"Hard work."

"You were struggling," Gwen said. "We couldn't see what you did, but you needed fifteen donations. Relax now."

Gwen helped her out of her chair. *Assiduous* would find his way to a good recharge spot on his own — one of the few tasks he could do without pilot guidance.

Her legs wouldn't support her, but Gwen's grip was firm. Haiki joined them, and together, they carried her to another room with a soft bed.

"Relax," Gwen repeated. "I'll stay with you. Sleep now."

She gazed at the ginger hair once again and closed her eyes, knowing she was being taken good care of.

CHAPTER FORTY-EIGHT

Emerging from hyperflight without need for another dona-tion felt good. Syreen grinned at Casey. "All clear."

"No trouble this time?"

"No trouble at all. We've left the chasm far behind. This part of space is stable, allowing an easy seven-sigma flight." She focused on her sensors, already picking up an incoming call. "In exchange, it's frequented. I must answer that call now."

"*Unknown ship, this is Moscow harbor patrol, Captain Tolstoj of* MSN Katharina *speaking. Please identify yourself and your origin, and state your business here.*"

The accent was barely understandable, but it was Common. She pronounced her reply carefully. "Moscow harbor patrol, this is the living ship *Assiduous* of the People. I'm Nav-igator Syreen, currently Duchy Fleet Commander in Charge. Port of departure was Kyris, destination is Crown, in order to deliver a guild message vault."

"*Navigator Syreen, please have your commandant reconfirm your port of departure. I read Kyris, K-Y-R-I-S, correct?*"

"Captain Tolstoj, I'm *Assiduous'* commandant. Navigator is the supreme rank among my people. I confirm Kyris. Yes, I traveled the chasm."

"*Navigator Syreen, according to what my teachers told me, you must be mad or brilliant — the chasm can't be crossed, they said.*"

"Captain Tolstoj, I'm certainly not mad, but your teachers were right. No ordinary ship can travel the chasm unharmed. However, those rules don't apply to a living ship with his

Navigator. Is there a merchant guild office at Moscow?"

"I'm not sure yet what to make of your story, but yes, there is. I will forward your arrival to Moscow Orbital Three and detach an escort to you. Please stand by."

Moscow Orbital Three was the largest space station Syreen had ever seen, dwarfing even *Assiduous*. The two light cruisers that had attempted to appear as if they were escorting her living ship were replaced by a nine men strong *honor guard* inside the station.

Following Mo's advice, she carried her guns again.

"You don't want to appear weak. It's part of the show."

Her guard hadn't been overly impressed by the guns, but her decorations had immediately caught their attention. They hadn't asked, though.

They approached a portal framed by strong red-and-silver pillars, the doors made from some almost-black material.

Guards in red and silver moved to attention upon their approach. The doors opened inward, and a solitary man stepped forward. He wore a red robe with a silver lining, the latter almost matching his hair, and bowed before her.

She saluted and smiled.

"Welcome," he said. "I'm guild secretary Ivanow, at your service. You had a safe journey?"

"Hardly," she said. "I'm Navigator Syreen. Traveling the chasm is anything but safe."

The secretary gave her a startled look. "The chasm? But . . . but where are you from?"

"The Duchy."

"The Duchy? But—that's impossible."

"Can we go inside?" she asked and gestured at her guards. "I'm carrying classified information."

"Oh, uh, yes—come in."

The honor guard stayed behind. Instead, four guards in red and silver guided them into the guild hall and into a small conference room. Two guards stayed outside, two assumed position on each side of the door inside.

If he trusts them, I'm fine with it.

The secretary waved at a chair. "Make yourself comfortable."

When they sat, he smiled at her and folded his hands. "Bear with me—I didn't recognize the code. What's the real issue here?"

She placed a small data vault on the table. "A copy of the Kyris guild rolls. The *complete* rolls, including the part that's never trusted to drones. I've promised to deliver one to the first guild member I meet, the second to the guild commissar at Crown."

Ivanow's gaze flicked back and forth between her face and the vault. "But—that means you really had to cross the chasm."

"That's what I said, yes."

He squinted at her. "There's one thing our experts are absolutely firm about. The chasm can't be navigated by any object larger than a message drone. The result is inevitable destruction. They say the structure of space itself is damaged beyond repair. These statements have been challenged for megacycles, at least, and been confirmed each time. Now you're sitting here and claim you're wiser than our brightest scientists—and yet, fact is you're sitting here. Can you explain?"

"Your experts are right. What they tell you is the sad and undeniable truth—the fabric of space itself is damaged to an extent that your technology can't navigate. Caused by too many reckless jumps at too low sigma levels for too long. Beyond repair as far as all your experts have been able to learn about it." She glanced at the guards at the door, who were uncomfortably shifting from one foot to the other. "However, their science isn't mine. Their rules don't apply to a Navigator of the People and her living ship."

"A *living* ship? What does that mean?" He scratched his

chin. "I may have read or heard something like that, but I don't remember. Can you give me another clue?"

"Have you ever heard of the Forgotten People?"

One guard wheezed. The other almost lost his balance. Ivanow forgot to breathe.

Syreen patiently waited until the secretary had digested her statement. A few deep breaths later, he was able to meet her gaze again.

"That's just old lore my parents told me," he said. "But . . ."

"But I'm one of these no longer forgotten people, I'm here, and my living ship is docked at this station."

"And there's this vault, which will doubtlessly prove at least the port of origin you claimed." Ivanow briefly closed his eyes. "But what does your sudden appearance mean? What makes old lore become current reality?"

She shrugged. "You're touching a sore spot there. I'm a foundling, an orphan. But from what I've seen so far, it's time for an enforcer to set some things straight. During the last twelve kilocycles, I had to witness violations of all three edicts."

The guard wheezed again, the secretary took another deep breath. "The surprises won't end. Violations of the edict — but what do you mean, *three* edicts?"

Syreen smiled, sensing his attempt to test her. "Three edicts, as laid down in your codex."

She recited, "Edict Number One proscribes deliberate damage to the fabric of space or destruction of stars. Edict Number Two proscribes deliberate destruction, sterilization or rendering uninhabitable of worlds, especially, but not limited to, kinetic strikes, large-scale application of nuclear or biological weapons, and systematic destruction of geological stability. Edict Number Three proscribes deliberate interference with the genetic code of intelligent beings."

"Those are not the words of the codex," Ivanow tried again.

"No. Those are the words from the original source, translated into Common. Your codex contains a simplified version."

The secretary nodded. "And you say you've witnessed violations of all three?"

"And found evidence of even more, yes. Careless four-sigma jumps where six-sigma would have been possible. Attempted and announced kinetic strikes against inhabited worlds. Genetic experiments—yes, I've seen it all. Until I reached the chasm, I had thought I'd seen the worst already."

"The chasm." The secretary leaned forward. "The guild established rules for safe travel. But we have no means to check what people do."

"That's meteor dust," Syreen interrupted him. "Pure nonsense. Of course you have means. On my side of the chasm, every warship records jump parameters. Merchants could do the same—and if you know how to protect credit chips or guild rolls against tampering, you can do the same with a trader log."

"But to make people use it—"

"You make it mandatory for everyone. Those who don't have such a log can't register with the guild, can't exchange credits, can't dock at stations. How long would it take to have such rules in place? A kilocycle, at max. Next, you set standards for standard routes. Where one pilot can make six-sigma, everyone can. Failure to do so results in penalties, unless there's recorded emitter damage. Easy—if you want it."

The secretary shook his head. "Easy, as you say—but a decision I can't make. Since you said you'd address the commissar, you may put your proposal to him. Perhaps he's willing to listen to a member of the Forgotten People."

And ignore my request, as she could read from his

expectation. *But there's more I'll have to tell him.* "He will listen, I promise you."

"Oh, of course. You've traveled far enough to trigger his curiosity. Now, let me check this vault."

Syreen patiently waited.

Guild secretary Ivanow frowned. A while ago, he had confirmed that the vault was sound. Now his mind was racing, and she didn't like his feelings.

"That statement about docking fees," he began.

"Yes?"

"I fear I can't accept such an obligation. That's beyond my authority."

She had learned enough about merchants to smell trouble.

"That's not the question," she said. "Secretary Jacomo showed me. The obligation is recorded in the rolls, and you confirmed the rolls are sound. The question is whether it's within your authority to cancel or deny such an obligation — after I've fulfilled my side of the contract by safely delivering the rolls. My delivery can't be undone. The terms can't be re-negotiated."

"Of course that's possible. That's regular business."

"Only if both parties agree. I won't."

He seemed to reconsider his options.

She showed him her predator smile.

He flinched.

"You're a merchant. You're an experienced man. You surely renegotiated countless contracts in your life. That's your way." She pointed at her chest. "I'm a navy pilot, trained for combat. I'm not particularly good at negotiations, but I excel in battles. Each of these stars is a successful kill, and some of those stars represent dreadnaughts."

"Dreadnaughts," Ivanow echoed.

"That's my regular business," she said. "I negotiate the

terms of surrender — once. There is no second round. Violating the terms of surrender usually results in a kill." She winked at him. "Some have tried to blackmail me, once. They only added to my decorations."

Ivanow's feelings told her he'd discarded any questionable ideas, so Syreen softened her smile. "Sorry, I've let myself be sidetracked. We were talking of your merchant way. I said I'm not interested in renegotiating the terms of my contract — partially because I can't rely on regular income. As I don't know yet if and where I might find a contract for my return trip, I must watch my purse. So — may I expect that question of my docking fees settled?"

The secretary knew when he had lost. "Of course."

CHAPTER FORTY-NINE

I could get used to this kind of travel, Syreen mused after another easy hyperflight. Even though she had seen evidence of damages here and there, the fabric of space overall was still solid in this sector. Perhaps merchant pilots were more concerned with their jumps hereabouts?

Crown was buzzing with travel, so she wasn't instantly noticed. When the call came, *Assiduous* had already assessed the strength of their entire fleet.

"Unknown ship, this is Crown harbor authority. You arrived at an uncharted jump exit. Please identify yourself and your origin, state your business here, and explain your reasons for violating our regulations for safe travel."

"Crown harbor authority, this is the living ship *Assiduous* of the People. I'm Navigator Syreen, currently Duchy Fleet Commander in Charge. Port of departure was Moscow, final destination is Crown, in order to deliver a guild message vault. We did not violate your jump regulations, as we did not arrive by hyperjump."

There was a long pause, much longer than light speed delay required. As she was easily sailing system-inward, she felt no reason to hurry.

"Assiduous, did you mention the Duchy? Please repeat."

Syreen sent a data package with her home system coordinates. "Crown harbor authority, I confirm the Duchy. Last port before Moscow was Kyris. Although you didn't ask, I confirm having traveled the chasm."

The next pause was even longer. The answer was an

unexpected broadcast. *"All ships, stand by. All ships, stand by. Outbound ships, proceed as scheduled. Inbound ships, prepare for evasion course and await instructions. I repeat, outbound ships, proceed as scheduled. Inbound ships, prepare for evasion course."*

Mo appeared in the door to the bridge.

She waved one arm. "Come in."

He waited for *Assiduous* to grow a chair up from the floor for him, then dropped into it. "How did they take your announcement?"

"With silence so far." She invoked a display of the system for Mo. "It's a busy place, with tightly regulated traffic, and I don't fit into their pattern."

"I've seen similar patterns in our sector, too. Very efficient."

"Here they are," she said.

"Assiduous, you are required to keep your current vector and double your current deceleration. You will be assigned an escort and guided to a quarantine zone. The authorities will decide on your appeal in due time."

Syreen glanced at Mo. "Quarantine? Do you know of similar procedures?"

He scratched his head. "Other than restrictions for planets like Gattaca, there's usually nothing station sanitization can't handle. According to guild regulations, free trade may not be obstructed by arbitrary authoritative procedures. I'd have to check, but I think putting a ship under quarantine requires a vote by the local guild board."

"Thank you." She activated her comm. "Crown authorities, I confirm my current vector. I confirm double deceleration to allow your much-appreciated escort adapting their vector. Your quarantine proposal is hereby rejected, as it wasn't accompanied by the required guild board decision. I expect to be treated appropriately for a priority one guild courier, beginning with priority docking."

And thanks to Jacomo for telling me how to deal with them.

Mo only smiled, until their reply came.

"*Assiduous, your guild message vault will be delivered by a high-speed intrasystem courier. Your complaint regarding quarantine has been registered.*"

The merchant made a sour face. She hushed him with a hand wave.

"Crown authorities, for your records, I did not file a complaint regarding quarantine. For your records, should I not be provided with appropriate directions for priority docking, I will approach the next available vacated docking position."

To her staff captain, she added, "This stubbornness is embarrassing."

"*Assiduous, your escort will guide you to your quarantine position, if necessary, by application of force.*"

"Boneheads." She shook her head. "Crown authorities, your threat of application of force against an enforcer has been recorded. I must advise you that any such action may be regarded as complicity and result in your world being placed under edict itself."

Mo stared at her. She pointed at the display and let the symbols of the four approaching warships flash. "This is getting out of hand. I'll give them a last try."

A single thought changed her comm settings. "Crown authorities, this is *Assiduous,* Navigator Syreen. I arrived here in peace, as courier for the guild and as enforcer of edicts. I was threatened with illicit impediment of free trade by quarantine. I was threatened with the application of force. Should you not return to reason and provide me with the appropriate priority course and docking instructions for a priority one guild courier, I will cancel my approach to Crown. Instead, I will spread the news that Crown is no longer a world honoring guild rules. This is my last call."

"Useless, if you ask me," Mo said.

She only smiled. The answer didn't take long.

"*Assiduous, your last message was broadcast. Please check your* comm settings."

A smirk grew in the merchant's face. "You broadcast that message?"

The Navigator nodded. "All frequencies, all directions. I guess I've got their attention now. I won't have that nonsense."

She let the warship symbols flash again. "They're sending warning messages. I shall not make any attempt to change course. Oops."

"What?" Mo asked, alarmed.

"A laser shot, meant as a warning. A far miss, but that's unacceptable. I must do something about them. Excuse me."

She focused inward. *Let's take control of these four.*

— What will we do with them? —

For now, we'll disable their weapon systems and jump drives.

— That's all? Done. —

Syreen switched her comm back to single receivers and waited.

"Did you shoot back?" Mo asked warily.

"No. I didn't go through all this pain of traveling the chasm to start a war here. We're here to follow proper administrative procedures — so that I won't have to resort to terminal punishment."

Syreen watched the escort ships' course. Keeping up their acceleration toward *Assiduous* didn't make sense if they still planned to align their vector with hers — their drives weren't powerful enough for it.

— They are preparing several course change maneuvers. I cannot see their calculations, but applied at certain points, some would be suitable for an attempt to ram us. We could dodge such an attempt, of course. —

Of course. Just make their drives fail should they trigger anything foolish.

— Their current course is foolish already. —

Okay, make that overly *foolish.*

Another incoming call interrupted her musings.

"Assiduous, *this is Crown port authority, Harbor Director Thorwaldsen. Guild Commissar Okamele is sitting at my side. We're authorized to speak for the Crown government and for the guild. Please accept our apologies — the harbor staff on duty wasn't properly trained for handling such extraordinary cases. My staff is preparing a priority access route for you. Please bear with us — we have to make sure other traffic won't interfere with your approach.*"

Nicely put. She glanced at the escorts' vectors again.

"Director Thorwaldsen, thank you for your personal intervention. There's no need for apologies, and of course, I'm glad your staff is taking diligent care of my safety. My current primary concern is the safe delivery of the cargo entrusted to me to Guild Commissar Okamele. I will send you drive parameters for the fastest approach — your staff may add the safety margins they feel comfortable with."

In fact, it wasn't the fastest approach *Assiduous* could handle, but the fastest she was willing to unveil. Nevertheless, it outclassed any ship in this system by far.

"Assiduous, *this is Guild Commissar Okamele. You said you traveled the chasm. Does that mean it is safely navigable? I'm asking for the sake of several border worlds we've lost contact with for quite some time.*"

Syreen took a deep breath. "I'm sorry, Commissar. The fabric of space all through the chasm is severely damaged. There is no safe passage."

"But you could cross the chasm, you said."

"I'd like to discuss the details with you once we meet in person — mending even enough structure for a single passage required substantial personal sacrifices."

"Mending? You repair hyperstructure?"

"Yes."

"By all spirits in space. Can you teach us how it's done?"

Syreen sighed. "Let's meet in person, and I'll explain."

CHAPTER FIFTY

Syreen studied her counterparts' faces and emotions while they struggled to digest her tale.

The bald harbor director's gaze stayed focused on her chest—whether more for her decorations or more for her female shape, she couldn't tell, but he seemed to be amazed and attracted by both.

The guild commissar simply stared at the data vault she had placed into his palm. His remarkably fluffy brown eyebrows matched his curls well.

"Well," Thorwaldsen said. "If my records about Duchy awards are still true, those stars mark starship kills. Right?"

"*Warship* kills." She smiled. "Everything from stingship to dreadnaught."

"Practice targets?"

"Real targets. Targets that shoot back, manned by real people—people who died when I shot their ships."

"Sorry, I didn't mean to—well, where would you find dreadnaughts in operation? Too big for escort services, too expensive in terms of maintenance and staffing. Even battle cruisers aren't worth the effort."

"I asked myself the same. However, the Association seemed less concerned about cost or staffing than about firepower."

"Unless they're about to start a war, that's just foolish."

"They started a war, beginning with blasting orbital stations away—without prior declaration of their war."

The director frowned. "That's a no-go. All other nations

would rally together and fight them."

"Against a fleet of dreadnoughts and battle cruisers?"

Thorwaldsen nodded. "I understand. Still, that's overkill. Standard cruisers are way more effective."

Syreen shrugged. "Unless you need the engine power to haul asteroids for kinetic strikes."

The guild commissar dropped the vault. It bounced on the table, skidded away from him and came to a rest in the center. "That's against the edicts!"

The Navigator turned to Okamele. "And that's why I'm here. I need a guild tribunal to formally rule on their violations."

Okamele nodded. "That's the proper way. However, you have to address your local guild commissar. It's his authority."

"The local guild commissar resides on the Association's central world."

The harbor director laughed. "There's your hot potato, Oscar. I told you no one dares to cross the chasm for trifles."

Okamele shook his head. "No, you were right. But invoking a tribunal—do you have any clue how much time it takes just to make enough guild secretaries agree on a date and a location? You might live long enough to see it happen, young officer. I daresay I won't."

His emotions radiated honesty—he wasn't trying to mock her.

"I assumed the tribunal would take place here, in the Crown system. I also assumed you'd just call, and they'd take the next ship to get here."

"The guild isn't built on assumptions, Commander. There are procedures to be followed—and then, there's the problem of travel. Some worlds aren't linked to the passenger network."

"What about merchant ships?"

"They usually don't take passengers, and those who do won't take more than two or three. Not enough room for a secretary and his staff."

She raised an eyebrow over the mention of staff. But after all, it was their guild, their ways.

"Okay. How many secretaries do you need, and where are their worlds? *Assiduous* and I can pick them up."

"Some of those worlds are difficult to navigate."

Thorwaldsen chuckled. "Who are you trying to explain that to, Oscar? The pilot who crossed the chasm?"

Okamele sighed. "Sure, Niels. But even Moscow — where she just came from — requires eight difficult jumps."

Syreen leaned forward. "No, it doesn't. The hyperflight from Moscow took less time than my approach within the Crown system."

"As far as I know, there is no safe straight vector, even if I assume your ship is powerful enough for such a long jump."

"Listen. I didn't say jump. I said hyperflight. In flight, I don't need a straight vector, only a sound path to follow."

"But who would decide when to change direction? I was told computers can't do that in mid-flight."

"I do. I'm a Navigator. I fly hyperspace on sight." Syreen decided a shortcut would be appropriate. *You'll accept my fact-based explanation.*

She focused on the commissar. "From what Jacomo told me of the guild, I expected to find more support for my cause here, at the heart of the guild. Is it because you deem my claim unjust — or because it means uncomfortable decisions and cumbersome bureaucratic procedures?"

"See, Oscar?" Thorwaldsen said. "Precise navigation, right on the spot."

The commissar sighed again. "What exactly do you expect? After the sentence, I mean. It would do the guild no good to declare an embargo and then be unable to follow up on it. Such an approach would undermine our credibility — and worse, it might break the guild — the only organization keeping the worlds together. We might see worse than the guild wars."

"I understand your concern. Please understand mine. I will move against the Association with or without your sentence, because that's my duty as Navigator, as an Enforcer's pilot. My mission is legitimate within the rules my people set, that's all I really need. However, your embargo would make my mission legitimate among your people, too — which may ease the aftermath that's to be expected. From my point of view, failing to act on a clear violation against the core of your rules will do worse damage . . . than asking me to act on your behalf." Syreen smiled. "I'm the only one able to cross the chasm again, anyway."

Okamele wasn't convinced, yet. "But if we send you, and you fail, the guild's reputation will suffer, too."

She shook her head. "Should I fail, reputation would be your least concern."

Thorwaldsen scratched his left hand. "Would you think the Association could eventually cross the chasm with their dreadnaughts?"

"I wouldn't put that past their leader, even if he had to send his ships all around the galactic center. But no, that's not the issue here."

The commissar glared at the harbor director. "Niels, of course we're worried about the population on the other side of the chasm, too. We can only hope they're wise enough not to provoke a kinetic strike — that would be tragic."

Tragic indeed. But again, he wasn't mocking. His concern was genuine, on each topic.

She turned to Okamele. "And sadly, you couldn't come to their rescue. No, that's not my point, either. From your own observations — would you regard the chasm as stable?"

"What are you up to?" The secretary frowned. "At the

beginning, we saw more and more routes become unnavigable. But lately, there haven't been reports about trouble."

"Because few dare traveling close to the chasm," Thorwaldsen said and scratched his hand again. "So we don't have reports on successful passages, either."

Syreen sighed. "When I told my story, I mentioned the repairs of damaged space structure, remember? I only indicated the difficulties I had. I didn't touch the overall situation in the chasm yet. The deterioration of hyperspace continues, even without ships passing. It's only a question of time until it reaches Crown, too."

CHAPTER FIFTY-ONE

"**N**o jumps, no faster-than-light travel, nowhere in this sector." Syreen kept eye contact with the guild commissar. "And it won't stop here. Ultimately, this galaxy will die."

Okamele shrugged. "Let's focus on the issues at hand. Wasting our time on a distant doomsday scenario won't get us anywhere."

So ignorant. So selfish. Why should I worry about their rules, if they themselves don't care?

Should I tell them there are no more than two megacycles left? Should I make them listen? Should I tell them about the single black hole this galaxy will become? Should I tell them I'm the only person between them and ultimate destruction? Should I tell them just one Navigator won't suffice to mend the damage? Should I tell them there's no way to find more of my people, as there's only me – and him.

Him.

Realization came like a shock. She swayed in her chair. Thorwaldsen caught her shoulder before she could drop to the floor.

"Are you okay?" he asked.

She blinked. "Uh – yeah. I . . . I only just realized the true scope of my duties."

One man, one woman.

No. Never.

Thorwaldsen stared into the strange woman's face. One

moment, she had looked so fragile, so vulnerable — and now, her eyes told of a grim determination he'd never be able to match.

He knew his own virtues and flaws. Braveness wasn't among them. He was a good organizer, he knew how to get things done and keep them in order. He had enough imagination to make improvements to poor processes — but what burden this young Navigator carried, he couldn't fathom.

But in a way, he knew she told the truth.

Okamele shook his head. What to do? For most of life, his path had been clearly laid out before him. Join the guild, become secretary, do good work, gain attention of other guild secretaries — only in a positive way — network with local governments, rise in the hierarchy, become commissar . . . make no mistakes, retire to one of the recreation worlds.

He'd done his best to mitigate the problems the chasm posed. He couldn't have done more for the people affected. He had saved merchants from risking their lives. He'd kept his sector peaceful, he'd kept his records clean. Or so he had told himself.

Until now.

Out of nowhere, this woman had appeared. Having done the impossible, having traveled the chasm, she had come to ask the impossible. Or so he had tried to tell himself.

Watching her face, observing her stance, knowing of her achievements, believing her testimony, his carefully built self-deception couldn't persist.

With a firm shrug, he shook off his negligence. Yes, in the past, he had worked hard to attain his current, comfortable position, to have an easy life.

But damn, I've worked hard to be the man I wanted to be — the one who always does the right thing, who does things right. I won't change these ways. It's just another challenge.

"Let's plan the trip first. Who we need and the fastest way to collect them all. I'll prepare advance messages for the drones. Let me gather some stuff for the journey, and give me a little time to brief my deputy. Once we're on our way, you can tell me more about your concerns, about your most important issue. Okay?"

"Okay."

He had the strange feeling of being dismissed — in his own office. He glanced at Thorwaldsen, only to find a knowing grin.

With the heat rising in his cheeks, he lowered his gaze to the table. A tap on the table summoned his deputy.

CHAPTER FIFTY-TWO

Guild commissar Oscar Okamele watched the golden curtain close behind him, just as it had opened upon his approach. Only now did he dare to stare at the brightly lit hall. Walls and ceiling seemed to be covered with the same kind of golden curtain, with folds and wrinkles. Even the floor shimmered in the same color.

Rows of round, olive colored containers lined the walls, except where he spotted the racy shape of a corvette. He was squinting at a larger object in the back when another man sailed down from the ceiling.

"Impressive sight, isn't it?" the man said. "Welcome aboard *Assiduous,* Commissar. I'm Mo, Syreen's staff captain."

Without thought, Okamele shook the offered hand. "Thank you, Mo . . ."

"Just Mo. Come, I'll show you around. That ship in the back is *Bumblebee,* our frigate. As you may have guessed, this room is hangar and storage in one."

"Oh—no." He gazed back. "No airlock? Isn't that impractical?"

The staff captain grinned. "Not for *Assiduous.* Either ship can enter and leave without a single breath of air slipping away. This way, please."

"Where?" Okamele only saw a seamless wall where his guide was pointing.

"This way. Come closer."

He did as instructed. The shimmer seemed to form a ring

around them — now that he had seen it, he was able to spot similar patterns in other places on the floor, and also on the ceiling.

The pattern above them seemed to come closer.

When he gazed down, he almost stumbled — the staff captain caught his arm to stabilize him. The floor moved away from them — or were they moving up?

"It takes some getting used to these elevators," Mo admitted. "But it's completely safe, I assure you."

The ceiling opened when they reached it, and closed under their feet. "Force fields?"

"Something like that. I didn't understand *Assiduous'* explanation and decided not to follow up on it. Different technology — or biology, as you see it."

"You can talk with — with the ship?"

"Of course."

They were walking along a corridor with the same kind of gold-veiled walls. "Isn't it — uh — kind of pretentious to put up so many golden curtains? Or do they serve some special purpose?"

"Curtains? Oh — no, they *are* the wall. Or skin. Whatever."

Okamele shrugged. "Whatever. The Navigator said we'd be departing soon. Should we find a seat eventually?"

Mo shook his head. "We were on our way the moment the door closed behind you. Syreen said we're doing a twelve-stop round trip?"

"Yes. We need to collect twelve of my colleagues. I assume we won't run out of space?" He tried to spot any doors along their way, but failed. In a way, he wasn't surprised when the walls suddenly parted to a spacious room with his luggage in the middle of the floor. "No furniture?"

"You can have any you like." Mo followed him inside. "*Assiduous,* two chairs, please."

Two bumps appeared in the floor, grew, and blossomed

into comfortable-looking chairs. He sighed. "That's indeed something I must learn to accept. Growing furniture. Scary. Like it could eat someone."

"*Assiduous* won't eat Syreen's guests."

Mo didn't further comment this, and Okamele didn't dare to ask. Instead, he dropped into a chair and examined his room. "I'd like to have a bed, a desk and a chair. After all, I'll have to spend quite some time on this journey."

Fascinated, he watched the room change again. "The ship listens to me?"

"*Assiduous* listens when directly addressed," Mo said, taking his own seat. "And a short while afterward, in case there's more need. Yes, I guess we'll need around forty tencycles round trip."

Okamele shook his head. "There are some six-jump legs along the way. I've learned each recalculation takes time. Hyperspace is dangerous."

His opposite smiled. "Syreen crossed the chasm. She knows about the dangers of hyperspace, and we're not jumping. We're doing each leg in one hyperflight. It's so much faster you'd hardly notice it before it's over, if not for her announcement."

CHAPTER FIFTY-THREE

Syreen felt regret pulling *Assiduous* from hyperspace. Hyperflight in stable territory felt so much better than in the chasm, listening to the stars around, and all.

However, now that they'd reached their destination, there was no excuse to linger in flight any longer. Nor should she remain in deep integration. *Assiduous* didn't need the deep link for deceleration, and the Banjo authorities would call soon enough.

No. Why leave the initiative to them?

"Banjo authorities. This is Enforcer *Assiduous,* Navigator Syreen speaking. I'm on a top priority mission for the merchant guild. Please clear space for a high velocity approach to Banjo Orbital Four."

As close to the planet as she had exited hyperspace, message delays were negligible.

"Navigator Syreen, you've broken every traffic rule by placing your jump exit that close. Prepare to surrender to remote control and welcome a boarding team."

That was to be expected. "Negative, Banjo authorities. As I arrived by hyperflight, rules for hyperjumps do not apply. My exit point was carefully chosen outside designated transit areas. My current deceleration and trajectory fulfill regular safety requirements. For the sake of peace, I didn't read your last sentence properly—too easily it could have been misheard as an announcement of a hostile capture. Worse, your transmission arrived without identification."

Which made it illicit. *No need to rub it in.*

Their next message was significantly friendlier.

"Assiduous, *Navigator Syreen, this is Banjo Navy Harbor Control, Space Marshal Tony Young speaking. Please ignore earlier communication attempts. You are cleared for a high velocity approach to Banjo Orbital Seven, docking bay Ares Seventeen. This is a high security bay, for your protection. Your most impressive deceleration parameters might trigger unwanted attention."*

"Marshal Young, thank you for your kind invitation. I'm adapting my course accordingly."

"Navigator Syreen, I appreciate your understanding. Now, as you mentioned guild business, I will make sure the Banjo guild secretary will be advised of your arrival."

"Marshal Young, please advise the secretary of Guild Commissar Okamele's arrival, too. He is my guest."

"Navigator Syreen, how can that be? He's was on Crown four tencycles ago – according to latest drone message relay."

"Marshal Young, we left Crown two tencycles ago. Hyperflight is significantly faster than jump sequences."

There was a pause. *"Navigator Syreen, I'm looking forward to meeting you. I hope you'll find the time to join me for a hot forwine. Just one more question – how should I rank a Navigator in navy terms? Just for the arrival ceremony, you know."*

She grinned. "Marshal Young, for ceremonial purposes you may consider a Navigator equal to a tenured captain, but you might as well make preparations for the Duchy Fleet Commander in Charge."

"Oh. Fleet Commander in Charge, okay. Wait – did you say Duchy? Northern Rim Sector? The system still operating skirmishers?"

"Correct. In case you're wondering, yes, I crossed the chasm."

"We are honored. I'm sure there's an epic story behind that. I'm looking forward to any part you may tell me."

CHAPTER FIFTY-FOUR

Syreen took the offered seat with a smile.

Marshal Young's office was spacious, with desk and chair at one end, a large conference table with twelve seats in its center, and a smaller table with two chairs at the other end — where she was sitting now.

The marshal followed. "Would you like a drink? Our local biribona juice is excellent. Or a forwine?"

"I'll follow your recommendation and try the juice, thank you."

He smiled and fetched a jug and two glasses from somewhere under the table. "You won't regret it."

While she watched him pour the juice, she briefly sensed for his emotions, and found no sign of malice or mischief. *Just to be sure. I can't take risks.*

"What would you say as a toast?" he asked and raised his glass.

"Duke's health."

"Duke's health."

They clinked and drank. The juice had a sweet, strange taste.

"I like it," she said. "Can it be ordered from one of the orbitals?"

"Of course, but I'll gladly provide you with navy stock. And whatever you need."

"I'll tell my staff captain, and he'll check our needs."

"Consider that message delivered." He nodded toward her chest. "Your decorations are almost as impressive as your ship's drive. It must be very powerful."

"It is. However, I earned my first stars with my skirmisher, and a few more with a corvette and later a frigate."

"Oh. Skirmisher against stingship?"

"Some. You know skirmishers?"

"I'm interested in historic shipbuilding, and Duchy skirmishers are among the oldest designs still in operation—for their effectiveness. Until today, no stingship design could match their performance. It's fascinating." He picked up his glass and tapped its rim. "One of the most fascinating designs is that of the Forgotten People's so-called *living ships*—where no one can tell what that term *living* exactly refers to. By the way, I guess your *Enforcer* resembles quite closely what I've heard of them. Was its build perchance inspired by their descriptions?"

She cocked her head. "If you have any sources on the Forgotten People, I'd like to have a look at them. *Assiduous*—my ship—is no copy or rebuild, though. He's one of them."

"He?"

"All living ships are male."

The marshal almost dropped his glass. Drops of juice sprinkled over his fingers and sleeves. "You say you're flying a real living ship? But—how's that possible?"

"Indeed I am. Regarding the *How*—I'm a member of the Forgotten People myself, a Navigator, qualified to pilot one of their living ships."

After a sip of juice, she went on, "I found him on an unregistered planet, with the aid of a historian who had come across an ancient star map of my people. That map mentioned the place where a living ship had been hidden."

Young shook his head. "A real living ship. Incredible. But—in that case . . . you know why it's called *living?*"

"Because he is alive. Conscious. A person in the shape of a ship, with a mostly organic body."

The marshal took a deep breath. "Can I—can I meet him?"

"Of course. Visit us, and I'll show you around."

"No secrets?"

"Lots of secrets. Secrets I can't unveil because I don't know of them. For example, how he works. I have an intuitive understanding, but I couldn't explain his aggregates—organs—or rebuild them. I can only explain what they do. Like hyperflight—we don't jump, we fly through hyperspace like you'd fly a shuttle to the next orbital. We can see where we're going."

"We?"

"*Assiduous* and I. We're linked together, like one ass and one mind, if you excuse the profanity."

Young smiled. "You make my imagination run wild, if you excuse my frankness. May I dare to ask if you'd allow me a closer look?"

"You're welcome aboard, if your schedule allows—our stay here is limited. As soon as Commissar Okamele finishes his business, we're on our way again."

"My adjutant will be sorry, but he'll make my schedule fit. One of the privileges of rank—as fleet commander, you know what I mean."

Syreen nodded. Okamele had briefed her on Young's rank—space marshal was the highest rank on Banjo and many other planets in this sector.

"Now. Why don't you give me a sketch of your story—enough to let me recognize where we can support you?"

"The short or the long version?"

"Whatever you feel inclined to tell me."

"The long one, then."

"Great. Should I order dinner for us?"

"Highly appreciated, thank you."

CHAPTER FIFTY-FIVE

Mo found Syreen on the bridge, sitting on the floor, her back against the pilot chair, knees pulled close, face buried between her crossed arms.

"Are you okay?" he asked.

She looked up. "Huh?"

"Are you okay?"

"Oh. Uh, yes, mostly. I'm tired. The long flight, the meeting, the visit—everything okay, but in sequence, it draws from my strength."

"Need a bite?"

"What? No, thanks."

"Why don't you take a nap?"

"We're leaving soon. I must—"

"No, you don't. Tell *Assiduous* where to go, and could he put up some panels, too? Yusef can take the watch until we reach the transit point."

She shook her head. "I'm too tired to think straight. Of course, you're right."

"Shall I take you to your room?"

Syreen gave him a weak smile. "Yes, Poppa. As soon as Yusef arrives, you can pick me up. *Assiduous,* put up seat and panels. Yusef will get clearance for us, and then you'll depart as planned. Wake me up five centicycles before hyperflight."

— *As you instruct.* —

Yusef heard soft steps and turned to the doorway. "No

incidents, and we're right on track. Mo took care of our newest passenger — the commissar isn't overly happy with his sudden summoning, but once he met some of the girls, he was full of glee."

Syreen smiled. "I can imagine."

"Okamele asked for you, too. Mo told him you're taking a nap, and the commissar said he was glad to learn that there's still something human about you."

Her smile grew wider. "If that helps, I'll gladly take another nap once we're departing from Finney."

"Not during our approach?"

"No — they might be nervous until we meet. According to Okamele's message drone schedules, we're still ahead of the advance notices there." She climbed into her seat.

Yusef watched the large dildo slip into her crotch and felt his own member stirring.

She hissed once when putting her legs into position, and a second time upon leaning back. After a brief moment, she looked up. "Crew, prepare for hyperflight in three."

Syreen closed her eyes. "You're staying?"

Yusef nodded.

"Okay. I'll leave the screens up for later."

Chapter Fifty-six

Syreen suppressed a sudden impulse to yawn and stretch. No doubt Yusef would have appreciated watching her, and she'd appreciated his attention, but there was work to do — and there was Chiara. She didn't want to threaten their delicate relationship.

"Finney authorities, this is Enforcer *Assiduous*, Navigator Syreen speaking. I'm on a top priority mission for the merchant guild. Commissar Okamele is aboard and sends his regards. Please clear space for a high velocity approach to Finney Orbital."

The Finney system was far less frequented than Crown or Banjo, but still busy. How busy were their authorities?

Judging from the sleepy voice, they weren't busy at all.

"Lady, there ain't no such thing as a velo approach, but we've got plenty of clear space around. Just stick to your path, and you're fine."

"As you say. Have a dock ready for me in four cycles."

"Four cycles? You're kiddin', lady — you only just dropped in!"

"Four cycles, as I'm going easy. I'll be there, watch your plot."

"My plot? Lady, you're mocking me — heck, what's that? You're no hauler?"

His voice no longer sounded asleep, she noted with amusement. "You're watching an Enforcer in action. Our vector will be aligned with your orbital within the next four cycles. This way, we won't interfere with your traffic or your quietude any longer than necessary."

"*By all ghosts in space — I've never seen such parameters. What kind of ship is that, lady?*"

"A living ship. Have you ever heard of the Forgotten People?"

There was a brief pause, followed by a series of expletives.

Syreen waited. A quartercycle later, the man called again.

"*Lady, this is Danny, Finney space control, harbor authorities etcetera. Welcome to Finney. I must apologize for my prior communication. You're assigned to docking bay Charlie One, and your high velocity approach is confirmed. Now, if you could be so kind as to enlighten me what the fuck is going on here?*"

"Man, what eloquence," Yusef commented.

She winked at him. "Danny, I'll gladly brief you once we're docked. It's a long story."

"*I'm sure it's worth the patience, but — well, lady, the suspense is already killing me.*"

"I'll have to resurrect you after our arrival, then."

"*Oooh lady, I'm looking forward to your kiss of life.*"

When Syreen entered the dock, a lone, dark-haired man in a green jumpsuit approached her. "Navigator Syreen, I presume? I'm Danny. Welcome to Finney Orbital."

She grabbed him by the shoulder, pulled him close, and kissed him. His eyes widened. A moment later, she found herself wrapped in a tight hug. *Who's resurrecting who?*

When he let her go, gasping for air, she smiled at him. "Welcome back to life."

Danny laughed and slapped her shoulder. "Gal, you're all right. Now — what can I do for you?"

"I'd like to get clearance done so that Guild Commissar Okamele can visit the guild secretary on Finney, and perhaps allow my crew to stretch their legs."

"Oh, that. Consider clearance done."

"Indeed?" She turned around. "*Assiduous,* tell them we're

cleared."

"Confirmed."

Danny waved at the ship. *"Assiduous* is a strange title—your second in command?"

"My ship. I mentioned that after leaving hyperflight."

"Oh, sorry. I didn't pay attention." He stared at the open door. "Sorry, Mr. Assiduous. No offense meant."

"No offense taken, Mr. Danny."

The space controller, harbor master, etcetera, was already too distracted by the girls filing through the airlock and past him to take any more notice of her ship.

Okamele came last. By the time he joined them, Danny had managed to regain his senses.

"Welcome, Mr. Commissar."

"Call me Oscar. You're Danny?"

"I am. Pleased to meet you, Oscar."

"The pleasure is mine. Oh, by the way, the docking fees are on the guild."

"On the guild? What happened—did you lose a bet?"

Okamele smirked. "I'm not gambling or betting. We're obliged to compensate for a most valuable shipment—across the chasm."

CHAPTER FIFTY-SEVEN

Okamele found Syreen on the floor of her bridge, reclining against a large chair with attached screens.

"This was the last secretary to pick up," he said. "You're taking us back to Crown?"

"As planned," she said. "And after your tribunal, whatever its outcome, I'll take them all home, as promised."

"You don't have to. They can take regular liners. Although I'm sure they'll miss *Assiduous'* attentive hospitality — and they'll miss your staff's passionate attention as well."

"You won't?"

He gestured down his body. "Look at this old man. I'm hardly an appropriate companion for any of them. Oh, I admit, I like them, I like them all, their cheerful attitude, their dedication to your mission and their kindness in everything large and small. It makes me wonder how you recruited them."

"They didn't tell you?"

"I didn't ask until now."

"They were, well, entertainers."

"I guessed so. They are very good at what they do."

"They've come around to being proud of it." She indicated a chair Assiduous had grown for the commissar. "Have a seat and I'll tell you how I picked them up on Gattaca."

"Gattaca — that name rings a bell. Wasn't that a quarantine planet?"

"It is — which is meant to conceal the fact that the local populace results from a violation of the third edict. Someone broke quarantine rules to set those women down. I broke them again to put things back in order. You want to hear the whole story?"

"Please." Okamele sat down. "The more I learn about the situation across the chasm, the better founded our decision will be."

CHAPTER FIFTY-EIGHT

Syreen wasn't sure whether the conference room had been chosen to intimidate.

Thirteen tables were arranged into the shape of a U, opening toward the door. Thirteen seats were placed around that shape, occupied by the guild secretaries she had picked up, with the commissar at the crest. All men wore shiny robes.

A single chair in the center was obviously meant for her. Accepting that place would force her to turn around a lot — and it would hide her face from the men at the outer ends while she faced the chairman.

So she picked up the chair and pulled it back to where it would stand if the table arrangement were closed. There, she sat down and waited.

Okamele tapped the table. "The guild tribunal is assembled. The identity of the twelve secretaries has been recorded in advance."

She knew their names anyway. There was no need to waste any more time with formalities than absolutely necessary.

"The applicant is present. Please identify yourself."

"I am Syreen, Navigator and member of the ancient race you call the Forgotten People, pilot and commandant of the living ship *Assiduous*, Enforcer of the edicts."

"Thank you, Navigator Syreen. For the records — the tribunal members visited the living ship *Assiduous*, thus giving witness to its genuine existence. The ship in turn confirmed accepting the applicant as his legitimate pilot and as member of his constructors' people." He waved at her. "Now, Navigator Syreen, would you please start by quoting the foundation for your application?"

She was glad of this question. Okamele had assured her he'd guide her through the process. She wouldn't fail by leaving out important details or confusing the tribunal members.

"Yes, commissar." She closed her eyes to focus her mind.

"Edict Number One proscribes deliberate damage of the fabric of space, like actions that could create a rift or destruction of living stars. Edict Number Two proscribes deliberate destruction, sterilization or rendering uninhabitable of worlds, especially, but not limited to, kinetic strikes, large-scale application of nuclear or biological weapons, and systematic destruction of geological stability. Edict Number Three proscribes deliberate interference with the genetic code of intelligent beings. These edicts were established by my people long before your people ventured into space, long before my people became forgotten."

She could sense his desire to comment and paused.

"Thank you, Navigator Syreen. Note that these edicts are the same as the ones in the guild codex, only the words are different — they resemble the original engraving, not our ancestors' simplification. It is not this tribunal's task to investigate our codex' history. For the purpose of the current application, we may simply assume the edicts are the same for both our peoples. Agreed?"

He gazed around and found no argument.

Syreen sensed no disagreement either, rather curiosity.

"Navigator Syreen, before we come to the cause of your application, please tell us why you apply to this tribunal at all."

This was the question each secretary had asked her several times during the journey. Why had she crossed the chasm? Why this tribunal? She answered them truthfully. Today, her answer was for the records, and thus more elaborate than before.

"It is my people's responsibility to guard and enforce the edicts. It is my people's responsibility to witness violations, bring them to the attention of an enforcer for judgment. It is my own responsibility as enforcer of my people to judge the violations I witnessed and decide on a proper course of action. As you decided to make our rules your rules, and as the violations were committed — although not ultimately ordered — by members of your people, and moreover my verdict will affect your people, I'm now seeking judgment by your people, by your rules."

"And are you willing to accept our decision?" Okamele asked.

Ah, that was the crucial question! Another question asked during their journey, a question she hadn't really answered yet.

She nodded. "Yes, I will. I will take your decision into account when I make mine — it is my responsibility to judge whether you honor the edicts or not." She paused. *And if not, whether I'm still willing to aid you or leave you to your fate ultimately.* "In any case, I will deal with the one other person of my people who's behind all this, and nothing you say or do can take this responsibility away from me."

"That sounds like you're expecting us to decide in your favor."

She shrugged. "Of course. From my point of view, the situation with regard to the edict violations is unambiguous. I can't see how the tribunal could reach a different conclusion. Open, in my eyes, are the measures you deem appropriate. In any case, I always listen to reason."

Okamele placed his hands on the table. "I understand your position, and I hope you understand ours — our view on the situation and the conclusions we draw will rely on your testimony as well as on the evidence presented to us."

"Sure, I'd expect no less."

"Thank you. Before we begin, let me ask my colleagues —

do you agree with the applicant's position toward this tribunal?"

Syreen felt their reluctance and smiled. "Come on. I'm not about to bite your head off just because you ask a question. Challenge me, that's what we're here for."

"Let me ask," the Banjo secretary said.

Roger Walker was his name, she remembered. He was the youngest of them all. Red hair, tall, dimples — he looked cute. *Not now. Focus.*

"Let me ask," he repeated. "You're asking for our decision, but in the end will you do what you like?"

"You could read it that way," she agreed. "I'm asking for your decision, your advice, and for your support, too. For your decision, because whatever I'll do will largely affect all mankind in this galaxy, one way or another. The merchant guild is the only interstellar organization not limited by political boundaries, that's why I'm asking you. I'm asking for your advice, because your experience may help predict the people's reactions to what we decide to do. I'm asking for your support, because I believe we have a joint cause. However, while I may rely on your advice and your support, I cannot drop my responsibility into your hands. I will honor your decision in all conscience, but only I can ultimately resolve any conflicts between your judgment and my duties. And, believe me, I won't like what I'll have to do."

Walker nodded slowly. "Would you explain your conflicts to us and give us a chance to help resolve them to our joint satisfaction?"

She nodded, too. "That much I can promise, yes."

"In that case, I can accept and understand your reservation. After all, you're not a guild member nor in any other way related to the guild."

She cocked her head and focused on him. "Correct, aside from my triple registration as star angel."

"*What?*"

CHAPTER FIFTY-NINE

The turmoil her casual remark created took Syreen by surprise. Excited exclamations came mixed with questions. Their mental emanations were a storm of disbelief, curiosity, fascination, and — admiration.

While she waited for the thirteen men to calm down, she listened to Crown's central star. It sang of sorrow and hope, of sadness and joy, of its longing for harmony.

I'll do my best to foster harmony.

Her mental statement resonated twice — with cheerful notes in the star's song, and also in the guild tribunal members, soothing their excitement and their pulses.

"You never mentioned that before," Okamele said.

"Does it change anything?" Syreen asked. "Regarding the tribunal, I mean."

"No, not really," the commissar said. "Not from the legal point of view, that is."

"What is it, then?"

He sighed. "You must know, meeting a member of a race considered long forgotten is more than extraordinary — a truly unique event. It's something none of us ever would have dreamed of. But every member of the guild shares one dream — meeting a star angel once in his lifetime. You've made our dream come true."

She sensed the other tribunal members' agreement, and she spotted wetness in the corners of some eyes.

Walker cleared his throat. "This moment should not easily be pushed aside. Important as your claim to the tribunal may be, would you spare us a few centicycles to tell your story?"

Syreen shook her head. "If you want to hear the story, I will tell it—taking the time needed. If you're fine with that?"

Walker nodded, and Okamele said, "Navigator, please go ahead."

CHAPTER SIXTY

The audience remained silent long after Syreen had finished her tale. This time, she refrained from listening to their emotions. It didn't seem appropriate.

Again, Walker was the first to speak up. "What a story. Thank you for sharing it with us. It helped me understand how bad the situation really is. It taught me a lot about you, too — most of which I'll probably become aware of long after you've left us. Plus it sheds some light on what Oscar told us — that you'll return there anyway, whatever we decide, and that you expect at least a chance to succeed. You have a remarkable record of achieving the impossible."

"Indeed." Okamele rose. "I admit I was wrong. When you told me you'd deal with this navy leader, I thought you were crazy. No one can break through the ranks of an entire navy, system, and planetary defenses, to pick a fight with a single person — or so I thought. However, from what I've heard today, you might indeed be able to reach Nysa and face that man — whatever the outcome may be."

She shrugged. "Been there, done that."

Seeing his puzzled face, she explained, "Yes, I traveled to Nysa before, incognito, or so I thought. I met their supreme leader, escaped his torturer, and left before he learned my true identity. Next time, I'll be better prepared."

"What torturer?" Okamele asked.

"His name was Paolo. He was proud of his skills — deservedly so." She anticipated Okamele's next questions. "I rid Nysa of his presence before I left. About his death, I feel no remorse. Not after what he did to me."

"He didn't inflict permanent damage?"

"He didn't worry about that, as long as I remained able to answer his master's questions. However, time heals all wounds."

His face showed disgust.

Yeah, I prefer not to remember. "Can we return to business, please?"

"Yes. Yes, of course. My apologies. I didn't want to—oh, no matter. Now—we've learned about your motivation, and we've got an idea of your claim. It's time to state your request in clear words and to present evidence."

"Sure." She waited until all tribunal members signaled readiness. "I'm asking to put Nysa—no, the Association as a whole—under edict until compliance with the codex has been thoroughly reestablished."

Okamele frowned. "That's a severe claim."

The Kambria secretary raised a hand. "But it's also a very straightforward and clear claim. Let us not discuss its appropriateness before we can review the evidence."

"Agreed," another secretary said.

The commissar nodded. "Well—your turn, Navigator."

"Okay. I will present different sets of data. The first is my original tac—the one I used when my home world was attacked. It doesn't show edict violations, but that's where the AP started. The next two are taken from my frigate and my corvette, genuine and untampered with. In addition, there are recordings taken from several captured ships. In the end, *Assiduous* will add his own recordings."

CHAPTER SIXTY-ONE

The dense silence seemed to demand being cut into slices. Thirteen men stared at the lone woman before them, long after the last recording had been played.

Syreen sensed the turmoil in their minds. Again, she reached out, comforting, soothing, calming—reassuring.

She spoke quietly, slowly, precisely pronounced. "It is my duty to enforce the edicts. It is my duty to reestablish harmony. I will make sure such ugly events will not happen again."

Okamele rose. "You and your ship alone?"

"That's all I have. It will be all I need."

To her surprise, he shook his head. "No. That's not all you'll have. Not if we have a say in it, and our voice is heard on this side of the chasm. You will get all the help we can give."

"What do you have in mind, Oscar?" Secretary Walker asked.

"You all saw *Assiduous'* huge hangar. Large enough to harbor a dozen frigates and a score of fighters. We'll make sure the Navigator will not return with empty hands—or an empty hangar."

Walker shook his head. "I'm still not sure where you're heading."

"I'm talking about watching her back while she's challenging the most dangerous maniac in history. I'm thinking of Crown's *Fumigator* class escort destroyers, and I'm thinking of a stingship wing—the *Finney Fianna* in particular."

The Finney Secretary—Kiernan O'Donnell, she remembered—smiled, rose, and bowed. "I'm sure the *Fianna* won't hesitate to serve you, Navigator."

Syreen frowned. "I'm sorry—this is going so fast. What about the tribunal?"

Commissar Okamele spread his arms. "Our decision has already been recorded. Your claim has been granted unanimously. Having seen the evidence, there could be no other outcome. Did you doubt that?"

She shrugged. "I expected an intense discussion."

Now he smiled. "I did, too—before I knew the facts. Now we all have some work to do to get the decision settled. We must provide you with proper records." He nodded toward O'Donnell. "Kiernan, would you please send our request for assistance to Finney?"

"Sure, Oscar. A top priority request, I assume."

"We're talking about the edicts, Kiernan. Codex priority."

"Codex priority, aye."

"Thank you. I will apply to the Crown government myself. Roger, will you please take care of our guest and applicant?"

"Of course, Oscar." The Banjo secretary rose and walked around the table arrangement. "Will you join me for dinner?"

CHAPTER SIXTY-TWO

Syreen placed her cutlery on the empty plate. "That was delicious."

"I'm glad you liked it," the Banjo secretary said. "Is there anything else I can do for you?"

She examined his temporary office. There wasn't much he could offer without calling for service again.

"Don't you have other things to do? Your colleagues left in a hurry."

"They will be preparing drone messages, calling in favors, pulling strings and such—it's not like we just can declare sanctions and nobody would ask questions. We've made our decision, and now we must make sure people will follow our cause, first of all the regional governments. Politics, you know?"

She sighed. "Yes, I know. And you don't have to—pull strings and such?"

He smiled and shook his head. "I'm in office for only three kilocycles. There are no strings attached yet—at least not firmly enough for such an important cause. The other secretaries will take care of my region."

"So you earned the job of being my nanny."

"I'm sure that wasn't what Oscar had on his mind."

"What do you think was his intention then?"

"To help you relax. You appeared quite tense in the end."

"Tense?"

"The more evidence you presented, the less relaxed and confident you appeared—I can understand, as I was about to jump from my seat and cry out my rage myself."

"But you didn't."

"No. I didn't want to miss any part of the story. And after-ward—I'm not sure, but when you looked at us, I felt some-how relieved. Yes—I felt relief. You're there, and you'll take care of our trouble, and everything will turn out well." He shrugged. "And while I was sitting there, enjoying my ease, you were facing that incredible burden of implementing our decision. I was so glad Oscar came up with his idea."

She eyed her empty glass, but only briefly. "You all seem to know what he was talking about. Is it common knowledge?"

"The Fianna are commonly known. They're the best sting-ship pilots on this side of the chasm, and that's not just a claim—they've proven it in every contest. Do you have con-tests, too?"

His words stirred a memory. "My flight instructor men-tioned something like that—but long before our time. No, we only had contests among the different squadrons."

"You scored well?"

"Very well—good enough to get away with other short-comings. So they are good?"

"They are very good. You'll see when you meet them."

She gazed down. "I'm not sure what to do with them. Where I'm going, stingships have a snowflake's chance in hell to survive."

Or not? With Assiduous' *coordination and her precognition, they might prove more helpful than anyone would expect.*

"I'm not sure if I should feel glad or terrified by your smile," the secretary admitted.

"Both," she said. "Glad that I can help them survive. Terri-fied by the prospect for our enemies. I will make good use of them. Now tell me about these destroyers—I doubt we can harbor any ships larger than a frigate."

"They aren't larger. We don't need warships around here,

but there's still demand for escorts. Just not to give any local bonehead bad ideas, you know? So the Crown navy launched a new design — small like a frigate, but with a destroyer's firepower. The *Fumigator* class is built to take out a pirate's nest with local defenses. Enough crew for three-shift duty and space for a small marine unit for boarding maneuvers, tough and with long-range firepower, if I remember right. The first new design in megacycles — the obvious reason is to save on crew pay and maintenance."

"I see." This time, she rewarded him with a warmer smile. "Surely useful for a strategy of small steps. Biting away from the edges."

"Something like that, yes. By the way, now you look much more at ease."

"I am. I see my course now." Syreen noticed his gaze idly resting on her chest — and not on her medals. "We should take our time to relax some more. I take it we're undisturbed here?"

"Yes, why? Oh."

She opened her jacket and unzipped her shirt. "Oh?"

CHAPTER SIXTY-THREE

Syreen licked her teeth. The canines were gone — good.
After a last glance at the exhausted man on her bed, she left.
Roger would sleep for the next four cycles, and after a few
hearty meals, they'd do it again, one, two, three times — like
they had done for the last five rest periods. His stamina and
creativity left little to ask for, and his blood tasted sweet, especially during or after sex.

His blood donation helped her during the shift.

The last four tencycles, she had watched twelve Crown destroyers exercising against each other or against simulated
targets. This time, they'd face a new opponent — a living ship.

After that exercise, she'd start practicing together with
them, but first, they had to learn what *Assiduous* could do, or
at least some of it.

I'm a naughty girl.

Aside from the overall exercise, the next tencycles would
show which crews would qualify for her support.

She had been invited to watch their initial briefing. Commissar Okamele had presented her claim, her mission, and a
summary of her recordings — including some of *Raydancer's*
combat reports, "so you know who'll be leading you into battle," as he had put it.

They knew what she could do with a corvette, and they had
been appropriately impressed. When Okamele had told them
she'd only take four of them along, the crews had glanced at
each other with determination. The race was open.

She still refused to set qualification parameters. She hadn't won her own battles playing by the rules, and she wouldn't choose her support for compliance with the Books. She needed inventiveness and courage, kept at bay by good judgment. How could she set parameters for that balance?

Smart decisions, skillfully implemented, whether successful or not, were what she was looking for. On their journey back, there'd be plenty of time to teach them what they needed to survive.

They'd fail today, and their reaction to failure would contribute to their scoring, too.

CHAPTER SIXTY-FOUR

Syreen climbed the platform in *Assiduous'* hangar with a smile.

Twelve ships, three shifts, with a captain, a pilot, and a gunner per shift, totaled to a hundred and eight men and women, and they all were silently waiting for her debriefing after the exercise.

Their minds radiated curiosity, anticipation, and restrained anger in some. Where their anger was directed, she couldn't tell without digging into the individual minds, and that was something she wouldn't do.

Nor would she soothe their minds—not yet. Their anger had to be put to good use.

"You had been briefed," she began. "You've watched *Assiduous'* performance at Klondike. You knew missiles were a bad idea. You knew what an EMP cannon does. You knew you'd lose, but you tried your best anyway. As to be expected, you lost the battle. You may ask—why did we do this exercise, if the outcome was set from the beginning? Because you must understand what a living ship can do, how different our performance is—how much more efficient we are. You must not only understand with your mind, you must understand with your hearts, your belly, your gut feeling, too. Only once you're able to tell what I can do and what I can't, where I might need help and where you're just getting in my way, you'll become useful."

She remembered her own first lessons. Painful truths served brutally straightforwardly, making her grit her teeth and clench her fists — making her struggle hard to do better next time.

No, other than the Fianna or these people, she hadn't participated in serious competitions. She'd had just one real test, a live-or-die style competition against the AP invaders.

"Actually, your interception setup was very good — you probably knew that. You could have stopped a battle group with battle cruisers and light cruisers this way, or perhaps defeated a dreadnaught. But you couldn't stop me."

"We should have scored," one of them mumbled. "The computer failed to register it."

She caught his gaze. "You're right, Captain Reed. You should have scored. Your shots were on target and would have hit *Assiduous* midships — if I hadn't dodged them."

"Who can dodge a pulse shot? You'd need faster-than-light detectors."

"Exactly. I sensed your shot the moment you fired it. There was plenty of time to dodge it. That's what a Navigator does, and, as far as I know, what nobody else can do. I'll show you."

A gesture produced a large screen. *Assiduous* presented the relevant details — Captain Reed's recordings synced with his own, showing his shot, and her change of course a fraction of a second later.

"I see it and I can't believe it," Reed said. "How can you do that?"

She shrugged. "If I only knew. Let's say I have an affinity with hyperspace. The speed of light doesn't count there."

"Strange."

"True. Much of what you've seen still feels strange for me, too. Five winters ago, I was nothing but a skirmisher jockey. Now I'm fighting an entire star nation with a large and powerful navy with just three ships, and in practicing that, I'm learning more and more about myself."

Syreen saw his urge to say something. She raised a hand.

"Just a moment. There are three things you should keep in mind. Firstly, I'm the only one who can command *Assiduous*. Secondly, I'm the only one with true battle experience. Thirdly, I'm aware of my youth, and I'm open to good advice, suggestions, critical questions — I had to learn fast to survive, and I'm eager to learn more. So, unless we're in the heat of battle, never hesitate to speak up and speak straight. I can take some heat."

Taking her hand down, she nodded at the captain. "Captain Reed, your turn."

"Thank you, Navigator. You mentioned skirmishers — isn't that an outdated design?"

"It wasn't considered outdated in the Duchy, but very effective — in fact, it proved very effective during the AP raid, although we lost in the end. I alone took out seventeen sting-ships."

"Is it true what I read about them — uh . . ."

"Yes. Sexual stimulation is part of the concept." She spotted another waving hand. "Yes, Lieutenant David?"

"Pardon me — you said you were a skirmisher pilot, but during the briefing, the commissar had mentioned you were first in command? How does that match?"

"Leadership is passed down to the highest-ranking survivor. I'm the last living member of Duchy Fleet on active duty. That way I became Fleet Commander in Charge."

"You mean, they're *all* dead?"

"The Association shot all our ships, our space station, even rescue pods. Yes, they're all dead. If there's anyone left of Fleet, it's because he'd already retired from duty."

"But shooting pods — that's against the rules!"

Syreen made a grim face. "You better understand they're not playing by the rules. You might survive a little longer if you're prepared for nasty surprises."

The lieutenant nodded, his lips pressed tight.

Her neighbor asked the next question. "You mentioned battle experience. It was part of the briefing, but I must admit, I focused on the edict violations. Can you give us another summary?"

"Of course, Lieutenant Cage." She pointed at her chest. "Each star represents a kill. I fought at the Duchy—these eighteen, including the dreadnaught. One pirate. One battle-cruiser, three light cruisers, twelve stingships at RAK-11."

She continued with Wagaki, Hawthorne, Second Stop, and the pirates between Le Mans and Kathmandu. "At Klondike, I rejoined with *Assiduous*. The whole battle, fought in five waves, resulted in seventy-two stingship and fifty-three tank kills, two of which were dreadnaughts."

Lieutenant Cage nodded and glanced at his neighbor. Lieutenant David shrugged.

The Navigator picked up their clue. "I'm not particularly eager to seek out such a confrontation. In that case, I simply couldn't leave the Klondike people to their fate. Otherwise, I prefer to pick a place and time more in my favor. Moreover, I'm not going back to kill brave soldiers by the score. I'm going back to discourage them from fighting on, to take their leader away, and to guide them back to decent behavior. My mission is to reestablish harmony, not to cause mayhem. Your task will be to watch my back and to discourage them from sneaking up on me. In addition, you will help enforce the sanctions."

"So we may eventually return home?"

That had been another female voice from the other side. She turned around and spotted the source. "Yes, Captain Scabbia. If I survive, I will carry you all back across the chasm."

Captain Reed spoke up again. "If you put it this way— what can we do to ensure your survival? What are the next steps?"

She smiled. "We'll practice exactly that. From tomorrow on, you're part of my fleet during our training. We'll practice until you know what you can expect from me and I know what I can expect from you, and what we can teach each other."

"Can you teach us to dodge a pulse shot?"

"No. Instead, I can teach you not to be in its core firing range in the first place. I'll teach you how to make each of your shots count. I'll teach you how to heat up a mug of for-wine with your lasers across ten light seconds. I'll teach you how to treat incoming missiles, and I'll teach you how to do intrasystem hyperjumps."

"Intrasystem jumps?"

She put on her predator smile. "I'm a Navigator. You'll learn what that term truly stands for."

CHAPTER SIXTY-FIVE

Thorwaldsen groaned when his comm flashed.

Another interruption! I'll never get my improvement concept done with all these distractions.

He waved an acknowledgment anyway. "Who is it?"

"Sir, Navigator Syreen is here and asks for a brief meeting. You said any of her requests should have top priority, so I—"

"Yeah, sure," he interrupted his assistant. "That's fine, send her in."

He pushed all thoughts about his concept aside. The Navigator wouldn't come without appointment for a mere trifle. Was she having any trouble with her exercises? So far, he'd heard only good news. After their initial defeat, the Crown destroyer crews were constantly improving under her guidance—at least that was what everyone told him.

There she stood in his doorway—a beautiful woman, but looking all business from head to toe.

"Come in," he said, rose, and walked around his desk.

"Thank you for your time," she began. "I won't occupy you any more than necessary."

"Spending time with you is not a question of necessity."

"You're nice. Another time, perhaps."

He sighed, trying to direct his gaze up, from her chest to her face. "Okay. What can I do for you?"

"You know of the Fianna, right?"

"Of course. They're on their way to us. They should arrive within the next five tencycles or so."

"They'll arrive here in about thirteen cycles. I'd like to give them a special welcome."

"Special?" He became aware of her mischievous smile. "What kind of welcome do you have on your mind?"

"I've just borrowed a stingship from Crown navy, and with it, I'd like to challenge their skills."

"With a stingship? Not with your partner?"

"He understands and supports my intentions. Stingships are no opponents for a living ship — such a challenge wouldn't reveal anything new."

He shook his head. "You know they're coming with their entire First Wing? That's eighteen against one."

Her pout was too cute. "You think that's unfair? Perhaps I should fly without shields, then."

CHAPTER SIXTY-SIX

Syreen's newest ride still felt wrong. She missed the touch of a strong tool inside her crotch. Of course, she had steered *Raydancer* and *Bumblebee* without, too — but now, she was riding a stingship, the second-smallest armed spacecraft after the Duchy skirmishers, not much more than reactor, engine, guns, and a seat, wrapped in a thin sheet of steel.

She'd had the better part of a tencycle to get accustomed to this model and its controls, improve its target computer to meet her standards, and get into interception position for the Fianna. Not much time, but she felt confident for the oncoming dogfight.

As announced, she flew without shields. Thorwaldsen had protested — once. Her glare had stopped him short.

"It's your hide," had been his only comment.

Now she sailed across the Crown system toward the designated entry area for ships from Finney. The star sang to her, telling her of the incoming jump.

The carrier *Fir Bolg* — basically an ordinary merchant ship refitted to carry the Fianna stingships and their maintenance equipment, licensed to bear small armament, and beaming a military signature — dropped from hyperspace precisely on time, and only a fraction of a light second off. No need to adapt her course and give her position away by activating her engine.

She patiently waited for the harbor director's move.

"Carrier Fir Bolg, *this is Crown harbor authority, Harbor Director Thorwaldsen speaking. This is a distress call for the drill.*

Switch to simulation mode and copy. Repeat, this is for the drill. The Crown system is under attack. We're requesting assistance from the Fianna for the drill."

"Crown harbor authority, this is carrier Fir Bolg, *Captain Ru-draige speaking. We've switched to simulation mode. Repeat, we confirm simulation mode. Fianna assistance is granted for the drill, please advise about the situation for the drill."*

Syreen shrugged. This *for the drill* drill seemed exaggerated.

"Carrier Fir Bolg, *this is Crown harbor authority. Situation for the drill is as follows — Crown is under siege by an unknown warship with unknown capabilities, supported by one frigate, one corvette, and a single stingship to control civil intrasystem traffic. We don't have readings of the latter, so you must assume it's blocking your way system-inward."*

The *unknown warship* was *Assiduous,* of course, and like *Bumblebee's* and *Raydancer's,* his transponder signal showed on everyone's plot. Only her own stingship didn't advertise its position.

"Crown harbor authority, this is carrier Fir Bolg. *Radio silence for the drill."*

Syreen braced herself. *Here we go.*

The carrier turned his side forward while maintaining his vector inward. This way, some of his freight doors were out of sight for anyone lying in wait between them and the planet.

This was a sensible move, and to be expected, as it was in the Books.

The surprise came next, when the entire Fianna stingship wing shot away from the carrier in a pattern that should have looked random, but the systematics of which a very skilled navigator could spot anyway.

This is smart indeed.

The Books proposed a tight formation, so ships could give each other fire support, and shields could be joined. Their current formation—and it was a regular formation, although appearing random, they couldn't fool a Navigator—allowed fire support, too. Unlike the tight standard formation, it provided a much wider basis for scanning. Most importantly, this way they didn't present an easy target. Against a single enemy stingship, this was close to the best they could do. Only a truly random pattern would have been better—but in turn, in such a pattern, they'd hardly be able to combine scanning results.

Their transponder signals faded when they switched to tightly focused transmission lasers—again something they couldn't have done in a true random formation.

However, this good idea was wasted on the Navigator. She already knew their positions, had locked them into her target solution, and was ready to strike out.

She had to be ready anyway. The eighteen Fianna stingships were flying system-inward with *Fir Bolg's* jump-exit velocity of almost a quarter of light speed. Her own stingship was sailing against them at a tenth of light speed. The difference totaled to a good third of light speed. Any shot at that speed was difficult enough, and within a few fractions of a centicycle, they'd pass each other. After that passage, they'd be between her and the planet, and her exercise task of keeping them away would become impossible.

She flipped a switch.

Reactor, engine, and guns came to life together. A volley of six carefully aimed double shots from her twin cannons marked six Fianna stingships as killed.

The guns needed a fraction of a centicycle to cool down—or would have needed that time if used at full power, so the computer had to simulate the heat—before she could shoot again. Her second volley marked six more Fianna ships, but not before they were able to return fire.

A feeling made Syreen pull her stick firmly.

Of the twelve double shots sent her way, seven were poorly

aimed. Five would have been on target without her dodge—and one pair came at full power!

Such a hit could kill her. *So the stakes have been raised.*

Her next volley wiped five Fianna from the simulation. One target remained, and the distance had shrunk to a few thousand legs—too close to dodge another shot.

Too close for the Fianna pilot to correct his aim, but not for her. His hot pulses missed her, but her own precision shots hit home—no longer limited to exercise power.

His wings were gone, and so were his guns. She flipped her ship around, ready to answer any possible retaliation.

Seventeen Fianna signaled exercise defeat, one sent out a distress signal.

"Unknown stingship, this is Commodore Quinlan, Fianna First Wing leader. I apologize for this terrible mistake. This will have consequences."

"Commodore Quinlan, this is Navigator Syreen. Apologies accepted. With all your forces eliminated, the exercise is over. Exercise over, please copy."

"Navigator Syreen, I copy, exercise over. We have an emergency situation now."

She smiled to herself. "Commodore Quinlan, considering current vectors, *Fir Bolg* should be in a good position to intercept and collect Fianna One-Seven within a quartercycle. I'm ready to offer a solution for Captain Rudraige, if necessary."

"Any support is welcome, Navigator. If you allow, we'll join the carrier afterward. With your current vector, I fear, we won't meet so soon."

"Go ahead, Commodore. We'll meet at Crown Orbital. I guess your pilot will need some time to overcome his shock."

"We all need time to overcome the shock of how you outclassed us. I can't put it any differently."

"I'll be there."

"Uh—how?"

She smiled again. They were in for another surprise.

"Captain Reed for Navigator Syreen. Come and pick me up."

A few centicycles later, a Crown destroyer dropped from jump close to her trajectory.

CHAPTER SIXTY-SEVEN

When the eighteen Fianna pilots entered Thorwaldsen's conference room on Crown Orbital, Syreen rose.

Their leader with the commodore sleeve stripes whistled, and they snapped to attention and saluted.

"Commodore Ray Quinlan, Fianna First Wing, at your service, Navigator."

She returned their salute. "At ease, Commodore. I'm not into formalities. Please, find a seat."

He remained standing while his pilots filed around the oval table.

"As I'm assigned to your command, I should now ask you to relieve me from my duties. I've failed terribly. I reviewed the recordings. Lieutenant Connell's shot was on target, and if you hadn't changed your vector right that moment — luckily! — you'd be dead now, shot by the very people who'd been sent to aid you. I can't find the words to describe my embarrassment or my relief to meet you alive."

You already found a lot of words. She smiled. "Let's not allow that accident distract us from what needs to be done. In fact, that little mishap helped me make my point."

One of the lieutenants tried a weak smile.

Quinlan took a deep breath. "I guessed you wanted to make a point, I'm only not sure yet what that point is. Could you help me?"

Syreen pointed at the table. "Take your seat, Commodore, and I'll explain."

He didn't take his gaze away from her, but somehow found

his chair without stumbling.

She dropped into her own chair. "Okay. Let me start by congratulating you for your outstanding performance. Instant battle-readiness, a perfect launch maneuver, your almost-random scan formation, the way you quickly cut your active lines — and, of course, your quick reaction to my attack, with five precise, on-target hits. Or, better put, they would have been on target if I hadn't dodged them. Not by luck, though, but because I saw them coming and acted accordingly. That's my first lesson — I can sense shots before they reach me, faster than light."

She gazed around the table. "You've already received my second lesson. I shot you all, very precisely. The point I wanted to make is — I know how to handle a stingship. I know what I can expect of you, perhaps even better than you do."

Her gaze reached Quinlan.

The commodore nodded. "Point taken. Indeed, when we left Finney, that topic came up — how can you lead us if you don't know about us. We were quite convinced — should I say proud — of our skills. Your attack crushed that cockiness. There can't be any doubt — with regard to stingship piloting, you've outclassed us. I think we're ready for some serious talk now."

CHAPTER SIXTY-EIGHT

Syreen gazed at the plot above her seat, showing her fleet's latest exercise results.

My fleet, pha! I'm stalling. I'm delaying our departure, pretending I need more time, but I don't. I didn't need these ships and crews in the first place. Their training is just an excuse to stay, to avoid the final confrontation with my enemy.

— Their actions appeared useful, though. —

Really? That's the first time you called our allies useful *— or anyone else aboard, by the way.*

— Not true. Our livestock is useful to keep you healthy and powerful, I never denied that. Our crew is useful to nurture our livestock, which will soon grow, by the way. —

What are you talking about?

— Offspring. Our livestock is procreating. I think it's called babies. I've been asked whether my facilities can support the birth process. —

And, can they?

— Of course. I'm well capable of monitoring and supporting all functions of primitive lifeforms. —

You just called them useful, and now you call them primitive? Wait, we're having babies?

— All my readings confirm eleven pregnancies. Recent procreative activities between our livestock and the warship crews suggest further positive results in the near future. —

Oh my.

— To address your initial concern — I agree with your implicit assessment. Our supporters' performances still show significant improvement, but approach a limit that further simulations cannot

overcome. They need live experience to make the next step. —

So it's indeed time to leave. I will inform Oscar and Niels and talk with Matt and Ray.

— I will advise the commissar and the harbor director offices of your desire to meet them. Commodore Reed and Commodore Quinlan will soon arrive in the mess. They're debating today's exercise. —

She didn't tell him it wasn't nice to eavesdrop. After all, they were all inside his body, so he was supposed to know what was going on, wasn't he?

When Syreen entered the mess, all conversation fell mute. The two commodores — one only recently promoted — turned toward her and watched her approach.

Reed smiled at her. "You've made a decision."

She nodded and dropped into a free seat. "I did. Today's exercise clearly showed that we're ready to go. So that's what we'll do."

Quinlan shook his head. "We were just talking about our performance, and we're not entirely satisfied."

Reed leaned forward. "We need more training with intrasystem jumps. Our calculations are slow and sloppy. I can accept slow or sloppy, but not both."

Quinlan placed both hands on the table. "We're still too slow. We need more drills."

Reed laughed. "You mean, your wing is still slower than her. If that's your goal, we'll never leave."

"At least we're faster than your tin cans."

Reed made a sour face.

Syreen spread her arms. "Gentlemen, please. You'll have plenty of time for exercises on our journey across the chasm."

The destroyer wing leader shook his head. "I thought we can't do safe jumps there?"

"But you can do the calculations." She winked. "Plus there's another leg before we reach the chasm. Maybe we should leave the slowest, sloppiest calculators behind?"

Quinlan grinned, until she added, "Perhaps your stingship jockeys should do some calculations, too?"

"What for? Their ships can't jump."

"They're pilots, aren't they? I had to learn jump calculations before I was even allowed into a skirmisher cockpit. Why? Because I must know what my targets can do or what they can't — when and where they might jump away from me, so that I know until when I can catch them. You don't?"

He sat up and made a serious face. "No. True, you've got us there. Jump calculations are part of our training, and we're supposed to include them in our refresher courses, but it's a task no one likes because no one sees a reason — saw a reason. Your reasoning is sound, and I'm sure once I relay your explanation, my pilots will work on that deficit."

His fellow commodore nodded and leaned forward. "Yes! Let's grab the opportunity, Ray. Since we're stuck together for the next umpteen tencycles, let's mix the teams. Your pilots get to do our calculations, my pilots and my gunners will do stingship simulations. Your people learn how a destroyer behaves, my people learn what a stingship can do." Suddenly, he dropped back and turned to the Navigator. "As soon as we know who's going, that is. You've got room for six destroyers?"

She smiled and shook her head. "Didn't you notice yet? Over the last tencycles, *Assiduous* has grown his hangar so that we can carry your entire wing."

He raised an eyebrow. "All of us, yes?"

"As I said before — we're ready to go. All of us."

"When?"

"As soon as I return from the station. I don't know — do you need preparation time?"

The commodore gazed around. "If it's urgent, we're on our way last night. If it's not, I'd like to give my people a last night off before we go."

Quinlan nodded. "Same for us."

Syreen rose. "Okay. Same time, next tencycle, we'll undock with whoever is aboard. Until then, do as you like."

Reed raised a hand. "May we invite your crew along?"

She smiled knowingly. "I'm sure the girls will appreciate that."

CHAPTER SIXTY-NINE

Mo intercepted Syreen on her way to the bridge. "Just a moment, please?"

"Sure, Mo." To his surprise, she linked arms with him. "Come along."

"You're quite relaxed."

She adapted her stride to his. "I am. We're going home, I've got my edict, I've got support, people are happy. I know there's some hard work ahead, where the girls must help me, and there'll be trouble once we're through, but now, I can see a path to the future. Yes, I'm fine."

He took a deep breath. Her scent carried a hint of forwine. "It's good to have a confident and happy skipper. Good for you, too."

"Of course. But that's not what you came for."

"No." He considered his next words. "That Crown man — Reed — he'd like to see the bridge."

"Let him."

"You think that's wise? He'll see — uh — everything."

"Mo." She stopped, unlinked her arm and placed her hand on his shoulder. "You should already know I don't care who'll see me naked. I don't care if they know of my tight connection with *Assiduous*. They already know I was a skirmisher pilot."

"But actually watching you . . ."

He felt compelled to look into her eyes.

"Mo, I can bear whatever they might think about that. What I can't have is them thinking I'm keeping secrets from them. So please invite him to the bridge next time. We'll always find a free seat for him."

That statement made Mo grin. *Assiduous* could grow as many seats as needed, anytime.

He shrugged. "You're the skipper. Oh—you'll tell us when you need the girls again?"

"Sure. Next stop is Moscow. We'll wave goodbye there and approach the chasm. From then on, I'll need support."

"Will we take the same route back?"

The Navigator paused. "I considered that. It would be the easiest way across. However, I think we can't afford to ignore the damage there. I must take a different route and mend some more fabric, save some more stars on our way, even if that costs us a few more tencycles for my recovery."

Mo still struggled to comprehend what she was doing when she *mended fabric*. It was much easier to grasp her concept of recovery—drinking blood and returning from dried-out corpse to blooming life. The way she did it—biting—seemed odd, but after so many odd things she'd done, it looked like a minor quirk. After all, it was quick, practical, needed no tools, and, according to the girls, caused no pain.

How had Jona put it? *As an entertainer, you've seen worse. Bondage, floggings and the like—Syreen's kiss feels sweet against the atrocities of our past. Her grateful smile afterward is the greatest reward imaginable.*

"I'll tell the others."

They stopped at the doorway to the bridge.

Syreen placed a kiss on his cheek and stepped through. "Transit in fifteen."

He smiled. "Good that you mention it. We might miss it otherwise."

"You would know."

He felt lingering warmth on his cheek and started to reach for it, but stopped his arm halfway up. Yes, perhaps she was right. He might not know for sure, but he could feel the difference.

"Good flight." He suppressed a sigh and left.

PART FOUR—RETURN

CHAPTER SEVENTY

Yusef stretched his arms and legs and smiled at Chiara. "You like it," she said.

"Yes. I like it." The last training had been challenging, but it had also been fun. Moreover, now that they were halfway into the chasm, focusing on his training helped him ignore their situation—without Syreen, they couldn't go anywhere, at least not if they wanted to arrive within a lifetime.

He sat up straight again. The mess was a place to relax, but among the many new navy people, he felt uncomfortable making himself too comfortable. He frowned at the thought.

Chiara frowned, too. "Even if it's dangerous."

"Life is dangerous. As a merchant pilot, I've always been in danger. Pirates, AP inspectors, destinations with dubious reputations—that's not easy going. Running a frigate is dangerous, too, sure, but at least I can do something about it. Be quicker, dodge dangers, shoot back if necessary. I like it because it feels like being in the right place—in a place where I'm in control of events." He placed one hand on the table between them.

"But you aren't." She leaned forward and caressed his hand. "No one can control the events."

He felt an urge to hug and kiss her—again, this wasn't the right place. Perhaps they should go to their room?

"It feels like being in control—at least to some extent. I'm scoring fine in our joint exercises." He felt a presence behind and glanced around. "Oh, hello, Matt."

Commodore Reed smiled. "Hello, Yusef. May I join you?"

"Sure." He gave Chiara an excusing smile and pointed at the next free chair. "Have a seat."

The destroyer wing commandant dropped into the chair, nodded at Chiara, and turned to Yusef again. "You've done very well today — if you weren't in *her* crew, I'd try to recruit you."

Yusef nodded. "Your praise is welcome."

"And well deserved. Would you like to fly one of our destroyers once?"

The pilot shrugged. "Why?"

"They have more firepower than your frigate."

"I don't need firepower. I like her swiftness."

"Flying different ships might give you a better feeling about their differences."

Yusef smiled. "You've got a point there. Yeah, okay, I'm in. When and where?"

Reed folded his hands. "Next stop? While our Navigator recovers?"

"Sure. Send me a manual so that I'm prepared — ouch!"

Chiara's pointy elbow, rammed into his ribs, clearly transmitted her opinion on preparations.

He smiled apologetically. "Okay. Let's go, dear."

CHAPTER SEVENTY-ONE

Physically as well as mentally exhausted, Syreen let her feet carry her to the mess and to the first free chair. A few raised eyebrows resulted from her nude appearance — she noticed them, but she didn't care. Nor did she care about the curious glances of the destroyer crew she had just joined at their table.

It was Haiki who turned around at another table, spotted her, and hurried across to join her. "Skipper, are you okay? Need anything?"

She smiled at him. *A meal, just anything, would be fine.*

The engineer tapped the table for her.

A steaming jug appeared first, followed by a dish with an enchanting spicy smell.

"Try this," Haiki said. "My grandmother's recipe."

The meal tasted as good as it smelled. More importantly, it brought her back to reality — or what her crew would have called reality.

After a few bites, she felt able to glance around the table and at the curious faces of two men and one woman, all in Crown uniforms. "Hello."

"Hello," one man answered. "I'm Jaime, and this is my crew. We're from the *Eleven*."

"Jaime, yes. Jaime, Penelope, and Anton. That swing-by around the asteroid. Great idea." She fed herself another spoonful.

"You remember?" Jaime beamed and glanced at his team. "Anton came up with the idea, and Penelope did it."

"Uh, Navigator?" Penelope asked and pointed at her chest. "Should I go and fetch your uniform?"

Syreen shook her head and quickly swallowed her next bite. "What for?"

"Uh, oh — isn't that in your regulations?" Penelope gazed at her teammates for help.

The Navigator sat up straight, tightening her chest. "I don't really have regulations aboard *Assiduous*. If I had, they'd require being appropriately dressed for the occasion. Safety gear where necessary, nude for my pilot seat — or for leisure."

"For leisure?" the female pilot echoed.

"Sure. You don't need clothes aboard. It's warm enough, there are no sharp edges, and if you want to make love, clothes are just an obstacle."

She felt Haiki's amusement. He was wearing his mechanics jumpsuit, probably because he had planned to dig into *Bumblebee's* innards.

"Make love?" Penelope repeated. Her glance moved around the Navigator's body.

Syreen's stern look made the Crown lieutenant pause. "Stop repeating my words. You're not a message relay. And don't pretend you never heard of or tried intercourse." *Because I know you did. Because I can sense your excitement. Because I can smell it — as you're already wet. The only open question is — who'll be the lucky one?*

Meanwhile, she could focus on her meal, and its donator. "It's truly good. What's it called?"

Haiki smiled. "Grandma called it *resurrección*."

After Haiki, Penelope, and Anton had left, Syreen found herself alone with Jaime.

The destroyer captain placed his elbows on the table and leaned forward. "You're not overly worried about discipline?"

She looked up in surprise. "Why would you think so?

Discipline is essential — where it counts, when you're at your job, preparing for your job, learning for your job. Off-duty is different. Off-duty, people need to relax and recover. People should be easy — as long as they return to duty on time and in shape."

"And — uniforms?"

She sighed. "Jaime, I was the Duchy's best skirmisher pilot. You may ask me about that topic again once you've checked your records on skirmishers."

He frowned. "I remember reading about skirmishers."

"If you do, you needn't ask about uniforms."

The captain seemed to be unhappy. He sighed, and his gaze came to a rest on her right nipple. "What are you really doing during hyperjumps? Matt — Captain Reed — mentioned something about repairs?"

Syreen leaned forward. "Jaime, we're not doing hyper-jumps, but hyperflights. The major difference is that I'm consciously watching our flight. You could say I'm flying on sight. During our flight, I'm examining the fabric of space. In some places, it's just thin. In some places, there's no fabric left, and I must patch it."

"Yes, but how do you patch space?" His gaze was still stuck to her nipple.

"Well, basically you pluck a thread each from the stars around and weave them together. At least that's how I see it."

"But — those stars are light years apart!"

She shrugged. "Those distances don't mean much in hy-perspace. I have no better words to describe it, I can only say one thing for sure — it works well enough to get us through. Without those newly woven threads, we couldn't cross the chasm."

"But how does it work?"

"If only I knew." She gently caressed her right breast with her left hand. "I know, though, that you're hard, and I'm wet.

So why don't you show me how big a load you can shoot inside my tight little pussy?"

CHAPTER SEVENTY-TWO

When Syreen left her room and turned toward the bridge, the Fianna leader stepped into her way. She stopped, hands on her nude hips. "What's up, Ray?"

He reached out both hands as if to grab her, but stopped before touching her, and dropped his arms with a sigh. "Sorry to say that, but you don't look well. You're worn out, and it's worse each time we see you. This must change."

She cocked her head. "Straight to the point. Who sent you?"

He gazed at her bare feet. "I sent myself, after talking with the others. You could say I volunteered." Looking up at her, he added, "Syreen—we don't care what happens to us. We don't want to see you fade away like this."

"You're not entirely honest with yourself." Syreen stepped up to him. "You do care about your people. You'd be a poor leader if you didn't. And you do care about yourself—you know you couldn't bear doing nothing. That's why you're here. Admit it."

Close as she stood, his view of her feet was obstructed by her tits. That didn't stop him from gazing down.

"You're right." He took a deep breath. "You're right about everything, and for all these reasons, I ask you to go easy on you. Don't break yourself."

Again, his hand rose, and hesitated. She took it and pulled it to her chest, over her heart. "Feel my heart, Ray. It's beating strongly. My skin may look pale, my limbs frail, my face gaunt, but I'm alive and kicking ass, and with the next flight,

I'll get us safely out of the chasm — as soon as you let me pass."

He shook his head. "I—I didn't know we were already so close to the other side. My calculations—"

"Told you we were two thirds through, correct. The chasm isn't as damaged on this side. I think I've found a safe route for us—well, and if there were two more legs, I wouldn't be worried either. It's easy going, compared to what's behind us."

Ray's hand stirred under hers, but she didn't let it go. Instead, she pushed it firmly over her left cup. After a short struggle, he gave in.

"If it was so hard, why did you do it? Didn't you have a safe route from your first journey?"

"True. But with each rebuilt connection, I could save a star's life."

"A star's life? But—those are just very big balls of fire!"

She dropped her own hand and sighed. "You've got no clue. If only you could hear them sing like I can. Each time I save one of them, their cheer almost breaks my heart. I can't do less."

His eyes widened. "The stars are singing?"

"If only I could make you listen."

CHAPTER SEVENTY-THREE

With every light year they covered, Syreen's worries grew. There were no more stars to save, no more threads to mend, so there was time to contemplate her next steps, while *Assiduous* sailed through hyperspace mostly on his own.

First of all, she had to decide where to go. The Duchy was out of the question. Kyris? With an AP navy welcome committee waiting for her return?

She wasn't eager to meet them there—not because she feared the confrontation, but because she feared for Kyris.

— It is wise to choose the place of battle yourself. —

I would, if I only knew a good place.

— A good place is where the enemy doesn't expect us, and where we can hit him hard. —

Do you know such a place?

— Not yet, but we both know who to ask. —

She imagined slapping her forehead. *Of course.*

— An enemy star system is preferable in order to limit their options for blackmail. —

Again, I agree. Although I'm not entirely sure how much their grand master cares about his own people.

— Any strike against his own worlds will severely damage his crews' morale, if not turn them against him, which would help our cause. —

Indeed. You're wise.

— I'm not, I'm just experienced. —

In that case, I gladly rely on your experience.

— You're welcome. In the meantime, I'd gladly rely on your

instructions. We've almost reached the last set waypoint. —

She checked their vector. Their next waypoint, well outside the chasm, was a strong yellow star without planets. They dropped from hyperspace and turned toward its surface.

Let's pause and recharge here. I will tell the others.

She emerged from deep integration, flexed her muscles, and rose from her chair. Her stomach grumbled, thus clarifying her priorities.

"Yusef, Mo, Matt, Ray, please meet me in the mess in a halfcycle."

Syreen gazed at her full plate and sighed. No, of course the men wouldn't wait for a halfcycle to meet her — they were too curious.

Nevertheless, Mo beat Ray to the chair closest to her and turned to the others. "No questions, no talking with her until she's finished, okay?"

The Navigator quietly agreed and started to eat.

"And what are we doing until then?" Ray muttered and dropped into the next free chair.

"Tell us your insights on the last exercise." Mo sat down, too. They all knew that Ray's Fianna had epically failed during that exercise.

Consequently, the commodore made a face. "You just can't shoot a planetoid with a stingship. What should we have done?"

"That's the question, isn't it?" Matt leaned back and grinned. "I admit, yes, the setup seemed unfair to me, too. I'm clueless. What were we expected to do? Admit a glorious defeat? Run away? Waste our fire on the last shot? Try to evacuate at least a dozen locals?"

Yusef shook his head. "No. We were expected to use our brains. If you can't win, change the rules, that's what she says."

Ray and Matt both frowned and shook their heads, too.

Matt folded his hands. "So, which rule would you change what way? Any clues?"

Yusef scratched his nose. "She changed the rules before. A frigate can't go dirtside? She did, because we had no shuttle left. If a frigate can operate outside the Books, what would a stingship wing do?"

Good Yusef—thanks for the giving them something to digest. Meanwhile, I may get on with my lunch.

"Go dirtside, too?" Ray tapped the table. "It's imaginable, but what would that be good for?"

Matt closed his eyes. "Wait a moment. Wait. How fast can our stingships go? Ultimately, safeties bypassed?"

Clever boy.

The stingship leader raised an eyebrow. "Without safeties? Uh, I think my techies said no more than three quarters of light speed—and they'd strongly advise against trying."

Matt held up a hand. "And what mass would a stingship at that speed be equivalent to?"

Ray frowned again. "Mass? You know that's a ridiculously large number with many zeroes."

Matt nodded and raised his index finger. "Indeed. That's the point. A planetoid like the one we faced has a ridiculously large mass, too. Do the math."

Ray produced a tac and did as instructed. "Beat me. Okay, but it's still a fraction of that rock."

Matt let his finger hover in the air, almost without trembling. "Multiply by the number of your ships."

Ray did. "Beat me. Close."

Matt nodded. "Now tell me—if you place your stingships dirtside and start pushing, what will happen?"

"They'll probably crush—no, wait." Ray shook his tac. "No—of course they can bear that force, if it's done gently. And if we align our vector, we only need a fraction of our power."

Yusef leaned forward. "You don't have to stop that

planetoid, just change its trajectory by a half degree."

The stingship leader was frantically operating his tac. "Wait, yes, aligned like this — by all ghosts in space, *that easy?*"

He leaned back and stared at the ceiling. "Oh my — girl, that's divine!"

Mo started to lean forward.

A small wave of Syreen's hand stopped him. She swallowed her mouthful and smiled at Ray. "You've got it. Tell me when you're ready to try it for real."

After a deep breath, Syreen pushed her empty plate aside. "Okay, guys — you may have noticed we're in an empty system right now. We've successfully left the chasm behind. Now I must investigate where we're going next. This system is perfect — a strong star, and no message drones passing through. It's not on any charted merchant route. *Assiduous* can safely recharge here."

"What are your plans?" Matt folded his hands.

"I must finish two missions." She glanced around. "First — I must deliver another message vault for the guild. Second — I must enforce the edicts."

Ray raised a hand. "What about the sanctions? Don't you have to announce them?"

Syreen smiled. "The primary announcement is in the vault. It will spread as fast as drone relays allow. However, we're not just carrying the vault, we're also authorized to spread the same messages, like merchants do when there's no drone traffic."

She turned to Matt. "I'm envisioning a three-step approach. In the first step, I will deliver the vault and spread the news. For the second step, I've found an archaic term in the Books. It's called *throwing the gauntlet*. The third step will be a frontal assault on the Association."

"What does that term mean?" Matt gazed around in search

of help.

Ray smiled. "It means issuing a challenge that can't be ignored. What do you have in mind, Navigator?"

"I'll hit them where they don't expect me, deep inside their territory, some place where they assemble their flotillas before detaching them—where I can catch them on the wrong foot and hit a significant number of their ships, preferably with only a skeleton crew aboard."

"And how would you see our role there?"

She watched Ray, Matt, and Yusef—they were curious, but most of all eager to be part of the action. "You hold the exits. I want to be sure no single ship will escape. Not even a merchant—Yusef, it's your task to make them stay until it's over. After that, they may spread the news of the edict and of our challenge."

Ray nodded at Yusef before focusing on her again. "We shall cover the whole system, then?"

"Yes. You'll spread out as needed, or group together where firepower is required. You'll probably do a lot of intrasystem jumps to be everywhere."

The Fianna leader frowned. "Our stingships can't jump."

"True." She grinned and waved at Matt. "His destroyers can. And each destroyer can easily take two stingships along, with their bodies tightly locked. *Bumblebee* can do the same."

Ray's eyes widened. "That works?"

"After a little modification to your emitter programming, yes. Yusef already proved it." She waved at her frigate pilot.

Yusef grinned. "*Bumblebee* took *Raydancer* piggyback through a seven-jump sequence without trouble. If it works with a corvette, a stingship will be fine."

Now both commodores grinned, too. Matt clapped his hands. "It'll be fun."

"Those bastards are in for a big surprise." The stingship leader cocked his head and scratched the table with a fingernail. "How many stingships per destroyer? Two?"

Syreen nodded. "Two are safe and easy. Three, only if balanced well. I would strongly advise against four."

He stopped scratching. "That would require between six and nine destroyers to carry us around. Matt, won't that interfere with your final tactical arrangements?"

Matt grinned and nodded. "It eventually will, once I've prepared my tactical arrangements. After all, I've only just learned what to plan for. No—I think we should consider this new option and modify our patterns. What if nine of my destroyers and Yusef's frigate regularly operate with two stingships as fire support? In exchange, your stingships can profit from our missile defense."

Syreen leaned back with her arms folded behind her head and waited. Would they need a hint?

Yusef was the first. "At Klondike, we used *Raydancer* and *Bumblebee* to triangulate targets and increase target precision. If you can couple your target computers, you can multiply your effective target range far beyond anything the AP could muster."

Matt shook his head. "It'll take kilocycles to integrate our programming."

Ray smiled and knocked the table. "True, and untrue. You're right, Matt—we couldn't do it. But you didn't pay attention. Yusef said they did it at Klondike. We already know they arrived at Klondike just ahead of the enemy with a captured ship. So tell me—how much time did they have to set up and integrate?"

Matt stared at him. "Bugger me."

Ray nodded. "See? By the way, you might have missed it, but there were stories at Crown about a little *misunderstanding* upon the Navigator's arrival. The port authorities sent out four interceptors. One even fired a warning shot."

"What?" Matt glanced back and forth between Syreen and

Ray. He radiated shock and concern. "How could they dare?"

Ray raised both hands. "Calm down. A misunderstanding, as I said. However, the port authorities were challenged with a riddle—the four ships returned with a modified programming that rendered their weapon systems and jump drives unusable, while their logs gave no account of any modification. Worse, all their backup programs aboard, even those stored offline, were modified the same way, so resetting their system wouldn't have helped at all. Only after docking could their systems be restored to proper operation. What do you make of that?"

Syreen smiled. *Smart. That's why the Fianna are the best—they're using their brains, and they're able to think outside of the box.*

The stingship leader didn't wait for Matt's reply. "I'll tell you—one very sophisticated cybernetic brain by far outsmarted their safety programming. I know of only two superior entities in the same system at that time, who moreover were the designated target. I suspect they had the means, motive, and opportunity. Navigator?"

Syreen clapped silently. "Guilty as charged, although you'd have a hard time finding evidence for the means. Indeed, I commanded *Assiduous* to disarm them—which proved surprisingly easy. I wouldn't dare try that approach with AP ships."

"Why not?" Ray frowned.

"Because they shoot first, ask later. They won't leave us as much time as the Crown welcoming committee did."

Matt shook his head. "A pity."

"Indeed." She winked at him. "Because it means we'll have to shoot them first."

Ray nodded slowly. "Of course. Which means we should practice. How long before we leave here?"

"A few tencycles." Syreen rose. "I still must choose our destination."

Chapter Seventy-four

The familiar feel of hyperflight gave way to the dullness of normal space. A bright orange star sang its welcome. Two of its three planets were inhabited — one for mining only, the other with the usual mix of agriculture, industry and arcologies.

Syreen had carefully picked the Danos system for its importance for interstellar traffic — located near the outer rim of human civilization, yet still well connected by four major trade routes and three more message drone connections, it was also of traditional importance for the guild.

It wasn't particularly important to the Association, so she hadn't expected to find a major AP navy detachment here, and she was proven right. The single AP frigate currently approaching a trader for inspection posed no threat to her mission.

This was the place to drop her hot meteorite.

The Navigator felt a hint of excitement, warm humidity between her legs, her nipples stiffening, and smiled.

"AP frigate *Batwing,* this is Enforcer *Assiduous,* Navigator Syreen calling. You will cancel your current approach, cut your engines, discharge your guns, and declare surrender. I'm looking forward to your confirmation within three centicycles."

Switch lines.

"Danos harbor authorities, this is Enforcer *Assiduous,* Navigator Syreen calling. I'm acting as priority one guild courier and thus request priority docking at Danos Orbital for a meeting with the guild secretary. To ensure safe delivery, I've just advised AP frigate *Batwing* to cut engines, discharge guns, and surrender. My reason is — the Association is at war with the Duchy, and my second role is still Duchy Fleet Commander in Charge, thus I cannot allow enemy ships operating close to my fleet. I assure you I have no intention to involve Danos in this conflict any further than necessary."

Now I have to drop the meteorite.

"I will now deploy three destroyers to escort *Batwing*. They are my allies, provided to me by the Crown government."

She watched Matt's ships file out. *Your turn.*

Syreen wasn't surprised that *Batwing* answered first. After all, her message to them had traveled the least distance.

"*Navigator Syreen, this is* Batwing, *Captain Walter Harrison speaking. We're just calculating a safe trajectory and will cut our engines as soon as sensibly possible. Our guns are discharged already. For the records, I declare surrender, but please, tell me what this is all about? We're escorting merchants and ensuring safe travel — to be honest, I don't understand my recent orders.*"

She checked her readings. He was telling the truth, his guns were cold. And he was right, it was sensible to change his course before cutting his engine, as he couldn't know if and when she'd allow him to navigate again.

"Pardon me, Captain Harrison. Past encounters with AP ships weren't pleasant at all, so I have to be cautious. It's nothing personal. If you're really interested in explanations, you may accompany me to Danos Orbital, where I will share the news with the local officials. Well, if they let me."

"*Navigator Syreen, I gladly accept your offer. How do you envisage my transfer?*"

"I'll send you a shuttle." She prepared a short message for Yusef and focused on the next incoming call. Danos, of course.

"*Navigator Syreen, this is Danos port authority. You have no right to open hostilities in our system. We're neutral. We have no business with your war, and we'd like to keep it that way — what? Not now, can't you see I'm talking? Crown, yes, I heard it, so what? Wait — what?"*

There'll be more, Syreen mused, and indeed, the speaker continued his not so private discussion.

"Yes, I can see the transponder codes are genuine, but that can't be. Impossible. And why here, of all places? Uh — was that line open all the time?"

Syreen grinned. "Danos port authority, yes, I can confirm your line was open. I can also confirm that it's impossible for ordinary spaceships to cross the chasm, which is what we did to pick up our allies. *Assiduous* is no ordinary ship, though. I'll gladly brief you on the newest developments once we meet face-to-face. I will bring Captain Harrison of the *Batwing* along. He was very understanding of my special situation, and he's curious to hear our story, too. Together with Crown Commodore Matt Reed, Finney Commodore Ray Quinlan, and my staff captain Mo, we'll be five visitors. I hope we don't cause any inconvenience."

While she waited for the reply, she checked Yusef's confirmation and *Batwing's* new course. The Crown destroyers kept respectful distance, but guarded possible escape routes.

Finally, the anonymous voice called again.

"Navigator Syreen, you didn't cause inconvenience, but a storm of curiosity. We're eager to hear more. Please, feel welcome, and leave us a quartercycle to set up your priority docking."

CHAPTER SEVENTY-FIVE

Syreen gazed and sensed around the table in the spacious conference room Danos Orbital had provided. Of course, curiosity was the predominating emotion, but behind it, she found a colorful mix.

Rear Admiral Panagiotis Passagios radiated respect and concern—he obviously disliked the presence of her large warship in his home system, as it clearly outclassed his few old-fashioned cruisers. His uniform perfectly fit his toned body, and his wrinkled face could have been cut from stone.

Harbor Director Nikos Solaris tried to put on a friendly face, but wasn't entirely happy for her blocking one of his primary transshipping bays. *Assiduous* had grown too large for one of the military docking bays. In exchange, Solaris had almost grown too large for one of the standard conference chairs.

The short man with the business suit had introduced himself as Giorgos Tarakis the Seventy-Third of Danos, and had asked her about the Duke's health—which she didn't know about. The other men showed respect to him, while Tarakis himself radiated an inner serenity she envied him for.

Guild secretary Alexios Spyritis, tall and haggard, was still fuming about the docking fees, and tried in vain not to show it. His slender assistant, Elena Ananke, simply held his arm to calm him down, which seemed to work. She had accepted the guild's obligation.

The Navigator had introduced her company before, and had declined to answer any detailed questions with regard to their mission in advance.

Now she rose and nodded toward Tarakis, then Spyritis, Passagios, Solaris, and finally toward Ananke. "Lady and gentlemen, let me begin with my primary objective. I traveled the chasm to allow an independent guild tribunal to judge recent violations of Edict Number Two, as established by my people and as laid down in the guild codex."

She sensed insecurity and puzzlement in four of their hosts, and turned to the fifth. "Miss Ananke, would you please explain the second edict?"

The assistant nodded. "Yes, Navigator. It forbids the destruction of worlds."

Syreen nodded back. "Thank you. My people originally defined it as the proscription of deliberate destruction, sterilization or rendering uninhabitable of worlds, especially, but not limited to, kinetic strikes. Together with the guild tribunal's ruling, I will provide you with all necessary evidence. Now you may ask yourself why I traveled all the way to Crown instead of asking the guild commissar responsible for this sector, located on Nysa?"

She sensed comprehension dawning on them, including Captain Harrison.

"Indeed. Kinetic strikes were exactly what the Associated Planet's navy tried to do twice. Invoking a guild tribunal on Nysa was out of the question. Now, let me quote the sentence. The independent guild tribunal on Crown unanimously voted for an allover guild embargo on the Association. Effective immediately, no merchant registered in the guild rolls may enter contracts with the Association, accept cargo to or from planets within the Association, or otherwise act on behalf of or to the benefit of the Association. Only current shipments may be delivered."

The AP captain wheezed, and the admiral whistled. The guild assistant only raised an eyebrow.

Tarakis turned to the guild secretary. "And what does that mean, Mr. Spyritis? Isn't every merchant free to go where he likes?"

Spyritis folded his hands and bowed slightly. "Of course, Your Highness. Every merchant might disregard a guild embargo, or an edict, as in this case. Our codex would require us to erase that merchant from the rolls. Merchants not on the rolls may not draw credit on the guild and thus cannot pay their crews or their docking fees on guild worlds. Merchants not on the rolls will not be considered trustworthy. Most will consider this price too high. However, the overall economic impact will be severe. A quarter of the goods traveling through Danos originate from the Association, and one tenth goes there. We will lose that business."

Mo harrumphed. "Excuse me, gentlemen. I've been a merchant for most of my life. I know the market rules. Each time a source runs dry, another will be found. Where demand dwindles, new clients can be found. Aside from true luxury goods, merchants will find new routes, and with all the AP nodes dropping out of the network, your business will most likely grow."

Syreen left the merchants to their worries and focused on Danos' central star to learn about new visitors.

The star wasn't singing of trouble. Three merchant ships would soon arrive, one of them from the AP. They'd be among the first to learn about the embargo.

She noticed attention directed toward her and turned to the admiral.

He tried to stare her down. "Excuse me, Navigator, but who do you expect to enforce this embargo?"

Syreen returned the stare. "I expect the guild rules to be very effective. Of course, every star nation feeling concerned is welcome to contribute to our efforts, but my plans are solely based on *Assiduous*, my living ship, on the two units I captured for Duchy Fleet, and on the units the commodores Quinlan and Reed command."

Passagios leaned forward. "Excuse me again, Navigator, but are you qualified for such a command? Do you have the necessary rank?"

Syreen only smiled. "I'm still Duchy Fleet Commander in Charge, remember? According to the Books, that equals a five-star admiral." She pointed at her chest. "Regarding qualification, I'm the one with by far the most battle experience in this sector, if not in the known universe. I'd agree that orchestrating a fleet isn't the same as fighting with a single ship, but you may ask my fellow officers about my performance during our joint exercises." She placed one finger on her chin. "However, I've never turned down good advice."

The admiral smiled. "You're smart. I'd be glad to help you wherever I can. While our current crews haven't been tested in real battle, our ships have, old as they are. You might draw useful conclusions from their logs, like our crews did during exercises." He waved at Captain Harrison. "However, I would prefer not to share the same information with a potential opponent."

The AP officer nodded and spread his arms. "Believe me, I'm as much appalled by the idea of a fellow officer ordering or executing a kinetic strike on an inhabited world as everyone else in this room."

She sensed his sincerity and nodded. "I believe you, Captain. There are many AP officers like you who would rather face a court-martial than accept such an order. However, your supreme leader doesn't ask for obedience, he just makes it happen."

She found disbelief around her — of course they didn't understand. They couldn't, as they didn't know all the facts. Not even the Crown guild tribunal did.

It wouldn't work. She pushed her chair back and rose, her

hands firmly placed on the table.

"What I'm telling you now is a secret only a few people in the AP know about, and even fewer outside their navy. The Association's supreme leader is not a human being, no more than I am. He's a rogue of my people, and he's able to control other people's minds — like I can. Unlike me, he has no qualms to use his powers for his personal gain. Ultimately, he's the one I must go for, although there are too many in the AP navy who follow him willingly."

Giorgos Tarakis the Seventy-Third of Danos shook his head. "Pardon me, Navigator — there's one thing I must have misheard or missed before. Did you just say you are no human being?"

She nodded, chided herself for her omission and mentally braced herself for the storm to come. "You did hear me right, Your Highness. Despite my humanoid shape, I'm of a people far older than humanity. I must beg your pardon for not mentioning my ancestry before. Until recently, my people were called the Forgotten People."

Chapter Seventy-six

Syreen had expected a lot of different reactions — awe, like in Captain Harrison, growing respect, like in Admiral Passagios, fascination, like in the assistant Ananke, cluelessness, like in Guild Secretary Spyritis, confusion, like in Harbor Director Solaris — but not the steel-cold determination their sovereign suddenly radiated.

He cleared his throat and rose. His local people quickly followed, and they dropped on one knee when he did.

"Ancient One, we are your devoted subjects. May your wish be our command."

Before she could figure out what to make of his statement, he rose again and faced his admiral. "Rear Admiral Passagios, salute your Fleet Commander in Charge."

The admiral went from knee to attention in a single move and saluted his sovereign with the right hand at his temple. "Yes, Your Highness!" His hand dropped for a brisk turn, and he saluted her. "Ancient One, my fleet is at your command!"

Whatever the current fuss was about, she knew how to handle a military salute, and returned it as sharply as she could. "Thank you, Admiral Passagios. Now, gentlemen, it's your turn to brief me what this is about."

The admiral glanced at Tarakis and nodded.

When she caught the ruler's gaze, she found agreement and hesitation. *Oh.*

She had to sit down first. Only then did the others follow.

They focused their attention on Tarakis. The ruler smiled and pointed at himself. "My family has a very long unbroken tradition of ruling this planet, but even our oldest ancestors can't claim to have met your people. Nevertheless, our history reaches almost as far back as the Duchy's, and the original settlers owe finding this rich and peaceful planet to a star catalog that was attributed to your people. In recognition of their indebtedness, they proclaimed your people, the Forgotten People, supreme leaders of our nation. Today, I may relay their infinite gratitude to you, Ancient One."

"Please." She shook her head. "I'm Navigator, or Fleet Commander, or just Syreen, but please don't call me ancient. That makes me feel like my own great-grandmother—if I had one. I can't be sure, as I'm an orphan and foundling."

Tarakis raised both eyebrows. "You never met your parents? How can you be sure of your ancestry?"

Syreen shrugged. "*Assiduous* told me when we first met. A living ship would never accept another pilot. Ask him, if you like."

"Sure, sure." The ruler looked back and forth between his guests. "I won't miss that opportunity."

"You shouldn't." She smiled. "Maybe I should tell the story from the beginning now."

PART FIVE—RETALIATION

CHAPTER SEVENTY-SEVEN

Commodore Reed had hoped for a few words in private with their Navigator, but couldn't come up with a good reason to send Captain Scabbia away, so she was still stuck to his heels when he intercepted *Assiduous'* pilot between bridge and her quarters.

She stopped, smiled, and straightened herself, which did wonderful things to her chest and his crotch, but didn't help at all to focus on his questions.

Now he was glad for his company — in the presence of another woman, he felt much less tempted to make a fool of himself.

"Matt — what can I do for you?" Syreen asked.

He tried to keep his gaze directed at her pretty face. "Uh — I'm just curious. You didn't ask for reinforcements at Danos, despite their, uh, generous offer of help. Why?"

"Oh, that's simple. We've spent a lot of time on our drills, so that everyone knows what to expect and what to do in certain situations. We can't afford to add new ships and crews to the equation and form a team all over again. Not if we want to keep the initiative, if we want to be faster than the message drone network."

He nodded slowly. "I see."

"There's another reason."

Reed cocked his head and waited. Scabbia shuffled her feet.

The Navigator smiled a bit wider. "They won't be able to meet your standards. Their ships are an outdated design compared to your modern *Fumigators*."

Captain Scabbia waved behind her. "You invited them to contribute."

"I did." The Navigator nodded and faced the other woman. "And I didn't turn down their offer, I only didn't take them into our team. I'm perfectly happy if they step in for Captain Harrison and offer escort services in this region. That's what I told the admiral — in private. He had to admit they'd not be ready to join us within the tencycle, and in fact, he was glad his crews wouldn't have to join the front ranks. He frankly told me their training results leave much to ask for."

Scabbia frowned. "What are they doing all the time? Wiggling their toes?"

Syreen shook her head and gazed back and forth between them. "Of course not. But until the AP started their attack on the Duchy, we had a long period of peace, with a few pirates our biggest worry. Pirates became bolder lately, growing from a mere nuisance to real trouble — I've witnessed a part of that trend. They did not compete with other nations — didn't have to, didn't want to, as that would've meant extra cost. It was the same at home. The Duchy had three old destroyers in operation, plus a few skirmishers. Very effective to protect our own system against pirates, ready to smoke out a pirate's nest, if need be, but no more."

"What about the AP crews, then?" Scabbia asked. "Better trained?"

The Navigator shrugged. "Somewhat, yes. They had a head start, surely had an opportunity for exercises before their strike. It's a large navy with more other people to compete against, and they're better drilled. However, they had to learn how to run their reactivated ships first. A few times, I could take them by surprise. I would no longer count on that, though. They're learning fast."

"No easy prey, then." The captain bit her lip. "Not that

we'd have expected such."

"Other than me, they had no real opponent, though, and of my AP opponents, few had an opportunity to pass their experience on." The Navigator's face clouded. "They never were easy prey, but you may expect to have an edge against them."

Reed leaned forward. "If they're half as good as Yusef, I doubt that."

Syreen shook her head.

He couldn't fail to notice how sweetly her boobs followed that motion.

"They're not. Yusef is a natural—you'll find few able to match his intuitive skills. I was lucky to meet him, and he was lucky to have me as his teacher—sorry if that sounds like boasting. His talent would've been wasted in a hauler. A frigate is just right—sufficient standalone firepower, and still navigable with one hand. He wouldn't want it differently."

"I'm glad I won't have to fight him." Captain Scabbia faced her commodore. "Well?"

Reed sighed. "Agreed."

"We'll soon know what our training is worth. If you'd excuse me now? I'd like to have some rest before we start kicking ass." The Navigator moved closer.

Reed gave way. When she had passed, his gaze followed her naked butt—until Scabbia smacked his. He started, turned around, and faced her raised eyebrow.

She smirked. "Need to let off steam, don't you?"

CHAPTER SEVENTY-EIGHT

Syreen eased out of hyperflight, all systems muted, all senses open, and gazed around. Five planets orbited Avessori, two of them inhabited—Avessori Two, with mostly favorable living conditions, had the largest population, while Avessori Three offered little atmosphere, dust, and rocks, and thus provided subsurface quarters for mining and military purposes.

She counted fifteen battle groups in space—fourteen of them orbiting Avessori Three, drives and guns cold, with minimal electromagnetic activity from any of the fourteen battle cruisers, forty-two light cruisers, and eighty-eight destroyers.

One battle group shielded Avessori Two, with three destroyers monitoring the frequent in- and outgoing commercial travel, the other ships—one battle cruiser and three light cruisers—following one of the stations in orbit, their drives prepared, their guns cold, too.

Sitting ducks, all of them.

She would have preferred to eliminate one or two dreadnaughts with her first attack, but those had left the AP territory, as far as the stars could tell her. So they were deployed somewhere else, fully manned, and ready for battle—they'd require too many kills, which didn't seem appropriate just to make her point.

She commanded nine *trios*—one destroyer with two stingships—plus three free destroyers.

A quick thought assigned the active AP battle group to her

fleet. One trio per AP destroyer, one trio per jump point, two trios and the remaining three destroyers for the rest of that battle group.

Together with *Assiduous,* she would take care of the scores of units around Avessori Three first.

Crown destroyers and Fianna stingships passed the hangar door in rapid succession — each one triggered a welcome tingle in her crotch — then grouped into trios, and jumped.

Only then did she activate her transponder signal.

"Avessori harbor authority, this is Enforcer *Assiduous,* Navigator Syreen speaking. Your star nation, the entire Associated Planets, has been put under edict by the guild until proper compliance with the guild rules has been reestablished. Together with this message, you will receive a full copy of the tribunal's ruling and the underlying evidence. Associated Planet navy units — you are to surrender to this Enforcer and its supporting units unconditionally. Merchant units — put outgoing jumps on hold until further notice. This is just a temporary interruption."

Each of her supporting units would issue a similar request, only from a much closer distance to their designated targets.

She had prepared a choice of her own intrasystem jumps, just in case. However, she very much hoped for a peaceful outcome.

Don't act foolishly. Not this time.

Increased energetic activity under the surface of Avessori Three shattered Syreen's hope. Moments later, shuttles launched toward the ships parked in orbit, diligently registered by *Assiduous'* sensors.

They don't think first.

— They need a lesson. —

In fact, they're asking for it.

Syreen adjusted their course, refined their solution, and jumped toward the planet.

A powerful pulse struck the first group of waiting ships, wiping their memories, their batteries, their entire electrical equipment. In quick succession, the other ships were treated the same.

Dead metal. Crews on those shuttles will have a hard time even getting in.

— Dead it may be, but useful still. —

You want to feed?

— It is an opportunity to good to be wasted. Better, if they're already stocked. —

You've got a point there. Would you mind waiting until the situation around Two is clarified?

— Of course not. —

She watched her supporters approaching the active AP units. The three traffic-guarding destroyers showed hot guns. They were changing their course to engage the oncoming triples instead of surrendering.

Bad judgment.

The stingships had moved away from the destroyers, forming a triangle with them. Their joint scanning results allowed very precise target calculations.

The Crown *Fumigator*-class destroyers fired their forward guns across three light seconds, and each scored a decisive hit into the AP ship's reactor section, penetrating shield, hull, and bulkheads like paper.

Impressive.

— Their guns need a cooling phase now. —

Of course. But their company's still available.

Two stingships each focused on the AP destroyer's bows. With reactor and shields gone, they had no trouble cutting away their opponents' forward armament.

Limp, gutted, outclassed. They should consider their options now.

Two of the three AP ships did — they signaled surrender. The third tried to flip his ship and get his aft guns to bear.

Two Fianna stingships fired again. One shot went through the aft gun section, the other through the destroyer's command bridge.

Any enemy skipper too stubborn to recognize sure defeat won't be of any help rebuilding a better Association, as Reed had put it during their debate about the rules of engagement. They couldn't leave enemies behind who refused to surrender.

Syreen directed her attention at the second planet. The battle cruiser and the light cruisers could mean trouble for her destroyers if they played well. With their drives ready, if they broke formation quick enough, they could win time enough to heat up their guns and come at her ships in groups.

Unless my teams keep their wits about them and jump to safety first.

Instead, the battle cruiser silenced his engines.

Interesting.

— We have incoming calls. —

I noticed. Replay them.

"Warship **Assiduous**, *this is Avessori Harbor Director Jakari speaking. I must formally protest against this unprovoked attack and reject your request for surrender. This system is well-protected by our navy.*"

— This one's from Three. —

"Enforcer **Assiduous**, *I'm Rear Admiral Carpenter, Associated Planets Navy, Avessori sector commandant. What do you expect to gain from this ridiculous request? We'll wipe you from space and have your ass roasted on a spit! This is your one and only chance to surrender your ship and appeal to our mercy!*"

She smiled. *What a nice guy.*

— He is completely oblivious to the current distribution of power. —

Indeed. Another call?

— Yes. This one is from one of Avessori's orbital stations. —

"Enforcer **Assiduous**, *my name is Remo Largo, guild secretary* on *Avessori. I confirm receipt of your message. Please allow me a cycle to read it before I can implement the edict. This is quite a surprise, you understand?"*

— Several merchants on inbound trajectories are calling, too. —

No details right now. I'll answer them collectively.

"Avessori Harbor Director Jakari, Rear Admiral Carpenter, those of your forces that didn't surrender yet were incapacitated. For the records, while Avessori itself wasn't actively involved in combat yet, your system with its supply and shipyard capacities is a legitimate military target in a war declared by the Association, so my current operation is in no way unprovoked. Until the Associated Planets' governments have reined in their forces and made them follow their own regulations, in particular regarding kinetic strikes against inhabited planets, I will assist the guild in enforcing the edict. Effective immediately, no merchant may enter contracts for shipments to, from, or within the Association. Current shipments may be delivered, but no merchant currently docked at any of your stations may depart with cargo picked up here while retaining his credit with the guild. Read the tribunal ruling."

She briefly checked her readings for signs of trouble. *None.*

"Secretary Largo, you may take as much time as you like to read, but until you confirm the ruling, no merchant still docked may leave this system. To all those on their way — have a safe journey, but honor the rules, consider the consequences of violating a guild edict. Outgoing jumps are thus open again. To all new arrivals — you may deliver what you brought."

— Now there is trouble. —

Just spotted it, too.

Surface batteries on Avessori Three had just launched a total of a hundred and forty-four missiles.

Stupid. Assume control.

— You know I dislike that. —

I know. But you may devour them right afterward.

— Oh. That's a nice prospect. Crunchy. —

Syreen entered deep integration and joined *Assiduous* in diving into the missile computers. Capturing their remote control was no big deal, done in an instant.

She marked twelve targets. A tingle in her thighs made her sigh. *Oh yes!*

Twelve waves of excitement rolled over her, each one sending a shiver up her spine—and a concussion pulse down to the surface, grinding buildings, batteries, equipment, and crews to dust.

Now we'll have our appetizer.

CHAPTER SEVENTY-NINE

M o watched the assembly from the side of the stage in *Assiduous'* mess, Jona at his elbow. All destroyer crews and stingship pilots had come, with the girls merged into their ranks. They were all smiles and grins, and when their Navigator climbed the stage, they whistled and cheered.

A single nod by her made them fall silent.

Syreen gazed around her team.

"We've taken the second step, and now there's no way back. We're committed. I know you're with me, but from now on, there are no easy victories anymore. No safe bets, no sitting ducks. From here on, we must carry fear into our opponents' hearts, and to that end, we must face and defeat units ready for battle. Battle cruisers with their escort ships, even dreadnaughts. Mistakes will be lethal. You read me?"

Captain Scabbia picked imaginary dust from her uniform chest. "We knew before—this wouldn't be the real thing. Avessori was to make a point, not to take risks. Sitting ducks, no more, and still impressive."

Commodore Reed smiled. "There was no more resistance after the missile snack."

"Couldn't be." Scabbia shook her head. "But that's not what we came for, what we trained for. We came for battle, for ships with hot guns which we'll crush, nevertheless. That's the real point we have to make. Right?"

"Right." Syreen focused on her.

Mo tried not to grin. *In fact, she already made her point on the ground installations, but you didn't notice that, did you?*

The destroyer captain turned to her peers. "We won't make mistakes. We won't do stupid things like engaging a dreadnaught in a broadside duel. The AP must learn what a *Fumigator* destroyer can do when driven like a nasty stingship."

The stingship pilots cheered, "Hear! Hear!" and "We'll show 'em!"

They showed a lot of positive enthusiasm, but Mo observed a touch of serious confidence in their faces. *You'll need all the confidence you can muster.*

The Navigator spread her arms and waited for them to calm down. "Well, folks, let's develop our battle plan now."

CHAPTER EIGHTY

The growing tingle in her thighs felt all too welcome.
I should feel sad.
— Why's that? —
We're going to kill many brave soldiers.
— That's what war is about. That's what I'm built for. —
That's not what I was born for. It creates discord.
— You want to back out? —
No, of course not.
— Why do you complain, then? —
I should feel sadness, not pleasure.
— We must be efficient. Pleasure is positive feedback for efficiency. Positive feedback facilitates more efficiency. —
Yeah, sure.

Syreen knew she'd need that efficiency now. She had to make it clear to everyone — she'd be able to enforce the embargo even against powerful opposition. Powerful equaled a large headcount in this case.
The taste of victory is bitter.
She entered deep integration.

Assiduous dropped from hyperflight much closer to the central star than the Books advised. Her crotch opened to spill ships. Half of the destroyers dashed away, carrying stingships along, the others remained with their mothership.

The pre-recorded message followed.

"Eiffel harbor authority, this is Enforcer *Assiduous*, Navigator Syreen. Your star nation, the entire Associated Planets, are under edict. Your forces will surrender or be crushed. Merchant units—your contracts will be tested against the embargo regulations. Any attempt to evade inspection will be suppressed."

The dreadnaught before her cut acceleration toward his jump point. Guns turned in her direction, missile ports opened, the opposite of an offer to surrender.

The first boson gauge torpedo cleared their path, leaving nothing but randomly distributed sub-atomic non-matter.

Six Crown destroyers delivered their salvos to one of the accompanying battle groups, breaking its battle cruiser into two parts. Two light cruisers were severely hit, too. One cruiser managed to dodge and escape a similar fate—for the moment.

At a quarter of light speed, there was hardly enough time for a second volley, but Reed's gunners managed to finish off the rest of the surprised battle group anyway.

An EMP from her legs and clit wiped out a second battle group's power.

Before the third battle group's crews could overcome their surprise, the Enforcer and the Crown destroyers disappeared into hyperspace.

They reappeared close to Eiffel to challenge another dreadnaught with its three battle groups. Another EMP took out two light cruisers, one battle cruiser, and three destroyers. Their second gauge torpedo eliminated the dreadnaught, and the *Fumigators* inflicted severe damage on two battle cruisers with precise hits across three light seconds. Their plan seemed to work out fine.

Until one AP cruiser scored a lucky hit. The Crown destroyer lost its entire aft section, including drives and guns.

That shouldn't have been a problem. The ship should have followed its course past Eiffel at its quarter of light speed, to be picked up later. Further salvos removed any danger from the remaining AP ships.

Once the third dreadnaught came up around the planet's horizon, the small ship's fate was sealed, though. A single hit from one of the big ship's guns vaporized Captain Scabbia's *Fumigator*.

Follow-up volleys hit the few rescue pods that had managed to escape the inferno.

The dreadnaught launched a few hundred missiles in quick, consecutive volleys. These missiles targeted any and all non-AP ships in the system, including merchants still trying to comprehend what was going on.

Another salvo reached for the frantically dodging Enforcer.

The living ship noticed a change in his pilot's mind and body — in their integrated mind and body. A wave of anger and pain echoed through their unity.

Their EMP fried large parts of the dreadnaught's equipment, a concussion pulser shot shattered its hull and casually brushed several of the smaller AP units aside.

The remaining Crown destroyers recognized the opportunity to jump away, to regroup and re-plan.

The living ship remained behind, decelerating with impossible parameters, seemingly oblivious of the numerous missiles, the battle cruisers and light cruisers escorting the last dreadnaught as well as the ones already left behind — or the planetary defenses.

— This is unwise. —

An imperative order forced the ancient artificial mind back into deep integration.

More pulser shots made the dreadnaught's hull ring like a Brobdingnagian bell, tearing apart its seams and wirings, mashing up its organic content.

The missiles changed their course, picked up new targets.

The living ship swayed to one side, barely dodging the shots of two battle cruisers, rolled around and tossed another electromagnetic pulse against them — right before the first missiles struck.

No AP missile reached its intended target, but they all scored. Battle cruisers, light cruisers, destroyers, orbital missile launchers, the dreadnaught's gun bays, were all hit multiple times.

Syreen slowly fought her way back to her own, conscious self. Stirred up by an orgy of consecutive orgasms, shaken by the thrill of kills, appalled by the outcome of her rage, she nevertheless accepted the result — horror echoed through the few radio calls she received from AP survivors.

A female figure leaned over her, offered her neck. She caressed the girl's cheek and gently pushed her away. *Not now.*

"Team, secure the system."

We will feed now.

— Where? There's so much scrap around. —

The dreadnaught.

— There are still emergency calls from inside the wreck. —

I know. They know, too. But by shooting rescue pods, they crossed a line. I must show them the price.

— I understand. But does that support harmony? —

You weren't so considerate before.

— Before, we had to deal with violators of the edicts. It's your call. —

When I learned to be merciless, I learned from you. What made you change?

— You. I was created to be merciless. I had merciless pilots before. But I never had a Navigator like you. You taught me harmony. I strive to adapt, and now I don't want you to follow my old ways. —

When she considered her options again, she found her rage faded, almost gone. Indeed, she didn't really want to follow his old ways.

Any resistance left?

— No, the remaining AP units surrendered to our escorts. —

Okay. We'll pick up those dreadnaught survivors and devour the rest. I'll deal with them personally.

CHAPTER EIGHTY-ONE

Even before Syreen entered the mess, misery and grief almost overwhelmed her. If she hadn't looked for the remarkably few hints of anger, she could easily have missed them.

There were no cheers when she climbed the stage. Her uniform felt uncomfortable, but this time, it had been impossible to show up without it and its decorations.

"Folks." She gazed around. Crown and Fianna people mixed with her own crew. The few AP survivors huddled together in a separate group.

"Folks. We're at war. In a war, people die. That's the ugly reality. In a way, this is good—because it makes people consider before going to war. But of course, once you're committed, there's no comfort to be taken from this point of view. Today, we've lost many good friends. We've lost some because this is what happens in a war. And we've lost some more because people weren't playing by the rules." She glanced at the AP crew again. "No offense meant. I'm not playing by the rules, either. In fact, by completely eliminating your first two dreadnaughts, I deprived them of any chance to reconsider, eventually surrender, or at least abandon ship. I'm feeling no remorse—the only way to survive against a dreadnaught is to destroy it with your first shot. That's what I did—I wiped out two strong, heavily armed warships. Wiping out rescue pods is a very different thing. But it's just a symptom of what we're fighting against—a power out of control, a nation and its navy devoid of moral limitations, no longer bound by their own regulations, without honor."

Her words struck the prisoners hard. They didn't dare to argue, though—they knew she had voiced the painful truth.

"Yet, here and today I won't blame anyone for what happened in the heat of the action. Any battle puts each of us under tremendous pressure. Mistakes happen. Some are more lethal than others—consider yourself lucky if you are allowed to survive your mistake. Today, some of us weren't so lucky even without making a mistake. Let us remember." She briefly closed her eyes.

"I remember Captain Jeena Scabbia. She knew of the risk, always spoke up without hesitation. I remember her sharp view on the situation."

She scanned her crew for a certain face. "Lucy, do you remember First Lieutenant Ulfing, her second in command? Enough to give us one memorable moment?"

The woman only briefly hesitated. "Yes, Navigator. I remember First Lieutenant James Ulfing. He once told me of a wonderful beach on Crown, where he'd take me one day."

When the tears started to flow, another girl pulled her close and hugged her.

Reed spoke up next. "I remember Chief Wilson. He was never short of an answer for any technical problem, and he really enjoyed a good beer."

One by one, they found words for their comrades. When they had mentioned the last of Scabbia's crew mates, there was a brief silence.

Syreen focused on the highest-ranking AP officer. "Major Bonfreid, who do you remember?"

The man looked at her in surprise, briefly, and then he began, with tears in his eyes, "I remember Sergeant Loffler. He would never accept less than my best effort in combat training. But he never hesitated to help a friend in trouble."

CHAPTER EIGHTY-TWO

The Navigator sat on the edge of the stage and rested her head in her hands.

Major Bonfreid stepped forward. "May I ask you a question?"

She looked up. "Sure. Go ahead."

He waved at his crew. "What will you do with us now?"

Many frightened faces turned to her, but some just examined the floor before their feet.

"I'll drop you off at Eiffel Orbital." She shrugged. "I've got no use for you aboard this ship. You may tell your superiors you're released on parole."

The officer shook his head. "You're letting us go? Just so? Why?"

"Why not? This is nothing personal between us. Your navy will need you once this conflict is settled."

He clenched a fist. "You're taking that easy — after killing so many of our men and women."

Now she fixed her gaze on him. "I offered your men and women an opportunity to surrender. That's more than your navy offered to the people of Klondike before hauling a big asteroid at their planet. I do not like killing. It's disharmonic and disgusting. But I'm the one who stands between you and the ultimate destruction of this galaxy as a whole, and I will do whatever's necessary to guide you — that is, the entire AP navy — back to honoring your own rules."

"I don't know what you're talking about."

"That's because you decided to shoot first, ask later. You'll have plenty of time to study all the evidence we've brought during your stay here, I'm sure."

Bonfreid shifted his weight to the left foot. "Why should I believe your evidence?"

Syreen smiled. "You shouldn't. But you should believe the evidence gathered by AP navy ships."

CHAPTER EIGHTY-THREE

Reed studied the Navigator's face for a while. The mess was empty except for the two of them. The crews and the girls had retreated to their rooms, some to catch some sleep, others to overcome their grief in different ways.

"You're worried."

"Yes." She leaned back in her chair, nicely presenting her bare nipples.

Reed was glad of the table between them, blocking his view of her thighs and pussy as well as hiding his stirring member. She probably knew anyway.

"What about?"

"Nysa. Although most of the Association's navy is spread out to shield their worlds, to report sightings of a certain living ship, and perhaps to catch its insolent pilot, they retained considerable forces behind. I know of at least eight dreadnaughts with their respective battle groups. Add those that never traveled hyperspace, and we're facing a formidable opposition."

He rubbed his thumb. "We'll need careful planning, then. More jumps, quick assaults and retreats. How many of those gauge torpedoes can you afford to launch?"

Syreen shook her head. "No idea. There must be a limit, otherwise we'd already have lots of them in stock, but that's not the point." She sat up straight. "What's our mission, Matt?"

He frowned. "Enforcing the edict. Uh, why?"

"Exactly." She pointed to a place on the wall. He didn't

know why, but he was sure it was exactly the direction to Nysa. "Exactly. Killing AP spacemen is not our mission, not even a secondary objective. It's an unwanted necessity — but to what extent? That's what I'm worried about. I'm prepared to annihilate any warships endangering our mission, once it becomes inevitable. Right now, I'm worrying whether it really *is* inevitable."

Reed cocked his head. "That's got nothing to do with Jeena?"

Now it was her turn to frown. "I'm sad about her fate, and that of her crew, but we all knew there was no guarantee. It was an open battle with very good odds for us — but just that. Odds. No, Matt, it's got nothing to do with Jeena, but it's got a lot to do with Bonfreid, and even more with those who weren't as lucky as he."

"We're at war."

"We're at war." She nodded. "We're at war, and we're entitled to fight and kill. But the true art of war is not having to kill."

"Which only works if the opponent is convinced that you're ready to kill." He put his palms together. "Which we've demonstrated at Avessori and Eiffel clearly enough."

"Or before, at Klondike."

"Indeed. But do you think that's sufficient to make them surrender?"

Syreen shook her head. "No. Not with some of these boneheads. My ultimate terms of surrender are easy — return to their rules regarding kinetic strikes and inspections, declare the war on the Duchy ended and release its rightful government, and perhaps provide reparations to the civil victims' families. However, I don't think they're ready to consider giving up yet."

"So we've got no choice but to fight."

She laughed. "Ha! We have lots of options. We're the ones

choosing place and time. We can strike somewhere else, or not strike at all." Her hands waved over the table, like wiping something away. "Of course, such actions won't get us anywhere in terms of our mission. No, I fear I must meet my opponent at Nysa, and do whatever is necessary."

Her last statement sounded strange to him—wrong. Oh, yes. *"We* must meet our opponent."

The Navigator made a stern face. "No. *I* must meet him, personally, face to face. You've got a snowflake's chance in hell of surviving that encounter."

She reached forward and took his hands. "I know. I took you along to aid me in this fight. You're brave and honorable, so you won't shy away from the prospect of a hot battle. You don't even want to have it appear that way. That's okay—I appreciate it. But my battle won't be fought with pulse cannons. At least not where I'm fighting. What I'll need is a powerful distraction, though. That'll be your task, and you'll be quite busy with it."

He tried to smile. "I'm curious."

CHAPTER EIGHTY-FOUR

Syreen felt close to bursting with power.

Without her connection to *Assiduous*, she'd be unable to keep her beast under control. Only his presence provided her with the necessary emotional stability — his presence, and the songs of the nearest stars.

Most of all, it was Nysa's tune of welcome that made her stick to her plan. Right into the enemy's heart, on her own again —

She sensed a mental nudge.

On *their* own this time, ship and pilot together, ready to place their challenge.

The Fianna and *Fumigators* were gone, inspecting merchants with regard to the edict. They were supposed to keep AP units busy, and, of course, to keep them away from Nysa.

Yusef and *Bumblebee* were gone, too, together with all of her crew and all of the girls. They couldn't help her now.

Syreen and *Assiduous* gently surfaced from hyperspace at the system's outskirts.

Now.

— We're together. Don't worry. —

"Nysa harbor authorities, this is Navigator Syreen aboard the living ship *Assiduous*. I'm delivering the guild edict in person, in case your government has any questions about it or on how to end it. Of course, I'm formally required to request your surrender, but I've collected sufficient experience from your navy not to expect it. So, if your *master* still wants us, he can come and get us."

Until then, we have to wait.

"This is Nysa Navy HQ, Commodore Talier speaking. Navigator Syreen, you are to keep your current trajectory and start decelerating immediately. Do not try to heat up your weapon systems or use your targeting sensors. Should you fail to follow these instructions to the letter, you will be eliminated."

Syreen smiled. *Yeah, sure, that'd make your master very happy — not.*

She triggered a moderate deceleration — moderate from her point of view, but still exceeding anything any AP ship could muster.

"Nysa Navy HQ, I copy. Current trajectory is locked, deceleration initiated. I will reach zero velocity within four cycles."

Plus, my weapon systems don't need heating. Not that it'd matter now.

— I don't like offering a stationary target at all. —

Hush. You know the plan.

— True. That doesn't mean I have to like it. —

That made her grin, despite their tense situation.

Nine dreadnaughts had already begun moving into advantageous interception positions together with their battle groups. Their targeting lasers tickled her skin.

Soon she'd be in a very unfavorable position — nicely put. In fact, even with *Assiduous'* superior maneuverability and firepower, they wouldn't be able to escape unhurt, if at all.

Yeah, I know. My plan depends on the opponent's cooperation.

— In crucial points. But you're my Navigator. —

The warmth she felt seemed to come from inside.

He'll let us wait. I'll take a nap now.

— A nap? That's bold. Sleep well. —

CHAPTER EIGHTY-FIVE

A mental nudge prodded Syreen awake.

– Visitors are approaching. They already demanded access. I told them of my hangar door and illuminated it. They will penetrate in five. –

Thanks. I'll meet them there. You're with me while I'm aboard, right?

– Of course. –

Thanks.

She opened her mental senses. *Yes. He's coming. I must go.*

While she climbed out of her seat, she considered dressing in her uniform, with rank and awards and all. *It might impress them for a moment, but in fact, I don't need it.*

Syreen didn't need textiles as cover, or to support her courage. Nothing could give her more feel of protection but *Assiduous* all around her.

She felt the visitors coming closer twice – by listening to *Assiduous'* senses, and by locating the master's mind. She could tell exactly when they would enter, and she knew when she'd reach the hangar. There was no need to hurry.

The Association assault shuttle penetrated the living ship's hangar door and set down on the hangar bay floor with a bump.

Syreen smirked. *Amateur.*

Wide doors opened, and a score of heavily armed and armored AP marine soldiers jumped forward to spread across the hangar. They quickly assumed favorable positions to keep the entire space under control without getting into each other's line of fire. Their guns were aimed at the sole nude figure deep inside the hangar.

A group of six unarmed men followed—six of his abominations. They radiated powerful mental commands to surrender. Syreen could have felt compelled to obey—had she not taken precautions against such a kind of attack. For the moment, she pretended to be affected.

The last man to leave the shuttle was the *master* himself. His stance allowed no doubt about his ultimate superiority. He knew he had won—he only had to collect the prize.

"So," he said aloud. "After all this time, you recognized your proper place in this universe, and decided to deliver yourself. I might even feel inclined to be gentle with you— and perhaps postpone your *education* for later."

A chuckle followed his announcement. His imagination was less funny—torture and humiliation were his favorite pastimes, he'd save them for later, to utterly destroy any false hope that could have grown in his victim in the meantime. The longer he postponed it, the sweeter the victim's horror would taste.

Oh, his mind was so easy to read! He had come to seize the ship, enslave its insubordinate pilot, and thus bring his claim for unchallenged sovereignty to perfection.

Her nudity only added to his amusement, unspoiled by even the least trace of doubt.

She spread her arms. "Welcome aboard the living ship *Assiduous,* master. After all these unfortunate turns and twists of fate, you've finally arrived at the very core of your desire."

He advanced with slow and easy steps. "I knew you'd give up and return eventually. I didn't expect it so soon, or so simple."

Syreen walked forward with swaying hips. "I knew you'd honor my invitation without hesitation. I counted on it." *Your male ego wouldn't allow you to stand back, right?*

His anger grew — obviously, she felt much too comfortable with her situation for his taste and clearly lacked the appropriate level of fear and servility. She'd further feed his anger. "Thank you for bringing so many valuable resources along. We surely can make good use of their nutritive value in the upcoming fights."

He shook his head. "You seem to be oblivious of your true situation. I will have to educate you sooner than expected."

On your knees! His mental command almost took her by surprise.

Almost.

She remained standing. "The true situation is — this is *my* ship, and aboard this ship, there's a clear line of command, with me at the top."

The master spread his arms. "I see you at the point of our guns, in a clear line of sight. Now, would you please acknowledge your defeat?"

On your knees!

This time, his command came so strong and sharp that she couldn't help but follow. Her knees protested against the sudden impact.

Ouch.

"I should dispose of you right away." He gazed behind. "On the other hand, you might be entertaining yet."

She struggled to relieve her hurting knees. "You would dispose of the very *relic* you've been searching for all this time?"

"Of course not." He closed up to her. "Where do you have it?"

Syreen smiled at him. *"I am the relic, you fool. Only a female of the People can control a living ship." On your knees.*

Her sudden instruction made him drop like a rock, his face pure disbelief.

She didn't like her next order. *Assiduous, take care of his marines. They're yours. His shuttle, too.*

— Yes, Navigator. —

"Take her down!" Her visitor fought her command, too, physically and mentally. *Release me.*

Syreen shook her head and rose. *Stay put.*

Next, she focused on his six monsters. *Come and offer me your necks.*

"Noooo! You can't take a *Searcher!*"

Ignoring his further protests, but not his mental struggle, she sank her fangs into the first Searcher. She didn't let go until all veins were empty. The dried carcass dropped to the floor, where *Assiduous* began to absorb it, like he had already begun with the stunned marine soldiers.

When Syreen had finished her meal and *Assiduous* had finished his, too, she eased her mental grip on the self-appointed *master.* "Do you have a name? I won't call you my master, as you aren't."

He closed his eyes and shook his head. *Bend!*

His attack took her by surprise again, primarily for its unprecedented strength, and her body bent and twisted in agony. She could no longer tell up from down, her stomach heaved, and her uncontrollable convulsions made one of her elbows snap—which sent even more pain through her already overloaded nerve system.

Worse, she had lost her own mental grip on him.

His words reached her like through a dense mist. "I guess you can hear me, anyway. You made a most severe mistake, and I don't forgive easily. You'll tell me all about your claim regarding the relic—I'm sure you're mistaken, and we'll sort that out together. Meanwhile, you will pay for killing my servants, one by one."

Bend!

She couldn't block his command, couldn't focus—each time she felt a hold, another wave of pain washed it away.

"You're still fighting. How entertaining. Please, go on—I like to see you wriggle." His voice seemed to move around her.

So he wasn't entirely focused? That should — *Ouch! No!*

Another bone snapped.

Even after all her girls' blood donations, she felt her own power fading. Soon, she'd give in to him. *Everything's lost. I'm failing.*

— No, you won't fail. —

Syreen felt a warm hug. The familiar sensation of her pilot chair wrapped itself around her, followed by pricks in neck and leg and the obligatory double penetration.

While her body was involuntarily pulled into position, while her broken limbs were set, her mind was as involuntarily drawn into deep integration.

Bend!

The master's command felt distant and insignificant.

— We are power. —

Bend!

— STOP THAT. —

The man's motions froze.

There was a sudden urge — to smash him, to break him, to toss him all around the hangar, to retaliate.

She fought it down.

We could do it, but we won't be like him. Our mission is harmony. He needs a seat.

Her opponent made a puzzled face when he felt the chair growing from the floor right under his bottom.

Sit down and stay there.

"You'll never get away with that!" he spat out. "You're cornered and outnumbered."

He had a point there. Had he?

Let's talk.

Her jaw muscles felt slow, but she managed to make them work without leaving deep integration. Her body knew how to speak. "Will they shoot at a ship with their master aboard?"

She knew the answer before he could voice it — yes, they would. Like her, he could survive in open space, and like her, he could recover even from the most severe injuries. So they could shoot the living ship into pieces and collect him from the debris afterward. What a prospect!

That part of our plan won't work.

She had four gauge torpedoes, and she didn't need a battle simulation to know those wouldn't do against nine dreadnaughts. If she wanted to use them.

We must stir them up.

— We could sacrifice one of our children to make Nysa flare. That would render their targeting unusable for a while, long enough for us to enter hyperspace. —

Our children?

Again, the explanation came from inside her. Those long rows of containers, lining the hangar's sides, were eggs, ready to hatch new living ships — or to cause a star to flare, to make it send out protuberances far through the system.

Such flares could wipe a planetary atmosphere away, rendering that world uninhabitable, and cause havoc to intrasystem traffic.

That's against the second edict. No.

— There are exceptions for an Enforcer. —

Maybe. There must be another way.

"You will die." The master spat out. "Your time has run out."

As if to underline his statement, she sensed some of the AP ships adjusting their positions, likely in preparation for a strike. What orders had he left for them?

— We must act now. —

We will.

CHAPTER EIGHTY-SIX

Syreen sang, and Nysa answered. She didn't need searing flares, she only needed electromagnetic disturbances. The equivalent of a swaying hip, performed by the central star, its magnetic field vibrating, messed with the AP navy ships' readings and made target and navigation computers fail.

That was all she needed. *Assiduous* dashed away, accelerating with parameters they'd never demonstrated before, thus evading most of the opponents' interception plans.

A few random shots in her direction were easily dodged. A score of oncoming missiles was affected, too, and missed their target by a few thousand legs.

Before the effects wore off, she had entered hyperflight.

— Nysa supported you. —

Yes, she did.

— But how did you do it? —

I'm a Navigator. Doesn't that explain everything?

— No, it doesn't. Or, put differently, that explanation isn't helpful. —

Well, I can't offer a better one. Let me check our guest now.

She mentally braced herself before releasing her link to *Assiduous*.

The former master stared at her. When she turned her head to him, he blinked. *Bend, bitch!*

This time, she could easily discard his command. Different than before, he couldn't wipe out her mental barriers by surprise, and without that element of surprise, she was much stronger.

"Stop that nonsense. I told you before—aboard *my* ship, I'm the one in charge."

"My fleet will shoot you to shreds."

"Not here. They can't follow us into hyperflight."

"They can jump as well as anyone."

"We're not jumping. We're in hyperflight, currently orbiting Nysa. In hyperspace, but consciously so."

He laughed out loud. "Nonsense! You're fantasizing."

"Why should I?" She frowned. He'd be difficult to handle. Whether she'd be able to teach him better ways in the future, she couldn't tell yet. Was it worth the effort, aside from removing him from the Association? Without him, she hoped, they'd eventually return to reason, so that she no longer had to deal with the embargo. So that she could return her allies to the Crown. "You'll learn soon enough. For now, I've wasted enough time on you."

Syreen returned to deep integration, to her *Assiduous*, and to hyperspace with its beautiful songs. She focused on Nysa, but found an entire choir, among them Nysa, Eiffel, Kyris, and even the Duchy's central star. They sang a new tune, a tune that struck a special chord with her.

Welcome, our daughter. Welcome, Syreen Starborn.

The End

YOU MAY ALSO ENJOY THE FOLLOWING FROM eXTASY BOOKS INC:

Lioness Tracks III: Lioness Assassin
Valerie J. Long

Excerpt

After a while, Elodie and I reached a livelier beach section. Here, we could be sure about receiving all from benevolent-interested to lecherous-voyeuristic male glances. We weren't by far the only topless women, and also not the only ones in good shape, but we had two decisive advantages—first, we were confident about our good looks. After all, we were training hard. Second, we had systematically been trained for nude appearances, so we were used to act cool even in the presence of the greatest lewd assholes—any Mamba candidates who had failed in this subject were dead. To know that neither of the men on this beach wanted to kills us was a tremendously relaxing thought, so we could stay easy—and that worked to our advantage.

The only important aspect was that people remembered our tits and asses and not our sunglasses-covered faces.

Doubtlessly, the disappointment was huge when we reached our bag parked in the sand and covered ourselves with tops and shorts. One or another sporty guy might even have appealed to me—but for one, those guys were already in company, and for two, we still had a mission to accomplish.

Our robust all-terrain car without roof or doors was parked not far from the beach. Elodie just tossed our bag inside before slipping behind the wheel.

I mounted the second seat and grinned at her. "Giddyup."

She smiled and activated the power supply, tossed a routine glance at the mirror, and drove off. With a silent hum, we rolled toward the main street and followed it out of town.

A little later, Elodie turned into a small access road. She stopped when the already familiar house with the large glass panes came into sight. A small sign at the roadside declared the rest of the road private property.

"Have a look at the map," Elodie told me—or potential listeners and lip readers.

I nodded and fetched a paper map—a concession to this remote area where a handheld computer wouldn't always have reception. At the same time, it was the perfect tool for us to hide from the guards' eyes.

The plan granted us three minutes to find the right way on the map. Three minutes for Tess and Sabine to get their protégé out.

Three minutes to find out if this mission would remain silent or result in a big shootout—in which case we'd have to find cover quickly. Protective suits didn't match our role, so the two of us didn't wear any. We knowingly accepted that risk.

After all, we were Mambas. Even naked more deadly than a soldier company, that was our motto. Protective suits were a nice add-on, but no mandatory part of our equipment.

Three hundred meters were way out of range for pistols and machine pistols, and at least a challenge for a rifle shooter. At the same time, it was a long distance for Tess and Sabine and their instrument.

"Something's stirring," Elodie reported.

I moved my head to be able to see something through my

little hole in the map. Indeed — covered by the scraggy bushes, three persons in sand-colored camouflage suits were sneaking up toward us. The single guard on this side of the building still was only watching us.

The approaching other team needed a distraction now. My cue!

I jumped out of the car, grabbed a tissue box from the rear seat, and hurried between the bushes to relieve myself there — at least it should look like that to the guard. After all, he shouldn't watch anything but my bare butt for a short time.

Meanwhile, Elodie tried to turn the car around on the narrow piece of road, the driver's side facing the house. Her awkward performance, turning the wheel while stopping, should allow our teammates and their protégé to climb the car unseen.

Elodie finishing her turn was the sign for me our people were aboard. I pulled up my pants, hurried back to the car, tossed the tissue box onto the floor and jumped into my seat.

Elodie firmly pushed the pedal. The car leaped forward spraying small pebbles away. With according verve, she turned onto the main road.

I glanced into the back. "Problems?"

"No," Tess replied. Everything went as planned."

"Are we safe now?" a soft voice chimed in.

"Stay low," Sabine answered. She was covering the rescued Dragon technology graduate with her body. "The criminals have connections to the local police. It's over once we're out of here. Don't worry, we've got all that covered."

Elodie already steered the car to the curb. A station wagon with tinted windows was waiting there. "You can change cars now."

Tess stepped outside first to have a look around. "Clear. Come."

Sabine rose, let her protégé sit up, and nodded at me. "Good luck."

"Same to you. Have a good flight."

Elodie waited until the station wagon had left, then she followed to the next crossing, where our ways parted. Tess and Sabine would take the researcher to our Tigershark and thus take her safely — and invisibly — out of the country.

We'd end our vacation like two ordinary tourists. No one should make a connection between us and the researcher's sudden disappearance. A close departure would only be suspicious.

ABOUT THE AUTHOR

I am Valerie J. Long, born in 1963. I live and work in Germany as an IT project manager. I like role playing games, and I like putting my ideas on paper. I like all kinds of Science Fiction and Fantasy, I like music, and I like making you bite your nails off.

www.ingramcontent.com/pod-product-compliance
Lightning Source LLC
Chambersburg PA
CBHW071300170626
46809CB00001B/294